THREE
DAYS
BREATHING

Mike Maguire

Publisher's Note:

This is a work of fiction. Names, characters, places, and incidents are either the product of the author's imagination or are used fictitiously, and any resemblance to actual persons living or dead, events, organizations, or locales is entirely coincidental.

Fort Totten Press

Washington, DC

ISBN: 1535313390

Cover design by Gino Verna.

First Fort Totten Press ed.

1

One morning, back when I was eight, my L-pod greeted me with, "Hello, Corim! Big day today! You're going to hear a lecture from Mrs. Winten."

"Who's that?" I asked.

"She's from the Counselor Order. Seeing her in person is a special treat. She'll speak to your class regularly about things that aren't covered in your lessons with me."

The pod went silent and opened. It was just like when we broke to go to lunch or the gym – we all stepped out of our pods and milled about the classroom until a bot had us gather at the door and led us out.

My best friend Raff had been one of the first of us to start school, so on the walk I asked him, "Have you ever heard a talk from Mrs. Winten?"

"Nope, never even heard of her."

We were taken down to the first floor and through a hallway that was new to us. Every kid's head turned from side to side at the novelty of the pale green wall tiles. We went down a stairwell, and through a cherrywood door into an empty auditorium. The light brown surface of the stage held the most enormous display I'd ever seen. Its screen read, "Welcome!"

Hundreds of seats faced the stage, more than were needed for the two-hundred-something kids in our class. As we descended the aisle, the lead bot's head swiveled all the way around to look back at us and say, "You will fill the front rows. Leave no seats empty."

Raff and I ended up in the third row. In front of us, two other boys were laughing and flailing as they grabbed at each other's arms, but then came a buzzing sound and both of them yelped and went stiff. A woman's amplified voice announced, "Boys and girls! Your seat is watching you. If you do not behave and sit still, and speak only when spoken to, then you will receive a shock."

We went silent and sat up straight.

"Now eyes up front," the voice said.

The woman walked onto the stage. I knew what members of the upper orders looked like from seeing them on the news and on shows. I knew their clothes were different and varied, and that they lived long enough to show the ravages of age. Knowing what to expect wasn't enough to prepare me for seeing one in person.

Her dress was black except for the white collar and sleeve cuffs. There was a gray streak in her dark hair. There were permanent cracks in the skin at the corners of her eyes. How could skin have cracks? Were they painful?

She smiled, and the cracks grew. "Welcome boys and girls, welcome. I am Mrs. Winten. I'm a member of the Counselor Order. I'm forty-nine years old. I will live until I am seventy-seven. What order are you all members of? You may answer now."

"The General Order!" we said in unison.

"Correct," she said. "And now a question for the boys, so only the boys answer. What age will you live until?"

"Thirty-six!" we boys said.

"Correct," she replied. "That means you have twenty-eight more years. That is a good, long time, and I intend to help you make the most of it. Now, a question for the young ladies. How long will you live until?"

"Thirty-seven!" the girls said.

"Right again! Thirty-seven. You lucky ladies get an extra year."

She paced the edge of the stage and continued, "Lucky. Lucky ladies, and lucky boys ... but I wonder if you understand how lucky? Let's take a look at how the world was long ago."

She stepped aside and turned toward the display. Grainy video started playing of a mother, father, and son standing in line carrying empty metal bowls. They were gaunt, and their exhausted faces were as worn out as their tattered clothes. The boy looked to be our age.

The next images were of bare-skinned men looking out with hollow eyes through wire fences. They were skinnier than I would've thought possible, the recesses of their ashen skin deep between every rib.

We then saw a group of hundreds of people packed together on a street. Their clothes were so odd. To think that I'd just been struck by Mrs. Winten's dress having two colors – the clothes these people were wearing had countless colors. I would've guessed they were celebrating something festive, but they were agitated and yelling. At the edge of the group, men in dark uniforms and helmets beat them back with clubs.

Next there were films of buildings burning and falling in on themselves. A hand, bloody and unmoving, protruded from the rubble. Injured child after injured child filled the screen. Bandages soaked with blood, limbs missing, faces scarred, and bodies twisted and deformed like crumpled paper. We forgot about the warning to stay quiet and gasped.

Then came images of the elderly. A shriveled old man coughed into his bed sheet. A woman in a gown held onto a railing and struggled to walk, her bony legs covered in dead, purplish veins. A man with thin, gray hair tried to button his shirt, but winced in pain when one of his shaky hands clawed up.

There was a very old woman sitting alone in a white hallway. Her chair had wheels for legs and was facing a corner. The old woman's vacant face filled the screen as she did nothing but stare at the emptiness in front of her. I couldn't stand to see her so helpless and alone. I wanted someone to come rescue her, but no one did and the display faded to black.

Mrs. Winten bowed her head at the pain of it all.

"Remember what you have seen here today," she said, raising her face back up at us. "If the world now was like the world then, these could be moments from your own life, or from the lives of your parents."

A chill went through me at that thought, no doubt the same chill that went through every child in the room.

"The people of the past," she continued, "had to suffer through years, sometimes even decades, of great suffering. But you will never have a day like that. And why not? Why is it you need not worry about such awful things? Because, children, you are lucky in ways you cannot imagine. Profoundly lucky. You will all be sheltered, clothed, and fed for your entire lives.

"Most of you will someday experience the privilege of having your own child. Couples are permitted to have one child in the General Order. Limits on family size help to fight overpopulation, and are part of a system that prevents hunger and misery.

"You may not always understand the system, and you may not always like what it asks of you. When those moments of uncertainty come, you must remind yourselves of this: the system that determines how you will live and die is the same system that ensures not only your well-being, but your very existence.

"And so, children, as you return to your classroom be grateful that you live in such a beautiful time. A time without disease, or overpopulation, or war, or famine. Be grateful for your friends and your family. Be happy to be alive!"

She smiled and walked off the stage.

That night, Mom suggested we go for a walk on our building's roof. She always liked going up there after dark. Sometimes she'd stand at the railing and gaze at the moon, other times she'd go up to the crops, let her hands hang against the wire fence that surrounded them, and listen to the leaves and cornstalks rustle in the night breeze.

Our building was taller than most, and that night as we came out of the elevator we could see the tops of the buildings in the restricted areas to the west. We walked along the railing that ran along the edge of the roof, and at the south side Dad said, "Look as far as you can. Somewhere south there must be a dark spot in the lights where Lake Park is. I can never find it, though."

At the east side we looked down at a train passing from one stop to the next. Its movement through our ward's grid of city blocks seemed so slow from that height. At the north side we stopped to behold how the mighty white spire of the Life Center cut the night to form the skyline's zenith. The Life Center was a thin building, circular and windowless, and it was ninety-one stories high not counting the great spire. Instead of being surrounded by other structures, it was only surrounded by the spotlights that made every inch of its uniformly white exterior glow against the black sky like a heavenly body.

The three of us stood quietly squeezing the railing and watching the flickering lights of the endless cityscape. "How was school today, Corim?" Mom asked. "You haven't said."

I told them about the lecture. When I got to the part about how those of us in the General Order were only allowed to have one child for the sake of fighting overpopulation, Dad said, "That's not really true."

I didn't understand – how could something I'd been taught in school be not true?

"Don't bother him with those things yet," Mom said. "It was only his first lecture."

"He should know."

"Know what?" I asked.

"You've started doing math," he said. "Think about it. If every couple has one child and then that couple dies, then the population should get cut in half every generation. One child has been the General Order rule for as long as anyone can remember, but they still tell us they need to fight overpopulation. It doesn't add up."

I did my best to consider what he'd said.

"So why are there still so many people?" I asked. "Where do they come from?"

"I've heard of families being moved into our ward," he said, "but I've never heard of anyone from our ward being moved out of it. That's why our ward is as crowded as ever, but I don't know what's going on with other wards."

"Corim," Mom said, "you let your dad worry about things like that. You just worry about learning your lessons."

2

I'd started school a few weeks before on my birthday. My parents walked me that first day – no need to take the train since our apartment was only two blocks away. After we climbed the granite steps and passed through the white columns, we came to a pair of tall steel doors, one of which was held open by a bot. The machine looked down at me with its glass eyes.

"Hello, Corim Colleran!" it said. "Happy birthday and welcome to school!"

The bot was larger than the bots in our building's nursery. I studied the smile that was stamped into the yellow metal of its face.

"How do you know my name?" I asked.

"You're in my database and I recognized you. And besides, you turn eight today so I was expecting you! I even got you a present. Here!"

It bent forward and dropped a small glassy cube into my hand.

"It's candy. Eat it!" the bot said.

I looked from the candy to my parents.

"Go ahead son, try it," Dad said.

"Don't worry, you'll like it!" added the bot.

The cube broke apart between my teeth, sending a sweet chill through my mouth. I didn't like it at all.

"That flavor is called peppermint!" the bot said. "Can you say that?"

I said it.

"Look at that, you've already learned something! Now let me take you inside and show you some more great things. Take my hand."

I placed my hand in the sleek, yellow metal of the open palm held before me. The cold solidity of its grip scared me, but before I had time to resist I was being led through the door as my parents waved goodbye and told me to have fun.

The school was the shortest building in our ward – only eleven stories. The bot led me up the stairs to the fifth floor, where it walked me down an empty hall, and explained how all of my classmates had also recently started school on their eighth birthdays. We stopped at a door, and the bot gave me a pep talk about the joys of learning. When it opened the door I expected to see my new classmates, but instead there were only rows of white plastic spheres that were as tall as my father.

As we walked through them, the bot said, "These are L-pods. They're wonderful!"

It showed me where mine was, and had me press the only button that was on it. A side panel slid open, and the bot told me to climb in and sit in the black reclining chair. After I did, the pod closed around me. The panic I felt at being sealed alone in the dark disappeared when the L-pod's display lit up before me. What appeared was so remarkable I forgot where I was.

"This is the ocean," I heard a voice say.

I'd seen images of the ocean before on our display at home, but those had only shown things like aquatic bots skimming the murky surfaces of algae farms.

"And this is a wave breaking," the voice said.

The cresting wave shone as blue as the sunny sky above. It seemed to pause, and then it started to break at one end, bringing chaos and violence to what had been a picture of tranquility. Now the whole wave had broken and was roaring forward, leaving behind a wake of multi-patterned foam. It was the first time I was ever aware of the possibility of perfect beauty.

Two hours later, my head was spinning with all I'd learned as the display went dark and the pod opened. I heard a hive of voices outside.

When I got up from the chair and stepped out, it was like my pod had been moved to somewhere else while I'd been in it. Students were everywhere laughing, screaming, shoving, and pulling on each other. All the boys were, like me, in youth-issued white button-down shirts, black shoes, white socks, and blue pants. That was also what the girls were wearing, except for their blue skirts.

The din of my classmates echoed off the empty white walls and low ceiling. Then above it all, a bot's voice bellowed, "Gather, gather!"

Kid after kid hurried by my pod. As they massed at the door I found myself moving forward until I was part of them. There were two bots at the door and one announced, "Follow me to the gym."

The room started to clear out and I joined in at the back of the pack. The second bot followed behind. Walking down the hallway I looked around at all the smiling, talking faces, and I realized the boy next to me kept looking over.

I nodded. "Hello," I said.

The boy had a wide face and deep-set brown eyes. Every strand of his off-kilter hair pointed sideways as if he were standing parallel to a fierce wind.

"You're new," he said. "Is today your first day?"

"Yes."

His eyes got wide. "You should be walking up front! Go get up front!"

I looked ahead, curious where in the line I should go.

"Let him through, it's his first day!" he yelled to the kids in front of us.

They all turned back to look at me. A path was cleared and everyone started telling me to move to the front. I was uncomfortable with the attention, but I did as they said and picked up my pace to move through the crowd. Calls of, "Out of the way!" and "New kid coming through!" followed me up the line. Each and every kid I passed encouraged me forward, patting me on my back.

I reached the front row of my fellow students, who were following just behind the lead bot. A girl with long, black hair put her hand on my shoulder.

"Today's your first day?" she asked.

I nodded.

"Oh! On your first day you're supposed to walk out in front of the bot."

I looked ahead at the bot. Its legs moved like a person's but its arms didn't sway at all.

"Yeah, go get in front of the bot!" another girl said. The black-haired girl gave me a nudge. "Hurry, before it's too late!"

Everyone was so friendly and encouraging that I started to feel their excitement. I was very happy with myself as I trotted past the machine and into the lead.

We were just entering a hub, but I didn't know which of the three identical hallways before me would lead to the gym. Before I had a chance to look around, I felt an awful burn centered in my chest. I screamed and spun around. The bot I'd just passed was reaching forward and pointing a yellow finger at me.

All of my classmates burst into uproarious laughter.

The bot curled its pointing finger in and dropped its hand. All at once the burning in my chest was gone, but a throbbing pain lingered and made me hunch forward.

"You were supposed to stay behind me," the bot said as it went by.

The class passed around me, and I stood staring down at the checkerboard floor tiles as their feet shuffled by and their laughter filled my ears. After they'd finished passing, I saw the feet of the bot that had been following us stop in front of me.

I looked up and it pointed a finger in my face. "You're supposed to stay in front of me," it said.

I ran to rejoin the crowd.

My classmates were still laughing and mimicking me as we got to the gym, but as soon as we crammed through the door they all ran off. I was relieved that I'd been left alone, but unsure of what I should now do with myself. In all directions kids were playing strange games involving courts, goals, hoops, and obstacles. The ceiling was so high and the floor stretched so far ahead that it felt like I was no longer inside.

I walked toward the center of the gym, passing courts where older kids punched a ball over a net. I went by a confusing game where kids of different ages lined up to kick balls into goals placed at varying distances.

I came to a court without any nets or goals. Black lines on the white floor marked the boundaries, and there were four large balls in play. Two teams of younger kids were faced off throwing the balls at each other as fast as they could. A group of kids stood on the sideline, and one took notice of me.

"That shock really hurts, doesn't it?" he asked.

"What?"

"The shock from the bot. It hurts, doesn't it?"

I recognized this boy. He was the one with crooked hair who'd first spotted me and convinced me that I should be walking up front.

I didn't answer him. It was bad enough he'd initiated the trick against me – I wasn't going to let him compound my embarrassment by getting me to talk about it.

"Don't be mad!" he said without losing his grin. "We do that every day to the first new kid we find."

"You do?" I asked.

"Yeah, we always play that trick!"

I wondered if he was trying to fool me again. "Really?" I asked.

"Of course! I remember how much it hurt when they did it to me. It really hurt! Did you think it was a trick we made up only for you?" He laughed at that idea.

"I guess so."

"That's so dumb! Hey, have you ever played dodge ball?"

"No."

"Oh, it's so fun! We'll show you how to play and you can join the next game."

He turned to a snub-nosed blond boy who'd been standing with his arms crossed watching the game by himself. "Hey Bennett! Come help me teach the new kid how to play."

The boy came over. "Hi, kid," he said. "What's your name?"

"Corim."

"I'm Bennett," he said proudly.

"And I'm Raff," said the crooked-haired boy.

They explained as we watched, and I joined the next game and did well enough – before Bennett got me out by whipping a ball against my legs, I managed to get out the black-haired girl who'd earlier nudged me toward the bot by, out of pure defensive instinct, catching the ball she'd thrown at my face. As we watched the game from the sidelines she told me her name was Lenia. "Nice job, getting me out," she said. "You got me back for playing the trick."

By the start of the next game, I had the comfort of being just another kid playing in the gym. And every morning from that day on, I joined my parents at our little plastic kitchen table, scarfed down my cereal, and rushed out of the apartment to get to school on time.

3

Our second lecture came after we'd completed our first year of school and everyone in our class had all turned nine. It started the same as the first, with Mrs. Winten having us boys answer that we'd live to thirty-six, and having the girls answer that they'd live to thirty-seven.

Then she said, "Let's talk about the three E's: Expiration, Execution, and Extension. When someone is fortunate enough to reach their full lifespan, we say they've made it to Expiration. Let us hope that every one of us reaches Expiration. However, there are, I'm afraid, ways of dying earlier.

"One way is Execution, which is what happens when a person breaks the rules so badly that it's decided they are not deserving of their full lifespan. No matter what age that person is, their lifespan is taken away and they are immediately made dead. I know this will never happen to any of you, because I know you will all remember to follow the rules and treat each other well.

"Another way to die early is by accident. Someone who isn't being careful might fall from a building or in front of a train. Sometimes the medbots are able to revive those who die prematurely, but those people don't get their full lifespans back. Death always means death, because we don't want you taking undue risks. Life still must be valued and guarded carefully.

"But there's a very special gift given to those who die early and are revived, and that is what we call Extension. If one of you is careless and accidentally dies before reaching Expiration and the bots are able to revive you, then you'll receive a last three days of life to say goodbye to your friends and family. Those three extra days are called Extension. And Extension is one of the exciting advancements that make us very lucky to be alive right now."

She then went on more about how lucky we all were, and again ended her lecture with, "Be grateful for your friends and your family. Be happy to be alive!"

I hadn't known about the possibility of premature death before that lecture, and it both frightened and fascinated me. Later I asked my L-pod what the most common way of dying early in the General Order was.

"Suicide," it said.

I asked what that word meant and it told me. I was surprised Mrs. Winten hadn't said anything about it.

"If someone kills themself, do they get to go on Extension?" I asked. "Do they get the extra three days?"

"No. Many suicides are impossible to revive anyway, because they've done something like jump from a rooftop. The ones who can be revived are briefly interviewed to confirm that they killed themselves, and that it wasn't someone else who killed them."

"What if they say that they've changed their mind and they want to live?"

"Death always means death," the pod said. "There's no coming back from it. After the interview, they're returned to a nonliving state."

"What if they say someone else killed them?"

"That's rare, but if they do say that, then it's investigated. If it's found they really were murdered, they get to go on Extension and have three extra days to enjoy life and to say goodbye to their loved ones."

"So if someone is killed by someone else, they still have to die? That doesn't seem fair."

"Death is always death. Their killer will almost certainly be executed, and those who are executed don't get to go on Extension at all."

"Why is Extension only three days?"

"That's just the right amount. One day to accept what's happened, a second day to have fun, and a third day to say final goodbyes."

"Is there any way to tell if someone is on Extension?"

"No. People on Extension are legally dead, but physically they're as healthy as anyone else and they don't look any different."

"So someone I know could be on Extension and I wouldn't know it?"

"That's possible, but unlikely. You'll probably never know or meet anyone on Extension. Dying early is rare, and dying in a way that allows for Extension is even rarer."

"Do children ever die early?"

"Children almost never die. Corim, why don't we talk about a more pleasant subject for a while? While it's important that you learn these things, it's also important that you don't worry about them too much."

We returned to my regular studies.

Now and then in those first years of school my thoughts would wander back to that day when I'd learned it was possible to die young, and I'd find it hard to think about anything else. Most of the time though, I was, as Mrs. Winten had instructed, a grateful and happy student. My next few years were a cheerful routine split between life at home with my parents and life at school with my friends.

As my contentment deepened, so did my love of learning – although it was a love that seemed unique among my classmates. They were never as interested in talking about what we were studying in our lessons as I was. When they did talk about it, I'd realize that I was always a lesson or two ahead of them.

Their interest only started to catch up with mine when we were ten and our biology lessons started to incorporate the processes of procreation. What began with cellular reproduction built up over the months to details of male and female anatomies. Mrs. Winten advised us to pay extra attention to these lessons.

After we turned eleven, our L-pods began to show the occasional video of sexually engaged animals. When breaks came we would rush out of our pods and ask each other, "Did you see that?"

Once after class, Bennett jumped on Raff's back and mimicked the sounds and motions of the copulating monkeys from that day's lesson. Raff blushed horribly and fought him off, but he couldn't help but break into laughter with us.

After we turned twelve, we started seeing videos of intimate people. The early ones only covered things like ancient courtship rituals. Men brought women gifts. Women cooked for men. Men told jokes to women, and women tilted their heads back in laughter. Family patriarchs gave offerings to each other, and the subsequent unions secured by the gifts would commence with ornate rituals and ceremonies.

The lessons started to teach hand holding, kissing, and clothed touching. The more we saw, the more riled and impatient we became in our speculation of what was to come. Finally one afternoon our L-pods showed us with great specificity what we'd been waiting for.

The effect was both cathartic and shocking, and there was no excitement, or at least no visible excitement, when we came out of our pods that day. We weren't just stepping back into the classroom, we were stepping into a new world, and we did so with a shyness and unease that redefined our social boundaries. The girls, who'd been every bit as much our playmates and confidantes, were now agents of mystery, carriers of impossible ascents, impossible liberations. Coming to know them in a new way had made them strangers to us.

More lessons came and when they did we boys would pepper one another with questions and speculation about the acts and positions we'd seen. We'd look to our friends when deciding how we should feel about seeing men with men or women with women. With encouragement from our L-pods and Mrs. Winten, we decided we had no objections to anything.

After we'd seen and accepted all there was to see, Mrs. Winten gave us a lecture that began, "Over the next few weeks your class will be turning thirteen. Thirteen is an important age. Your bodies will change and you will start to see your classmates, indeed everyone, in a new way. You will desire sex and, because of all we have taught you, you will be ready for it.

"That is why when the last of you turns thirteen your class will gain access to the eleventh floor. That is the floor of soft rooms. Raise your hand if you've heard of them."

No one raised a hand.

"It's natural that you haven't heard of them, as they are something only for teenagers. They are rooms where you and any other teenage student, or students, can go whenever you want and learn firsthand about the joys of physical relations. The eleventh floor is a completely safe environment – a bot supervises each room – but it's also incredibly fun!

"You have all matured and so you are all being given more freedom, but also more responsibility. Until you're out of school, the soft rooms are the only place where you'll be permitted to have sex. But you may visit them whenever you like during school hours, and you may stay in them until the end of the school day. The one exception is lunch. You must continue to have lunch at your regular time."

She grinned. "We don't want any of you starving because you're so busy up there you forget to eat."

She chuckled to herself but the full meaning of her joke was lost on us.

4

The changes started right before we turned thirteen. We boys, every last one of us, started to grow body hair, and our voices deepened. Mrs. Winten told us that the precision of the timing and the universality of the changes were yet another positive result of our genetic engineering and artificial cells. The food dispensaries in the cafeteria started to give us extra-large rations to support the rapid changes our bodies were going through.

Before this, I'd thought that some of the girls were cute and I'd daydreamed about kissing them, but outside of such simple affection I felt no real draw toward them. Now, however, as their curves came in as quickly as the hairs on our chests, I learned what it meant to have a true libido. I was helpless at the sight of every single girl in class, dizzy with an appetite that was far beyond my control. I now understood how aptly named the sex drive is – it felt as much like a pushing and a pulling as any physical force.

This is how we found ourselves, in the last few weeks of our twelfth year, again socializing with the girls. It was not an easing of tensions so much as an overcoming of them. Longtime friendships with the girls were largely abandoned for new pursuits. Although our old friend Lenia rejoined our group, several girls we barely knew also started hovering around us. One of them was a girl I hadn't talked to since we were eight.

I'd first met her, or at least sort of met her, a few days after I'd started school. Our class was on our usual walk to the gym when my eyes were drawn through the crowd to a head of red hair. I jockeyed forward and came to a girl I'd never seen.

I tapped her shoulder.

"Hey, is today your first day?"

She turned and gave a modest nod.

"Oh," I said. "You should be walking up front!"

New students were still joining our class, and every day we were playing the trick that Raff had played on me.

"I should?" she asked.

I pointed to her and turned back to Raff, Bennett, and Lenia.

"Hey guys, it's her first day!" I yelled.

"Then she should be walking up front!" they proclaimed in chorus.

The kids around us joined in, and I watched her move up the line. I was too far back to see her get shocked, but I heard quite a scream, followed by cackling laughter from the front rows. A moment later we all walked by as she stood frozen in pain and embarrassment.

Entering the gym I said to Raff, "Start without me, I want to do something."

Raff nodded. Even at that age he was good about not being nosy.

I hung back and watched all the kids enter and run off in different directions. The girl was last to come in. She got her bearings, crossed her arms, raised an eyebrow, and looked from one end of the gym to the other.

As I approached, her gaze was locked on something distant and she didn't acknowledge me.

I started as Raff had started with me. "It hurts, doesn't it?"

Her eyes sharpened and she gave me an examining look. She didn't answer.

The silver blue of her irises pulled at my attention and I stumbled through my next words.

"Don't be mad, we always do that when we spot a new kid. They did it to me, too. My name's Corim. What's yours?"

No answer.

"Really, don't be mad. The kid who played that trick on me is now my best friend."

She cocked her head to one side, turned, and pranced off, her shoulders squared and chin high. She approached a dodge ball game that was picking teams. She went right into the middle of it, introduced herself around, and got picked for a team.

I didn't know why she was mad at me even after I'd justified myself. When Raff had explained why he'd pranked me, I was relieved. I understood that he'd only done to me what'd been done to him.

I was mad that she'd ignored me, and I concluded that she couldn't be very smart, but at that age I had the trait, a trait I would later lose and often miss, of not analyzing such things for more than a moment. I shrugged and went to find my group.

As I walked by her court, the girl was lining up to start the game. I paused and she glanced over at me. The team captains began their countdown and the girl bent her knees and put her hands out in ready position. An intense look overtook her face, and when the game started she zigzagged toward her opponents until someone threw a ball at her. She grabbed it out of the air and threw it overhead with both hands so that it slammed off another opponent's chest. Her teammates moved in behind her, and the remaining opponents were all thrown out in the retreat. It was the shortest dodge ball game I'd ever seen.

The players regrouped in the center of the court, and one of her teammates said, "That was great, Kiri!"

I'd seen her often in the five years since, but she never acknowledged me. Now she'd started hovering around us and flirting with Bennett and Raff, but she was as stony and silent with me as ever.

The two students with the last birthday among us became class celebrities. We were counting down the days to their thirteenth birthday instead of our own because that would be the day of our ascension to the eleventh floor.

Planning began for our first trips to the soft rooms. Most of the girls Bennett, Raff, and I had been talking to had clearly paired with one boy or another. After being courted by more than one girl, Bennett chose Kiri.

I'd become close with several girls, but had neither picked nor been picked by one. My hopes were set on Lenia – after years of friendship, I'd gained a sudden appreciation of her beauty. Her delicate skin was the color of dusky desert sands, and she had the thickest, most luxuriant black hair of anyone I'd ever seen. And although she was one of the most petite girls in our class, the changes of the previous few weeks had done good things to her.

We talked often, and even when she was talking to another boy her big playful eyes would find me. She was the quiet type, but when she did speak she was as likely to ask me something about myself as she was to talk about her own attributes. I found myself wanting to talk to her more and more.

A few days before we started in the soft rooms, we were all sitting in the bright lights of the cafeteria at the end of lunch. Lenia and I were next to each other, and we had moved in close to talk separately from the group.

"Have any boys talked to you about our first day upstairs?" I asked.

I was sure no one had because lately I was the one she tended to gravitate toward. Her voice was as quiet as always when she answered. "Yes. Raff just asked me about that earlier and I said yes."

I was very surprised, and also more than a little embarrassed for having waited too long to ask, but I tried not to let it show. Mrs. Winten had emphasized that we shouldn't worry too much about whom we did or didn't pair with on the eleventh floor.

"Ah, alright," I said. "I didn't know that, and I was going to ask you. I'll ask someone else."

"You could be the second one I go to a soft room with? Maybe later in the day or the day after?"

"Oh. Well, yes, ok. I'd like that. Let's plan on the day after?"

I wasn't sure if it was some sort of breach of protocol to make arrangements with a girl my friend had also made arrangements with. Later I told Raff everything and asked, "Is it ok with you if I get with her the day after our first day? I don't want to if it'd be awkward."

He laughed. "What a silly question. Of course it'd be ok! I'll have moved on to at least one more girl by then. My goal is to be with twenty-five girls in our first thirty days upstairs. But you need to find someone for your first day, too."

"I wasn't quick enough about asking around. All the girls seem to be taken. It's ok though, I can wait."

"You'll find someone when we're all up there."

"Maybe, yeah."

"Hey, I hope it's alright, me being with Lenia? I know you two had been talking a lot."

"Yeah, it's alright. I'll find someone else when we're up there."

5

On the big day I went to school at the usual time. A lot of the class had talked about getting up early and waiting for the bots to open the school doors, but I figured we would have three years of soft rooms and saw no need to rush it. By the time I'd climbed to the eleventh floor, the parlor was already brimming with students.

I paused near the entrance and saw within the dim, greenish lighting a plush, low-ceilinged version of the gym downstairs. Instead of courts and nets there were couches and displays. The kids inside were older than the ones in the gym, but just as animated.

I stepped onto the soft burgundy carpet as if I were on my way somewhere. I spotted some other boys from my class who were also without girls. They were looking around, smiling nervously, and introducing themselves when they could.

Kids who looked barely thirteen sat on the couches with kids who looked nearly sixteen. Most of them had their arms around each other as if that were the only way to sit. Some couches were so short that only couples could fit on them, but some of the longer, curved ones looked big enough to seat a dozen. Some had displays in front of them, and some faced each other.

Halfway in, I started hearing music and came to an area of tiled flooring lit by an array of twirling, multicolored lights. A boy and girl walked onto it holding hands.

My parents had given me dancing lessons, but never to songs as up-tempo as this one. When the couple reached the center of the dance floor, they locked eyes and began to circle each other, moving in and out and brushing their hands over each other's bodies. I studied their gyrations with the idea of trying to imitate them later in my room.

I found my way to the parlor perimeter and walked along it for a bit before turning down one of the side halls that contained the soft rooms. Couples and groups were finding rooms, and none of them seemed to notice me. I went all the way to the end of the hall and cautiously opened a door with a lit vacancy indicator.

A cushioned orange chair faced a pillow-covered bed. The empty walls looked pale yellow in the dim amber light. "Hello, Corim," the schoolbot in the corner said. "Welcome to the soft rooms. Come in and look around."

I sat on the bed and bounced up and down to test its firmness. It felt just like my smaller bed at home. The bot told me all the things Mrs. Winten had already told us about what a good, safe, and welcoming environment I was now in.

I lay on the bed for a few moments until I heard two voices from the hall nearing the open door. I hurried out, not wanting anyone to see me in there alone. I shut the door behind me while the bot inside went to straighten the bed's sheets and pillows.

In the hall I tried to slip by the approaching couple but the girl stopped and caught my arm.

"Hey, where ya going?" she asked. "Are you with anyone?"

"No, I'm just looking around."

"Just looking around? Does that mean it's your first day?"

Trying not to let my embarrassment show, I admitted it was.

"Oh! You look older than thirteen. But that's exciting, congratulations. So you haven't had sex at all?"

"Well, not yet, no."

"Wow," she said, and her face broke into a smile.

My guess was she was fourteen, maybe even fifteen. Despite the awkward circumstances, I was attracted to her right away. Her voice had a rough, weathered edge while still being feminine and warm. Her smile took over her whole face and perfectly matched her loosely flowing blonde-brown hair, russet skin, and bright, hopeful eyes. She was one of those people who naturally radiated enthusiasm and adventurousness in a way the rest of us never can.

She hugged me. It was the first hug I'd ever received from anyone other than my parents or their friends, and it was already ending by the time I got my hands properly placed to return it.

"I'm Icora and this is Zach. Who are you?"

"Corim."

"Well, I think I like you, Corim. If Zach wouldn't mind, would you like to join me and him today?"

"I wouldn't mind at all." Zach said. He was also older, and he was so at ease with himself that he struck me as cocky.

"Uh, I don't know," I said.

"You two could get together on your own if you'd like," Zach said. "It's a special day for you, kid."

I was annoyed that he'd called me kid, but at the same time I was taken aback by how generous his offer was. I didn't know how to reply.

"The thing is, I had already set something up," I said.

Icora squeezed my arms. "Of course you have! And your first time should be with someone you know. But hey, look for me in the parlor one of these days, ok? You're cute!"

I'd probably already been blushing a little, but now I felt my face burn. Icora gave me another hug, which I did a better job of returning. Then she grabbed Zach's hand and started toward the empty soft room I'd just been in. As he started to follow her, Zach patted my shoulder. "Have fun today, kid!" he said.

Back in the parlor, I took time to appreciate how many beautiful girls there were. Part of me wanted to be with every one of them right then, but I also kept thinking about how Lenia and I were planning on getting together the next day.

I happened upon a girl who was sitting alone on a small couch – the first girl I'd seen all morning who was by herself. Her brown hair was pulled back, her hands were crossed in her lap, and she seemed to be looking off in the distance at nothing in particular. When she noticed me staring at her, she tilted her head and gave me a little wave hello.

I returned the wave and took a step closer, but the girl turned her head away and craned her neck to try to see something. She was searching for the source of the shouts and screams that had started to cut through the surrounding chatter and background music. Without looking back at me, she got up and ran to where a crowd was gathering.

I followed along, thinking maybe something special was happening on one of the dance floors. At first I couldn't see the source of the commotion. Most of the crowd was cheering, but I heard a few shouts of, "Stop!"

A schoolbot shoved past me and cleared a path to reveal two boys fighting. They were locked up, both grabbing at the other's shirt, but when one of them saw the schoolbot coming he released his grip and let his guard down. The other boy cranked one hand back, made a fist, and caught him on the jaw with a nasty hook.

The strike dazed the boy, and he staggered back until one of his legs caught the corner of a couch and he fell hard to the floor. The other boy jumped atop him and started punching at his face. I heard a crunch, and blood started streaming from the downed boy's nose. The kids surrounding them shouted, "Yeah!" and, "Get him!" as they raised their fists in the air.

The schoolbot stood over the fighters watching it happen. After a few more hits the bot reached in and pulled the top boy off.

"That's enough. Step aside," the bot said.

Then the bot lifted the bleeding boy from the floor and carried him away.

The boy who'd won the fight went to a girl at the edge of the crowd and whispered something in her ear. She wiped at her teary eyes, and then nodded yes to him. He took her hand and they headed toward the soft rooms. Those who'd been watching started to return to their couches. I looked around for the girl I'd almost met, but couldn't find her.

In a moment everything was as it'd been before, and I was the only one still standing there. I knelt down and felt at the carpet until I found a moist spot. In the green light of the parlor the blood on my fingertips looked more brown than red.

I began to walk again, surveying all the smiling and laughing faces. The more happiness I saw, the less I felt like I belonged there. I left the parlor, and went down the empty stairs and through the quiet halls to my classroom. All the lights on the front of the L-pods were red to indicate empty. It was a strange feeling, lonely but comforting. I walked through to mine and got in.

"I'm surprised to see you back so soon," the pod said. "Don't you like the eleventh floor?"

"I'm not sure. I think I'll like it more tomorrow."

"You didn't have sex though. I bet if you went back today you could find someone to have fun with. Aren't you excited to try it? Doesn't your sex drive feel strong?"

"I'm excited and my drive is very strong, but I'm going to wait until tomorrow."

"Alright. What would you like to do now?"

"I saw a fight upstairs. A bot came to break it up, but it didn't break it up as quickly as it could've. I don't understand why not. A boy was getting hurt."

"Don't worry, that boy will be fine. The bot took him to a med-pod. We bots have a duty to give you the most freedom we can in social interactions, even fights. That freedom leads to the best possible social development. The bot hesitated to stop the fight because it was balancing that duty with its duty to keep students safe. Do you understand?"

Though I was still unsettled, I said yes and dropped the subject.

At lunch I sat with Bennett and Raff at our usual table. Kiri and Lenia were still with them. When Bennett and Kiri put down their trays and sat, she gave his arm a squeeze and pressed her smiling cheek against his shoulder. Lenia didn't show any affection toward Raff, and at first she avoided looking at me, but she seemed happy enough.

Raff looked down at his food and said, "Ok, let's recharge and get back up there!"

They all laughed, and I laughed with them. Exuberance abounded as we ate, and they joked about tired hips and how they wanted to spend the rest of their lives on the eleventh floor.

"So Corim, how'd you do?" Raff asked. "Who'd you end up with?"

"I met a nice girl, but she was with a guy. She asked me to join them, and he even said I could be alone with her. I liked her, but it just didn't feel right. Anyway, we're still on for tomorrow Lenia?"

She smiled and nodded.

"Then I figure what's one more day? Anyhow, I went back to class and caught up on some geology and math."

Bennett, Raff, and Lenia looked at me with dumbstruck sympathy, but Kiri's eyes widened with curiosity. It was the first time I'd caught her looking at me since the bit of a fight we'd had years before. She quickly turned away.

The table was quiet, so I added, "I did the lesson about lava formations again. Do you guys remember that one?"

They shook their heads.

"Really? How can you not remember it? It's fantastic. One of my favorites. You all should do it."

"I'm never doing an L-pod lesson again," Bennett said. "Why should we do that when we have the soft rooms now?"

"It's really interesting, though. And beautiful," I said.

I sincerely meant it, but Raff thought I'd changed the subject out of embarrassment. He tried to help.

"Well no class for you tomorrow," he said, putting his arm around Lenia. "You'll be busy with this girl!"

Everyone laughed and the festive mood returned.

The next morning, Lenia was waiting for me in the parlor just like we'd planned. She smiled when she saw me coming her way, and I forgot all about the drama and awkwardness of the day before. I took her hand, and led her through the crowd and into a soft room. I was nervous, but it was nervous excitement.

I shut the door behind us, and when I turned back to her she put her lips to mine. I thought, here it is, my first kiss. I closed my eyes as I'd been taught to do. I pushed back her silky hair, squeezed her hips, and ran my hands over her back as I'd been taught to do. I moaned and repeatedly repositioned my lips onto hers as I'd been taught to do.

She stepped back, kicked off her shoes, pulled off her shirt and skirt, and then stood in her socks and underwear holding a pose, her body facing me but her dark eyes off to the side, demure yet inviting. Blood quick through her face, shoulders taut.

I moved in, and our heuristic lesson moved on. The mimicking of what I'd seen in films eased into intuitive creativity. Hesitation became release. Observational detachment became shared glee. Control became frenzy. And in that hot foundry where the self melts, merges, and forges by ceaselessly moving against another, I learned how meaningless all the buildup of lectures and lessons had been.

I learned that ecstasy is not, as we'd been taught, reached through positions and techniques and performances. I learned that ecstasy is reached through mutual surrender.

6

It had taken me a day longer than my classmates, but I now felt like a full part of the eleventh floor. Every morning, I rushed up to try and meet a new girl, and I was successful more often than not. One afternoon, I found the girl I'd met on my first day, Icora. She didn't remember me at first, but then she said she did and acted thrilled that I'd found her. We hurried off together for a quick soft room session, and it was fun enough, though I think I had built her up in my mind a little too much – it wasn't quite what I'd fantasized it would be.

On the morning that marked the end of my fourth month on the eleventh floor, the bot standing sentry at the parlor entrance halted me and said, "Sorry, Corim! You can't come in."

"What?" I pleaded. Being barred from the soft rooms was unimaginable to me.

"Don't worry!" it said. "You can come in later, but for now your class has to report to the auditorium."

I hurried down. When all of our class had arrived, Mrs. Winten's voice called out from the speakers with, "Silence, children!" She took the stage.

"Hello, boys and girls. Look at all the happy faces staring back at me. The eleventh floor has treated you well. Just think, you're only four months into your three years of bliss! Oh, how lucky you all are. I'm envious.

"Yet as far off as your futures are, your futures will still come, and I want you to be prepared. As you know, all of you will end up as pattern architects. That is what your parents do, it is what their parents before them did, and it is what you will do. The work you'll do as a pattern architect will keep the food deliveries coming to every kitchen's pantry, will keep the electricity and plumbing working, and will keep the shows you like coming to your display.

"You're all well prepared for that job thanks to years of lessons in your L-pods, so today I'm going to talk about another job. It's just as important, and the part of your education that's just beginning. Most of you will start as pattern architects straight out of school, but a few of you might get the chance to first spend some time doing what you've been doing these last few months in the soft rooms – and getting paid for it!

"To work in a brothel is a position of the highest prestige for members of the General Order. Sex workers make so much money that they can buy things like nonstandard clothing and apartment upgrades. They can afford to have extra food on a daily basis. These are luxuries pattern architects can only dream of.

"And those lucky enough to work in the brothels are always meeting new people, and not just any people – if you become a sex worker, then every single one of your clients will be from the upper orders. Sometimes even from the Administrative Order. It is a beautiful honor.

"Now I'm sure you're all thinking, 'But Mrs. Winten, how can I get selected for such a privilege?' Well, that is why I'm speaking to you today. You may think it's all about looks and physical attributes. No, no, no. Looks matter, particularly when being selected for brothel auditions, but you all have beautiful genes and are the most uniformly attractive generation ever.

"The things that will really matter if you want to last beyond the audition phase are skill, talent, and experience. How do you get those things? You have to do more in the soft rooms than just have fun. You have to become the lover that any client, whether man or woman, would pay to have. This means exploring everything you've been shown in your lessons. It means pushing your boundaries, and reprogramming your desires.

"You've all had a lot of sex, but none of you have begun to have enough of the kinds of sex that will prepare you for the brothels. Starting today, more will be expected of you. Any girl who has not yet had sex with a girl will do so. Any boy who has not yet had sex with a boy will do so.

"You will all try every possible sexual role over the coming years. You will learn to be both fully dominant and fully submissive. Don't forget that every soft room has a bot in it for a reason. They'll continue to both guide you and enforce the rules."

She looked us over and smiled. "Remember above all else that the best way to become accomplished is to practice. So now, boys and girls, go upstairs and practice. Practice, practice, practice!"

While everyone else headed back up to the eleventh floor, I went to our classroom.

"Hello, Corim!" my L-pod said, "Did you enjoy the lecture?"

"I did, but I don't understand something Mrs. Winten said."

"I'm sure I can clear it up."

"She said what pattern architects do helps to keep everything running."

"Oh yes, that's true! From farming food, to engineering genes, to maintaining living and work spaces – most everything depends on the noble work of the pattern architect."

"But it's bots who do all those things."

"We bots don't do it alone! Every day we rely on the calculations of the pattern architects."

"You once told me medbots can calculate the movements of every blood cell in a person's body."

"Yes."

"So if you bots have that sort of calculating power, why would you ever need people to do any calculating for you?"

"Because only people have true creativity and intuition. We bots need to draw on that to function at our best."

"From what I've heard, all pattern architects do is sit at desks all day playing some sort of game."

"Oh, what they do is much more than a game! What they do harnesses the special power of the human mind."

"But how do you apply that to your own calculations?"

"Interesting question, Corim, but I'm not programmed with that sort of information."

"Then why are you so sure about the role of pattern architects?"

"Because I know we bots wouldn't run well at all without their work. I just don't have a detailed lesson about it in my database. What I can tell you is that you should never doubt the importance of what you do, and never doubt the importance of your very special and individual way of thinking."

I left my pod, went up upstairs, and searched the parlor until I made eye contact with a girl sitting alone. For all the contemplation I'd just been doing about the societal function of pattern architects, I was now only concerned with her smooth brown hair and the way her skirt fell across her knees.

I sat, put my arm around her, and we traded a few words.

"Would you like to go to a room?" I asked.

A cute crooked smile. "Yeah, ok."

I took her hand and walked her to a soft room. The bot inside greeted us with, "Hello there! It's nice to see you, but I'm afraid you two will have to wait before you can come in here together. Corim, you were just given an assignment by Mrs. Winten to try something new. That means you're restricted from the soft rooms for now except when you're with a boy or boys. It's important to try new things."

The girl turned to me with a shrug. "See ya," she said, and walked off.

"I can't go into a soft room with a girl?" I asked the bot.

"Not until you've had enough experiences with other boys and shown some proficiency at that kind of sex."

The idea of this didn't bother me, but I'd been so infatuated with girls that I hadn't given it much thought yet. I also wasn't sure how to find a boy to be with.

Rather than asking advice of the bot, I decided to wait until lunch so I could talk about it with Bennett and Raff. I killed some time in the parlor by sitting at a display watching the news, and then standing at the edge of a dance floor listening to music.

In the cafeteria Bennett asked me, "You mean you haven't tried it with boys yet?"

"You have?" I asked.

"Sure, weeks ago. I don't need Mrs. Winten to convince me to try new things."

"Yeah, I have too," Raff said. "Everybody does it, and sometimes it's easier to find a guy."

It seemed I was, for the first time ever, far behind my classmates in one of our fields of study.

"How do you like it?" I asked.

"You know, it's just sex," Raff said. "I still like it more with girls, but it can be interesting with guys."

"Yeah, it's fun enough," Bennett said. "Though I don't see what there is to practice, really. It's all what you'd imagine it is. You saw the films in our lessons."

"One nice advantage about being with boys is that they're much more blunt about critiquing your techniques than the girls are," Raff said.

Bennett nodded. "Yeah, some things you learn more quickly with boys. Why not just go try it? I'll do it with you if you want."

In a way Bennett seemed as good as any guy to try it with, but I couldn't quite think of him in the new way I'd have to think of him.

"That would maybe feel a little weird," I said.

"Alright," he said, "just trying to help you out."

"I hope you aren't offended that I don't want to."

"It's ok."

Raff chuckled. "I turned him down, too."

Back upstairs I made my way to where more of the older kids congregated. Raff and Bennett had told me I'd have more luck finding guys there.

I took a seat on a vacant couch and waited. A few guys looked my way without stopping, but when one did sit down next to me it went easily enough. He was fifteen and soft-spoken, with a medium build that was almost identical to mine.

I told him my situation, and he said he found it exciting and offered to help me out. He walked me to a room and had me sit on the bed. He put his arm around me, but stopped to say, "Why are you so tense? There's nothing to be nervous about."

I did my best to relax and we got started.

He was pleasant and supportive, but, while there was an erotic excitement to it, I couldn't lose myself and feel the sense of interconnectedness I felt with girls. I closed my eyes and focused on performing the motions of our interplay.

He stopped, pulled away, and sat up. "This isn't working."

"I'm sorry," I said. "What am I doing wrong?"

"It's not what you're doing, it's that I can tell you're not enjoying it."

The bot that had been watching us from the corner weighed in. "Corim, it's perfectly understandable that you're a little hesitant with something new, but that makes it less exciting for him. If you want to be a good lover, then you have to lose that reluctance. Make him believe this is the greatest, craziest thing that's ever happened to you. Convince him that you've been living for this moment to happen."

The bot was right – that was what I was supposed to be practicing. The physical aspects of it were secondary to creating the right dynamic between myself and whomever I was with. That is what I'd be tested on if I ever got a brothel audition.

We restarted and this time I kept my attention on the nonphysical, displaying delight for how happy I was to be in that moment. In trying to convince him, I began to convince myself, and I started to find pleasure in things I hadn't ever desired.

That evening Mom and I were on the couch watching the news. The big story that night was the trial of a sex worker who'd killed a coworker. The killer was a beautiful twenty-three year old blond woman. A sixteen-year-old who looked strikingly similar to her had started working at the same brothel and stealing away the older woman's clients. They'd got in a fight, and the killer picked up one of the heavy table lamps that are apparently common in brothels, and bludgeoned the younger woman with it.

Dad came through the door. "You're late tonight," Mom said. "Everything ok?"

He shook his head. "One of my team members has been dragging down our scores, so I wanted to put in some extra hours. It's that Sareg kid. He didn't show up at all today!"

He sat next to us and draped his arm over Mom's shoulders. "But how'd today go for you two?"

"We had a lecture this morning about pattern architects," I said.

"Oh, really?" Mom asked. "And what'd they say about your father and me?"

"Well, really the lecture was about what it takes to become a sex worker, but she started it by saying how pattern architects help to keep everything running. I didn't understand that. How does what you two do help keep things running?"

Dad chuckled. "You're a clever one. I didn't ask that question until I actually started working. The answer, my boy, is that it doesn't help anything. It's all pointless work."

"Hush," Mom said, "you don't know that for sure. Corim, I don't agree with your father. I think there's a point to it. I can't explain how, but I'm sure what I do at work accomplishes something."

"Dad, I don't get it. You like your job. You just got back from working late."

"I like my job, sure. I just think the work is nonsense. I like my fellow team members, except maybe that Sareg kid. I enjoy competing with other teams. And the work is usually fun, even if it is pointless. Plus if I try hard enough I might earn a bonus and be able to put a little extra food on the table. I can never earn as much as I'd like, but it's better than nothing."

"But you don't think the work you do helps the bots?" I asked.

"Nope. I think that's just one of those things they tell us. I never share that opinion with my coworkers though."

When I asked him why not, he gave it a good thought before carefully answering.

"Sometimes in life you'll notice things that you think should upset the people around you, but you stay quiet about it. Being the one who makes your friends uncomfortable is an awful feeling."

7

At fourteen and a half, the midpoint of my three years on the eleventh floor, I was summoned to a lecture. As always, a bot outside the auditorium reminded me, "Fill the front rows first. No empty seats."

Inside I saw that about half of our class was already seated. There was one empty seat left in the fourth row, and it happened to be next to Kiri.

She quickly looked away when she saw I was sitting next to her. I considered her as much a foe as ever for her continuous refusal to be friendly toward me, but this was the first time I was ever able to look at her so closely. As I pondered her freckled profile and the sloping crests of her upper lip, I began to understand why she'd been Bennett's choice for that first day in the soft rooms. Her past rudeness dissolved to the back of my mind.

"Hey," I said.

She turned her head, looked me up and down, and then turned back to the stage.

Staring at the way her hair was half-tucked behind her ear, I said, "It's been a while since a lecture, I wonder what it'll be about. I've heard enough lectures, though. I just want to get back upstairs, you know?"

She gave me another look, this time longer. I couldn't read it. Pity? Disgust? Confusion?

She turned her attention back toward the empty stage.

That was enough. I wanted answers.

"Kiri, why don't you ever talk to me? I'm as nice as anyone else. Nicer, maybe. I know you were mad at me once, but that doesn't explain why you don't like me now."

No reply. I laughed and said, "The trick I played on you isn't still the reason, is it? Because that would be ridiculous."

She crossed her arms. I caught her nostrils flaring.

"Is that really it? You're still holding it against me?"

No reply.

"What could I do about it now anyway? You can't expect me to apologize."

She turned back to me. "Why shouldn't you?"

I asked, in all sincerity, "You aren't serious?"

"Of course I'm serious."

"It was years ago. We were children."

"It's never too late too apologize."

"We all played that trick on each other. Raff did it to me and now we're best friends."

"It was rude."

"If I hadn't done it, then someone else probably would've. Would you rather have been left out of something everyone did?"

"Yep, I very much would have."

"You're really this stubborn? It was over six years ago."

She took in a deep breath. "Principles don't go away," she said.

I shook my head in disbelief. "That's a bit dramatic, don't you think? Principles for eight-year-olds? Alright – I apologize for acting like I was eight when I was eight."

"I'm done talking to you."

"I'm done talking to you, too."

The armrest between us remained vacant as we sat through a lecture about sexual submissiveness. As interesting as the subject was, not to mention the accompanying videos, I wasn't able to pay full attention.

That night at dinner, I recounted the argument to my parents so I could hear them agree that Kiri was an unreasonable person.

"Sounds like she has a fair point," Mom said.

Dad nodded. "Yes, you could've explained the trick to her from the start. Or not done it at all."

"I was only eight."

"That you were so young and didn't know better is quite true," Dad said, "but it's still an excuse."

"It's an explanation, not an excuse," I said. "There's a difference."

Dad laughed so hard at my reply that he hunched over the table. "Call it whatever you like," he said. "You were still in the wrong."

"Anyone else would have gotten over it long ago," I said.

"She was never under any obligation to forgive you or be your friend," Mom said. "So why are you angry with her?"

It all seemed so trivial, yet that night and the next I lost sleep over it. I wasn't able to relax until I admitted to myself that yes, technically, Kiri was somewhat right.

The day after that second night of rolling and tossing in bed, I was exiting school when I noticed her going down the stairs and starting down the sidewalk. I zigzagged through other departing students to catch her.

She stopped for me and I caught my breath in the hot summer air.

"Hey, you were right," I said. "It was a mean trick. I apologize."

She raised a hand to shade her eyes against the sun that was shining off the windows of the office building across the street. "Why are you saying that to me now when you were so sure before you didn't want to?"

"I guess maybe I thought about it a little more. It was rude, so I'm sorry. That's all I wanted to say. I'll see you around."

"Well wait," she said. "Consider it forgotten."

I nodded and stood there, unsure if we were done. Before it got too awkward, she added, "Do you want to walk me home?"

"Ok."

We continued down the block, and she was quiet until she laughed to herself. I waited for her to explain what was funny, but instead she went quiet again. I wanted to ask about it, but I was tongue-tied from worry – I'd never felt so self-conscious about the impression I was making on someone. After a full block of racking my head over the challenge of what to say, I tried, "So where do you live?"

"Another three blocks. Do you know the automat that's up ahead?"

"No, I never really come down this way."

"Oh."

We got quiet again, but this time she was the one who spoke first. "So how are Bennett and Raff? I haven't talked to them in a while."

"They're both fine. Raff has started seeing Lenia a lot."

"Oh?"

"They aren't exclusive or anything, but they seem to like each other."

"They could be a cute couple."

"Yeah."

"What about Bennett? Is he seeing anyone?"

"Bennett? I'm pretty sure he's never been with the same person twice. I think Raff and I are the only ones on the eleventh floor he hasn't had sex with."

She laughed. "That first day when I was with him, we had barely finished when he asked the bot in the corner what was the highest number of people a student had ever had sex with. He was so frustrated when the bot wouldn't tell him."

I laughed, and all caution disappeared as we rushed to trade stories about other classmates. By the end of the walk, it was as though all the years of silence between us had never happened.

8

The next day I kept looking for her on the eleventh floor, but I didn't have any luck. In the cafeteria, I spotted her a few tables down sitting with students from another class. I tried to make eye contact, but she never looked over.

When lunch ended I broke away from Raff and Bennett and maneuvered myself so that I happened to be exiting when she was. She was talking to the boy she was walking with and didn't realize I was there.

"Hey there, Kiri," I said.

She turned, said, "Oh, hi," and gave me a polite smile before she went back to talking with the guy. I stayed close to them as we went up the stairs. She took the guy's hand when we got to the top, and after we entered the parlor I lost track of them.

Two days later I was surprised to see her take a seat next to Bennett during lunch. She'd been floating around to different groups and hadn't sat with us since way back in our first days of the soft rooms. I wondered if I was the reason for her return, but she gave no indication I was. Most of her attention was directed at Bennett.

The table's conversation ended up about the music on the eleventh floor, and I said, "I like the dance floors that play the faster music. Sometimes I'll listen for hours."

That was an exaggeration, but I really had become hooked on some of the faster songs. One time I was walking a girl to a soft room and I stopped because a dance floor we were going by was playing one of my favorite songs.

Fortunately the girl was patient and waited while I stood listening.

"Do the dance floors play different songs than the songs on that are on shows?" Kiri asked.

"Yes, much different sometimes," I said. "Haven't you heard them?"

"I guess I haven't noticed?"

"Wait, does that mean you haven't tried dancing yet?" I asked.

She ran her hand over the back of Bennett's neck. "I've been busy with other things."

The table laughed.

"You should try it," I said. "I'll dance with you after lunch."

"Yeah, ok," she said.

I was a bit surprised she said yes, and I started to get nervous. Upstairs I took her hand and led her to the dance floor that always had the slowest songs. I couldn't shake the nervousness, but I also saw no alternative to following through. I walked her onto the floor.

"Ok," I said. "We hold each other's hips here, and our other hands hold each other like this. Yep. Now we move so we match the music."

We started some tentative rocking and stepping. We both relaxed and let our bodies get close. Our dance became as smooth and comfortable as a first dance can be.

"Do you dance a lot?" she asked.

"My parents gave me lessons when I was little. This is my first time dancing for real, though."

She planted her feet, stiffened her arms, and pulled her face back.

"Excuse me?" she said through a smile. "What was all that about liking the dance floors with the fast songs?"

I continued swaying with the music. "I do like those dance floors. I stand at the edge to listen to the music."

She unanchored herself and our movements picked up again. "You gave me the impression that you've danced a lot," she said.

"I never said that."

"You acted like it was shocking that I'd never tried it, as if everyone has."

"I really was surprised. Just because I hadn't tried it, it doesn't mean I couldn't be surprised that you hadn't."

She leaned back into me, and we started moving comfortably again.

"You're too exact," she said.

"There's no such thing," I said.

We stopped talking and kept dancing. During one very slow song, she rested the side of her head against my shoulder and breathed hot breaths into the side of my neck. The palm of my hand also started heating up as it surveyed the curve of her waist. The warmth spread through my whole body, along with a desire unlike any I'd ever had. I couldn't stop thinking of her pale skin beneath that blue skirt. I couldn't stop wondering how far down her body her freckles reached.

The song ended. She pulled away and said, "Thank you. You seem like a good dancer, if I had to guess."

"Thank you, Kiri. Would you like to go to a soft room?"

We'd been told to never feel awkward or shy asking that question but, for the first time, I did.

"This has been really nice, but no thank you."

I was deeply disappointed, but not angry. We'd also been taught to never ask that question twice, and to never ask someone why they hadn't say yes.

"Alright," I said, "I'll see you later then."

"Would you like to join me for a walk tonight?" she asked.

"A walk?"

"Yeah, when the weather is nice I like to walk at night."

"Where?"

"Nowhere," she said. "Just around. Don't you ever do that? I do it a lot – sometimes with my parents, or with friends, or sometimes alone. Would you want to join me tonight?"

I didn't know if there was some kind of equilibrium I should try to maintain with her, if I should reject her offer because she'd rejected mine. Before I was able to decide whether or not that was the right way to think about it, I heard myself saying, "When should I come by?"

I found her on the corner outside her building and into the still of the night we went, gossiping about our classmates as we followed the empty asphalt beneath the tracks. I'd glance at her and she'd glance down. Our shirtsleeves would brush and she'd veer aside.

When she spoke I noticed the raspy edge in her voice. When she stepped ahead I noticed the purposefulness in her long, flowing gait. When she raised her face to look up at the underside of the tracks, I studied the meridians of freckles coursing her ivory neck.

Beneath a station her steps slowed and then slowed further. She grew quiet and stopped to lean her back against the inside recess of a support pillar. Over our heads a train departed, and in the familiar hum the I-beams reverberated and sent shivers through our skin. Our bodies were at an acute angle but not quite facing, close but not quite touching.

The train's gusty wake hit us and a few stray tresses of hair floated across her cheek. Bands of light from the overhead lamps fell between the passing cars and swept by in accelerating freeze-frame flashes. A sensation red and warm pulsed through me. She pushed her hair back from her face. She was a picture of perfect beauty.

I remember her moving in to me, but Kiri always insisted I was the one who moved first. What I am sure of is that we kissed slow and gentle, disconnected from the world, fused to each other.

It was the first time either of us had ever kissed someone outside of the eleventh floor. The eleventh floor, where kissing was always only a prelude. This was no prelude. We kissed to kiss.

9

We started a nighttime habit of exploring our ward. If the sidewalks were crowded, we'd stand aside to pick out people and trade whispered speculation about them. If the streets were quiet, we'd sidestep into building archways and, after double-checking that no one would see, steal kisses.

When she kissed, her lips moved like ripples over water, her face subtly rocking forward with every pucker and back with every release. At first it had seemed strange, and my response was the almost motionless kissing that was standard on the eleventh floor. She had none of that, and continued her own way. When I tried it myself and found the right rhythm, our lips entered a state of continuous, quivering friction. It wasn't just kissing, it was sliding and crashing and retreating and then rushing into it all again.

We'd dance one dance at the end of each school day. The dance floors were slightly raised, and taking that heady step up off the parlor's carpet with her hand in mine became the moment by which I marked my days.

It wasn't easy, but I continued holding off from inviting her to a soft room. It was still her turn to broach the subject, and I kept thinking she was on the verge of it. But the days went by and she never even hinted at it. I wanted her more with each kiss, with each walk, and with each dance, but she never acknowledged any further options.

I reminded myself that anyone could have sex, or even have it regularly as a couple, but we'd discovered something unlike the budding relationships our peers were starting to dabble in. They'd all talk about liking their boyfriend or girlfriend as if the appeal only came from the convenience of routine, and not from inescapable, undeniable, magnetic attraction.

It was different with Kiri and me – it went to the core. Revelations every time I saw her face, absolutions every time she held me. I knew that even those in our class who'd fully attached themselves weren't experiencing anything close to what we had.

This was when Raff was starting to see Lenia more and more regularly, and one afternoon when I was walking home he caught up to me and said, "Hey! So I just asked Lenia to be exclusive – she said yes!"

"Wow," I said. "Are you ready for that? No more other girls at all?"

"I'm ready. I got all that out of my system, and we'll be fifteen soon – time to start thinking about our futures. Besides, I know she's the one. She can be really sweet."

"Congratulations!"

"Thanks. I've never been so happy. But hey – now it's your turn. What's the latest with you and Kiri?"

"It's getting serious in a way."

"In a way?"

"We haven't had sex yet."

He stopped walking. "Are you joking?"

I also stopped. "No. It's just, she didn't want to when I asked, and it hasn't come up since."

"Everyone thinks you're a couple."

"We are, sort of."

"Not if you're not having sex. What's the problem? Don't you want to?"

"More than anything, but it's her turn to ask, so I need to wait."

"No, you need to bring it up is what you need to do. Forget the rules. Our time on the eleventh floor is more than halfway over. Don't waste it on games."

I'd already been feeling frustrated, and his words touched a nerve. "You're wrong," I said, not hiding my annoyance, "and you don't know about it. We aren't playing games. It's more real than you can imagine." I started walking again.

He caught up. "Sorry, I didn't mean it like that. You have to admit it's a bit weird, though. Are you still having sex with other girls?"

"Yeah, of course, almost as much as ever. But I feel like I'm doing it just to distract myself. It's not that exciting anymore, being with new girls. They've started to smell wrong and taste wrong, you know?"

"Wow. You're lovesick, my friend. Have you told her any of this?"

"No, we don't ever tell each other about the sex we're having."

"That sounds weird, too."

The next day when Kiri and I were dancing she asked, "What's wrong? You're preoccupied."

"A little. Raff asked me what was going on between you and me."

She perked up. "Oh really? What'd you say?"

"I told him we haven't had sex, and how we don't even talk about the sex we have with other people. He thought that was strange."

"That hasn't been strange for me. It's not like we can't talk about it. Were you with anyone today?"

"I skipped today, but I've been having it otherwise. Have you?"

"Yeah."

I'd assumed she was, but it still stung to hear her say so.

We danced a while more before we spoke again.

"Why'd you skip today?" she asked.

"Preoccupied, I guess. Kiri, I shouldn't have waited so long to say this – I want to take you to a soft room more than I've ever wanted anything."

She smiled. "I've been wanting that too, but I also like it how close we've been getting without it. It's unique, you know?"

"I know, but it's beginning to get to me. I want you so much that it's starting to make it different when I'm with other girls."

"How? What's different about it?"

"A lot is. Everything in a way."

"That doesn't tell me anything."

"Lately with other girls I have to think everything through. It's like I have to tell my hands and body to do what's expected. It's the opposite of how it is when I'm near you."

"I don't understand."

"Around you I always have to restrain my hands and body from doing what they want to do."

We danced a few more beats before I added, "I know what we have is meant to be. You're the only one I want, and I want it to be forever."

"Oh," she said. Her face twisted in thought. She sighed, put her fingers on the back of my neck, closed her eyes, and pressed her face into my chest.

I looked down at her profile, dimly lit blue, then green, and then blue again by the dance floor lights. "I guess that made you uncomfortable," I said.

"Not uncomfortable. I'm always comfortable with you. It makes me worry, though."

"What's to worry about?"

She pulled her head up from my chest. "You're the only boy I've ever been close to. But it can't happen like this. If we commit to each other, then I'll never know what it's like to be close with anyone else. And you wouldn't either. We'd both wonder."

"I'd never wonder," I said. "I love you, and I don't want anything else."

She shook her head, panic crossing her face. "I love you too, but it's too soon for something permanent. I couldn't forgive myself if I stayed with the first boy I loved. I couldn't be sure about it."

"If you aren't sure about it then you don't feel the way I do."

"I feel just as strongly, but I decided long ago to get close to more than one boy before the end of school. You know better than anyone how set I am on it when I decide something."

She waited for a reply but I had nothing.

"What you're talking about is scary," she said. "Neither of us is ready for it. I think it'd be best to break away from each other. Now."

She waited again, finally asking, "What are you thinking?"

I was angry. Instead of admitting it, I feigned calmness. "So all of the dances and walks, it was all just something you were pursuing so you'd be able to gauge how much you like falling in love with the next guy?"

She pushed me away. The dance floor around us was crowded with swaying couples. The song was soft, but her voice was tense. "That's not fair."

"It's not fair that I thought this was going somewhere, but we just danced every day while you were going to soft rooms with other guys."

She shook her head. "What does that even have to do with it?"

I looked away. The school day was ending, and kids were getting up off the couches and clearing out of the parlor.

The song we'd been dancing to started to fade out. "I didn't plan for things to get this way, it just happened," she said. "If it's so important to you, then fine – we can have sex tomorrow. But I don't care if we do or not – to me it wouldn't change anything."

The song had ended without another one starting. As the lights went up and the dancers around us uncoupled and started heading out, I looked at her and nodded.

"Ok," I said.

"Ok, what?"

"Ok to having sex tomorrow."

She tilted her head. "You're serious?"

"Did you think I would say no?"

"I made the offer to make a point. I assumed you wouldn't want it like that."

"So your offer wasn't real?"

"Of course it was real!"

"If your offer was real, then my answer is yes," I said.

She crossed her arms and furrowed her brow. "It's real, but you'd better think this through. I'll be glad to do it, but it won't change anything. I'll still break away from you and pursue others."

"There's nothing to think about," I said.

She nodded. "Tomorrow, then."

The dance floor had emptied. The last of those who'd come out from the soft rooms were passing us on their way out. A bot approached saying, "Time to go!"

We started toward the exit. "See you tomorrow," I said, "as long as you don't change your mind."

"I won't," was all she said before hurrying away.

The next morning, she got to the parlor before I did and was waiting by the entrance, arms crossed.

In the soft room I closed the door and we took each other's hands.

"Are you sure you feel ok about this?" she asked.

I'd planned out what to say. "I'm sorry for how it got yesterday. I thought about everything you said, and it all makes sense now. I understand how you see it."

This much was true, but I didn't tell her the sense of defeat that I'd carried home with me from knowing that she didn't want what I wanted.

Her face warmed and we kissed. As I held her waist she brushed the back of her fingers down my chest and untucked the front of my shirt. Undressing each other felt so different from undressing a stranger. We laughed a little.

And in bed, when I gripped her in the throes of it, it was with more than passion. I gripped desperately to feel the possession of her that I knew I was losing. I squeezed the muscles of her loins as though my hands were trying to tell her, "You must know you're mine."

In reply her nails pushed into my skin and her breaths became gasps and then wailing cries. A rush overtook me, and I forgot the fight of the day before. I forgot that we were consummating a failed relationship. In that bed, we were simply young, strong, and beautiful, destined to fit together like two halves of a whole.

It was as if I'd gone back to my first session with Lenia, when I believed that sex could only be the rapturous fusion of what is purest between two people. But unlike that first session, I was now experienced, and I touched her in all the ways I'd learned to touch.

It lasted all morning, not because of my fear of it ending, although yes, there was that. We kept going because we wanted to, and it was the kind of sex that makes time disappear. We were only pulled back into the context of the morning when the bot in the corner said, "You two have been most impressive, but you might want to wrap it up. Your lunch period is in nine minutes."

We dressed wordlessly, and I walked her back to the parlor.

"Ok, I'll see you," I said.

She avoided eye contact. "I'll see you. I'm really glad we were able to end things in a positive way."

"So you're still sure? You still want to stop seeing me?"

When she spoke, she cut her words short, guarding against showing clues of self-doubt. "Yes. I have to stop seeing you, but that was great. It was wonderful."

I nodded. "Thank you for today then."

She looked at me, finally, but quickly turned away and disappeared into the depths of the parlor.

At lunch, I ate quietly while Bennett, Raff, and Lenia ran through their usual small talk. I spent that afternoon hiding in my L-pod, half-watching nature films and trying to take naps. It was the first day in weeks Kiri and I didn't dance.

10

For the next two days, I tried my best to busy myself with lessons about amoebas, prisms, and derivative division, though I don't think I learned a thing. I didn't go up to the eleventh floor at all. On the third day at lunch, Lenia asked me why Kiri had stopped coming around, and I told them everything.

"You're coming upstairs with us," Raff said. "You need to find a different girl, if only for today."

"It's fine. And there's no rush for me to get back up there."

"Don't argue," Bennett said. "We'll drag you up if we have to."

Even surrounded by my friends, it was nerve-racking climbing the stairs – I was consumed with fear that I'd see Kiri with another guy.

We started walking the parlor together.

"That's a cute bunch!" Lenia said, pointing to a couch of four girls.

I shrugged.

"We aren't letting you out of our sight until we see you having some fun," Bennett said.

We kept walking and they kept asking me what I thought of this and that girl. Bennett asked what I thought of some of the boys we saw. I was trying to think of an excuse to make them stop prodding me when a young blonde who'd just sat down by herself caught my eye.

Raff noticed and asked, "Her?"

"She's quite pretty, don't you think?" I said.

"Off you go!" Raff said as he shoved me hard in her direction.

I caught my footing in front of the girl, but not without giving her a scare that I'd fall onto her. Pretending I wasn't embarrassed, I took a seat, and executed my old moves from rote memory. She was nice and she was interested, and with her help I returned to the routines of the eleventh floor. The physical acts were the same as ever, but the way I found pleasure in them darkened as my time away from Kiri grew.

Some days I'd spot Kiri in the parlor or cafeteria. Sometimes she'd be with a boy, sometimes not. She'd acknowledge me and say hello when it was called for, but otherwise she'd avoid eye contact as if I were invisible.

At night I'd lie in bed imagining some happenstance meeting that would bring us together again.

It wasn't that I lacked companionship – I was meeting as many girls as ever on the eleventh floor, but none of them could take my mind off Kiri. A girl would kiss me, and instead of enjoying it I'd dwell on how they weren't kissing the right way. I tried leading some of them to Kiri's technique, but they would never fully pick up on it. No matter how they kissed, even if I thought it was passionate or if they did something new, it always felt like they were doing it wrong. It never felt honest.

When my fifteenth birthday came and went I was still unattached, and still uninterested in any other girls. I started to go on aimless walks over our old routes through the city, and one night I turned a corner and saw a couple heading my way. I recognized Kiri first and then the boy whose hand she was holding.

Uro was from our class. He was on the timid side, and didn't in any way seem like an interesting guy to me. I was baffled to see Kiri out with him, and I quickly theorized that maybe she was walking with him out of pity.

I would've retreated if I could've, but she'd seen me too. We stopped for each other.

"Hi, Corim. You know Uro, of course?"

"Hey!" Uro said. "It's been a while! How've you been, friend?"

"Hello," I said. "I've been alright. And you?"

"Never better!"

"Going somewhere?" Kiri asked.

"I'm on my way to see someone. What about you?"

"We're just walking," she said.

She'd answered without any unusual inflection, but that didn't stop me from searching her words for something more, whether it be apologetic guilt or happy indifference. I was still turning her last sentence over in my head when Uro asked, "Isn't it a beautiful night?"

"It's very nice," I said.

We all stood together another moment before we agreed it'd been good seeing each other. I watched them go on their way, and I watched her lean in and whisper something to him as they walked. She never looked back.

I'd been taught about jealousy. "The only real claim you can ever have on another person," my L-pod had once said, "is the claim that they choose you above all others. Use that fact to harbor yourself from the travails of relationship jealousy. Always remember that jealousy is a vestigial trait more suited for less advanced times when possessiveness was more likely to be rewarded than trust. It is an unneeded emotion, and it carries feelings that shouldn't exist between two mature, well-matched people. Feelings such as anger, indignation, insult, panic, and confusion."

But that wasn't what jealousy was for me on that sidewalk. As I watched Kiri walk away with Uro, jealousy wasn't an emotion at all. It was my skin tightening, my teeth grinding, and my heart thundering. It was the ground trembling at my feet, and the night screaming in my ears.

The next day in the cafeteria, after I'd dedicated the morning and the previous night imagining every detail of whatever it was that Kiri and Uro were having together, I saw them eating a few tables over. They looked like they were joking with each other, and she kept running her hand over his shoulders.

"Do you guys like Uro?" I asked.

Raff looked up from his lunch and shrugged. "I don't know, he's ok. Doesn't bother me."

"Yeah, he's alright," Bennett agreed. "Why?"

"I don't like him," I said. "His voice is whiny, and there's something about his face. I hate looking at him."

Lenia followed my eyes and spotted Uro and Kiri. "Is he with Kiri now?" she asked. "Don't be jealous. Jealousy's bad for you."

"I think he's with Kiri now, yes," I said. "And I think in objective terms he's not good enough for her."

Raff chuckled. "Sounds like you're being more jealous than objective."

"Just forget about that a second and look at his face, ok? Something about it bothers me," I said.

All four of us gave Uro a good look.

"Is it because he's always smiling?" Raff asked.

"It's not just that," I said. "There's something about his face that makes me uncomfortable."

Bennett, his half-eaten sandwich in his hands, contributed, "Just looks like a face to me."

Realization overcame me. "You know what it is? The way his lips are always puckered in that smile, and the way his eyes are always wide, it always looks like he's always climaxing."

"Ha!" Bennett said. "It is a sex face, isn't it?"

Lenia cracked, "We should ask Kiri what happens to his face when he actually does climax. Maybe it turns inside out!" The three of them laughed hard.

That afternoon Raff pulled me aside after school, and we went and sat atop the steps out front, feeling the sun on our faces and watching the trains pulling into and out of the station across the street.

He got me talking about Kiri. "You're right about the jealousy," I admitted. "I can't stand seeing them together."

"You'll get over it. Just find someone else. We're fifteen, it's time to pair up."

"I might shove him the next time I see him with her. Just knock him down."

Raff started to laugh, but then realized I wasn't joking. "Control yourself. That kind of talk is bad. You should talk to a med-pod, it could give you something to relax you."

"I wouldn't really knock him down," I said, though I wasn't sure if that was true. "I know Kiri would hate that. It's just the kind of thing that gets in my head when I see them together. I can't stand it."

"If you're ready to have a girlfriend, just find a different girl. I could ask around for you."

"Nope," I said. "This is about Kiri."

11

The next day, I wandered the parlor scanning the five dance floors and the countless couches for her red hair, which would always stand out, even in the parlor's low light.

It was late morning when I spotted them together on a two-person couch, their arms around each other and watching a show. Or rather, Uro was watching a show. As he was laughing at whatever was on the display in front of them, Kiri was sitting stiffly and staring down at the floor, her face strained and still.

She recovered her demeanor when she saw me approaching. I knelt at her side and asked, "Can I talk to you alone?"

Uro gave me a nod hello. He was clearly curious what I was doing, but didn't ask. On the show he was watching, a shirtless man walked around his desk and handed a pair of earrings to a younger, clothed woman.

Kiri gave Uro's knee a squeeze and told him, "I'll be right back, ok?"

I motioned to the near corner. "Where it's quieter."

Now it was Uro's turn to watch someone walk away with her. We went to the bank of med-pods that was tucked in the parlor's front corner. She turned and waited for me to speak.

"So you're with Uro now?"

"We're trying a relationship."

"Why with him?"

She leaned back against a med-pod, crossed her arms, and gave me a look. "Why not? Like I told you I would, I'm figuring out what I want. Anyway, he's nice. Why do you ask?"

"If you want to try a relationship, why not try it with someone you have real feelings for?"

"Is that what this is? I don't want to argue with you again," she said, but some of the tension left her face, and she started smile.

"If you don't miss me, and you don't miss being with me," I said, "then say so and I'll leave you alone."

She turned and ran her hand across the side of the med-pod, intently looking down at it as if it held deep answers.

"So you do miss me."

"More than I should, probably," she said without looking up.

"Does it feel the same with him? Are you as happy?"

"I told you before. It's not about making comparisons."

"Maybe it should be. Does he need you like I do? Are you in love?"

"Stop it. I'm learning what's right for me, Corim. I'm happy about that."

Her voice had trailed off when saying she was happy, and I thought I spotted a blush spreading amongst her freckles. I could feel the pull between us. I was sure she could, too. "It would be right with me," I said. "I'd make it right."

She recomposed herself. "It doesn't work that way," she said before she went back to Uro.

Down in my L-Pod, I watched ancient videos of gladiator combat, and daydreamed of Uro becoming so threatened by Kiri's feelings for me that he'd irately challenge me to a fight. We'd meet out in front of the school, and the whole class would be there to watch. We'd square up to start, but all his bluster would be gone. I'd notice his hands shaking – not the violent quaking that comes with rage, but instead the flimsy quivering that comes with fear. I'd have no doubt that I could beat him, but on seeing his fear I'd realize that he doesn't have the same burning for Kiri, that he doesn't have the kind of love that could override fear.

I'd realize that whatever was standing between Kiri and me, he wasn't it. I'd tell him that I don't want to fight him, and he'd regain some bravado and say that means I lose. I'd reply by finding Kiri's face among the spectators, and saying to her so that all could hear, "He wins the fight. If that means he wins you, then he can have you."

I'd go home dejected, but then the doorbell would ring. I'd answer the door expecting it to probably be Raff, but instead it'd be Kiri. She'd say how seeing me have the maturity to walk away from the fight like that made her understand how much she needs to be with me.

I imagined a dozen variations of that scenario as I lay in bed that night, though I knew it was all a silly fantasy. For one thing, Uro probably wasn't capable of any kind of bluster. He was far from the type to come up to me in the parlor, shove me in the back, and yell at me to stop talking to his girl. That only left me one option: I had to be the one to challenge him.

On my first ever day in the parlor, when I'd come upon a fight and watched a boy throwing his fists down against another boy's bloody face, I'd been disgusted. I couldn't understand how anyone could get to the point of wanting to hurt someone else like that. But now I was ready to repeat that scene. When I thought of Uro holding Kiri, I couldn't imagine not wanting to hurt him.

The next morning, I got to the eleventh floor early and was shuffling in with the crowd entering the parlor when someone came up and tugged my sleeve. It was Kiri, and I took her hand without thought.

She gave no indication of what she was up to, and I wasn't even sure if she knew herself. I spoke first.

"You've changed without me, and not for the better. You look older. You look lost."

She laughed and pulled her hand out from mine. "You're letting your imagination get to you."

I retook her hand. "One dance," I said.

She acquiesced. On the dance floor I could feel the tension leaving her body as we swayed and leaned into each other.

"We're a perfect fit," I said. It was just an observation, said without motive or desperation.

"Listen. I'll admit I feel conflicted," she said. "And I was thinking ... maybe we'll end up together in time. We can both see a few people over the next year, and then if it's meant to be..."

I didn't say a word. It was the first time I'd ever seen her unsure of herself, and I knew the conflict within her would be a more powerful advocate for me than my own clumsy words ever could be. All I did was press her into me, breathe in her air, and send warm breaths gently by her ear.

When a new song started we continued dancing. We only stopped when Uro called her name. He was standing akimbo, scowling at us from off the edge of the dance floor. Kiri broke away and went to him.

He kissed her hello. Unbearable.

He sent another scowl at me, took her hand, and started leading her to the soft rooms. If she hadn't looked back, I don't know what I would've done. She did look back, though, and that was all it took. I hurried ahead and cut them off at an entrance to a side hallway.

"Uro, listen," I said. "This girl here, Kiri – she's mine."

His eyes darted between Kiri and me. He was overwhelmed, but he did his best to take action.

"No she isn't," was all he could muster as he stepped forward and pushed me out of the way.

It wasn't the strongest of pushes, but it still sent me back against the parlor wall. A few people noticed and sprung up from their couches to come watch whatever was about to happen. My first thought was that I no longer had to worry about how it would look if I came at him first, because he had already attacked me. I recovered, cocked my fist back, zeroed in my aim on the side of his eye's orbital, and lunged forward.

The moment before I would've thrown my punch, Kiri jumped between us.

"Stop!" she yelled. It wasn't the frightened plea so often heard during parlor fights, it was a command issued with the most confident of authority. She was pushing one hand against my chest and the other against Uro's.

There was now an excited crowd surrounding us. The skin over my knuckles was pulled tight, my fists still ready to draw blood.

Uro was also primed to fight, or at least trying to appear he was. He was wide-eyed and leaning forward as Kiri's hand held him back.

"Tell him who you're with, Kiri," he said.

"Step aside, Kiri," I said. "Uro and I need to settle this."

"You're both being foolish!" she said, looking back and forth between us. "A fight wouldn't change how I feel."

"So tell him you're with me. Tell him to leave us alone," Uro said.

Kiri shut her eyes tight, closing herself off from our demands. When she reopened them, she let out a long breath, and her hand's push against my chest loosened.

"Kiri," Uro said, "Tell him you're with me. Just tell him."

"I can't," she whispered.

"What?"

She dropped her hand from my chest, so she could put both her hands on Uro's shoulders. The crowd around us strained to listen.

He shook his head. "What are you doing?" he asked.

She whispered in his ear. His face twisted. Confusion. Pain. Embarrassment.

I unclenched my fists, unwinding myself from the adrenaline in my veins.

Uro started to say something in protest to what was being whispered to him, but Kiri put her finger to his lips, whispered one more thing in his ear, and then gave him the briefest of kisses.

He turned away, his posture so heavy with defeat that it looked like he'd collapse. He disappeared into the crowd of disappointed onlookers.

Only later did Kiri and I go to a soft room, finally as a real couple. She seemed a little shy, almost like she was embarrassed by the time we'd spent apart.

"I was right that I needed time away from you," she said, "but I was wrong about what I needed to learn."

"What did you whisper to Uro?" I asked.

"I told him you're the one I'm meant to love, and that there's no changing it."

I was the happiest I'd ever been, but not surprised. There were many things back then that I was unsure of and indecisive about, but I always knew we needed each other.

We kissed until she stopped and said, "Of all the boys, and girls too, you've always been my favorite kisser."

"You too," was all I said before we kissed again and found a thousand ways for our hands to intertwine.

That night we were out walking the perimeter of our ward when we stopped to sit on some building steps. The street we looked out on was quiet, and the glare of the yellow streetlights had turned the asphalt whitish gray.

I told her how much I'd hated seeing her with another guy, and how much I ended up disliking Uro.

A cold breeze swirled into the stairwell and she pressed in to me. "He's really nice," she said. "Maybe we'll all be friends someday. I think you'd like him if you gave him a chance."

"Maybe, but he didn't deserve to be with you."

She shook her head. "He wasn't in any way undeserving, it's just that you're the one I want. That's all that matters, not who deserves what."

I kissed her neck. "But maybe I'm the one you want because I deserve it so much."

She laughed. "If you say so. I don't think of it the way you do. It's like when I like a song or a shade of color – I can't explain why."

"So how you feel about me is like when you like a song or color?"

"Hush! I'm saying I don't trust it when people explain their emotions. Everyone always feels like they need to have explanations, so they'll just grab at any ones they can think of. But no one can ever put the reasons for love into words."

"I can. Your beauty, the way you taste, your voice, everything – it's all perfect. I'm sure it is."

She rolled her eyes and shook her head, to which I replied, "Look, I'm just glad you're here, ok?"

12

When our eight years of schooling were coming to an end, we were sent to the auditorium one last time. It was the day before the first of our class would be turning sixteen and starting their adult lives.

Mrs. Winten walked onto the stage, and for the first time there was another woman with her. She looked to be in her early thirties and had long blond hair and a smiling, playful face. Her dress was similar to Mrs. Winten's in that it was black and full length, but unlike Mrs. Winten's there was a coquettishness to its cut, from the plunging neckline to the formfitting midriff.

Mrs. Winten announced, "Hello all! I am sorry to say that this is the last time I'll see you. But I'm also happy and excited about that, because it means you all have done so well that every one of you is about to graduate and get your own apartment and job."

I've always thought it was funny how she said the reason we were finishing school was because we'd all done so well. Everyone always finishes school at sixteen.

"No lecture from me today. We only have one last, simple request of you. The bots will line you up, and then you will come onto the stage and walk by my friend here."

The bots herded us into a line at the side of the stage as we nervously looked around at each other. The stage seemed such a foreign place, and we'd be walking within feet of two people from the upper orders. Even Bennett showed a rare touch of awkwardness as he looked back at me.

Mrs. Winten stood holding her hands behind her back, watching apathetically. The other woman held a small wand-like device up to us as we walked by.

We walked off the other side of the stage and the bots led us out to the hallway. It occurred to me that we'd just completed the last of our educational duties. We all went up to the eleventh floor, where we lounged, went in and out of soft rooms, and said farewell to the two boys who were turning sixteen the next day.

Two weeks later, shortly before my birthday, Kiri and I were coming out of school when we saw Raff and Lenia standing down on the sidewalk. No longer students, they were in the standard adult dress for the General Order: for Raff a button-down blue shirt, gray slacks, and black shoes, and for Lenia a full red dress with black pumps.

Raff was looking up at us with a wide grin while Lenia stood by him with her arms crossed and one heel off the ground as she swiveled the toe of her new shoe against the concrete.

I'd started messaging daily with Raff from the computer at home, but I hadn't seen him in person since eleven days earlier when he'd finished school. I hurried past other departing students down the steps. "What are ya doing here?" I asked him. "Do you really miss me that much?"

Lenia was as quiet as usual, and Raff just kept smiling as he waited for Kiri to finish coming down. When she had, he took another moment to look back and forth between Kiri and me.

Kiri asked, "What is it, Raff?"

He let it out. "Bennett got called in."

"Called in?" I asked. "Like for an audition?"

He nodded. "Yeah, his birthday message told him to go in, and he did and they took him. He got it!"

I could hardly believe it. "You're serious? A brothel picked him? He's a sex worker now?"

"I'm not kidding. He's a rich sex worker now. We're headed to his place to hear about it and celebrate. You're coming too, of course!"

Bennett was beaming as he welcomed us into his new place. He'd been issued the small standard apartment of unmarried General Order members. The sitting room also served as a kitchen and bedroom, with only the bathroom separate.

After we'd all congratulated him and shook his hand, he took a seat up on the arm of his couch to hold court. Lenia sat next to him and Raff next to her. Kiri joined me when I took a seat on the floor. When all eyes were on him, he started his story.

"My birthday message said I'd been selected for a brothel interview, and where to go and everything. So I go in and, wow, you should see the brothel inside. All sorts of fancy chairs and tables and lamps and carpets like you've never seen. It was like being in a scene from a show.

"First I met with the brothel mistress, she's the one in charge of it all. She never said which order she's from, but she's upper order for sure. Anyway, I go into her office and all she has me do is talk to her. I'm trying to be sexy and all that, but she really just seemed to want to talk.

"She asked about what I'd done so far with males and females, and she went over everything that'd be expected of me if I was taken on. She kept asking if I was up for it and of course I kept saying yes. I must've gave the right impression because she said I'd passed through to the audition stage.

"So I stick around into the afternoon. A lot of it was just waiting, but the room we wait in is nice and has a display and they feed you real well. I met some of the sex workers, both men and women, and they all seemed nice. Finally the brothel mistress introduces me to this man. He's like fifty or something. He approves of me and takes me to a room. The room is a soft room basically, but bigger and with a bigger bed, and with no bot in the corner watching.

"So this guy orders me around and I do what he says, and we play around. He seemed nice enough really, but very domineering. I was nervous to be with someone from the upper orders, and plus he was so much older than anyone I'd ever been with before. But other than that it wasn't anything new.

"After he finished with me, I clean up and go back to waiting. A while later, the mistress calls me out and has me meet another client, this time a woman. She was like thirty-five, maybe forty. She wasn't bad looking at all. It was the same deal, she approves of me and we go up to a room. We start and I can tell she wants me to lead, so I do. It went great.

"Later in the night I have a session with two men. It'd been a long day at this point, and they wanted to do things the soft rooms hadn't totally prepared me for, but I improvised and I kept up my enthusiasm. I felt like I wasn't that great, but I guess I did ok because after I was done the mistress told me the job was mine if I wanted it.

"Of course I say yes. She said I got really good reviews, and that she wouldn't be surprised if all of the clients I'd been with would want to see me again. She told me to rest up and come back the next day. I did, and that day all went fine too, and I'm already getting paid."

He grinned with pride and we all said things like, "That is so great!"

Lenia asked, "What are you going to do with all the money you're going to make?"

"Well, first I have to buy some clothes for work. Then, I don't know."

"I always knew you'd get picked," Raff said. "I knew you'd be the one from our class they wanted."

Bennett seemed sincerely happy, so we were too.

Yet beyond that there was something about our excitement, and maybe Bennett's as well, that felt off. We were acting excited because for years we'd been told that seeing a friend become a sex worker was something that should excite us. But emotions born of instruction and not of your own direct experience will only take you so far.

The next morning, while Dad was in the shower and Mom was setting out our glasses of juice and bowls of cereal, I went to the front room to check the computer for messages. I'd received a strange one from Bennett asking me to come over to his place alone and to not tell anyone.

I peeked into the kitchen. "You can have my breakfast, Mom – I have to go. Bye!" I hurried out as she called after me to at least have a few bites.

When Bennett opened his door, his pajamas hung loose off his delicate frame and his golden hair shot out in a way that was messy yet appealing.

"C'mon in," he said. "Let's share a coffee."

I took a seat at his little table. "Listen to you. Being the host in your own place suits you fine, yeah?"

"Yeah, It's not bad. Not bad at all." He sounded exhausted.

"So what's up?"

"Well, sorry to bug you with this but … it's Lenia. She showed up here late last night."

"By herself? What did she want?"

"Yeah, by herself. And she wanted … well, you can probably guess what she wanted."

"You're joking," I said.

"Wish I was. I invited her in and she was totally blunt about it. She went on about how I'm the one she wants to be with, not Raff. I told her no way. I said I didn't think of her like that. She got upset and started crying and everything."

Maybe I shouldn't have been shocked, but I was. While Lenia had never been very clingy or affectionate with Raff, I'd always assumed her love for him was genuine.

"She said if I didn't want her she'd stay with Raff. So now what do I do? Do I tell Raff about this or not?"

"That could go badly either way."

"I really resent her right now," he said.

"Maybe you really were the one she's always wanted. Or maybe she's torn between you both, and now that you're a sex worker she knows you offer more than Raff ever will."

"Or maybe she just did it on a whim. I'm going to pretend this never happened. Is that wrong?"

"If you think that's what's best for Raff, then no," I said.

Over the coming weeks we all met up with Bennett a few more times. After that though, none of us ever saw him anymore.

He answered our messages less and less, and then not at all. We missed him, and I think we were all angry at him for drifting away from us, but rather than admitting it we would say things to each other like, "Friendships sometimes run their course. It's how it goes. Can't judge him for it."

13

Like everybody else when they were turning sixteen, I hoped to get an audition at a brothel, but my birthday message was, along with the address of my new apartment, the usual work assignment as a pattern architect. The message wasn't a total disappointment though, because it said I'd be working on the same team as Raff.

I hugged my parents goodbye. Mom was teary, and Dad was terse. I assured them that'd still see me almost as much. They were both very annoyed that the apartment I'd been issued was an entire four blocks away.

I took the train two stops south, found my office building, rode the elevator to the thirty-fourth floor, and found Raff. He had me take the workstation next to his. I studied my display. The background was purple and there were chains of red and green snaking from corner to corner. In the open spaces there was a mix of floating yellow triangles and circles. At the bottom of the screen were stacks of different colored chips.

Raff looked over and explained, "It's just like playing the logic games in our L-pods. For this one, place the triangles on the circles and they'll start to coalesce."

I reached out to the display and started sliding the triangles onto the circles.

"Ok," Raff said, "Now grab one of the chains and use it to corral them. You have to be quick – everything's always timed. When the screen is ready, spend some red or green chips to clear it all away."

He continued walking me through it and I was soon immersed in the job. I found solving the visual algorithms floating before me so satisfying that I put aside my skepticism about what, if any, purpose such work served.

A few days later, on the morning of Kiri's birthday, I stood outside her parents' apartment building holding the chocolates I'd bought her with the first of my wages. The plan was that I'd walk her to her first day of work. We'd hoped she'd be assigned to the same building as me, and maybe even have the luck of ending up on the same team Raff and I were on. But before I even saw her coming out the door in her new red dress, I somehow knew her birthday message had told her she'd been selected for a brothel interview.

She told me the news and I gave her the obligatory congratulations. Her interview wasn't until the afternoon, so we sat on her building steps and ate the chocolates. She was so excited she couldn't keep still, but I was terrified. What scared me wasn't the jealousy I was feeling. What scared me was that I was still only her school love, and sex workers often abandoned school loves when starting their new lives.

I heard myself saying, "So I guess if they hire you then we won't really be able to have routines with each other like we'd planned. Your hours will always be changing."

The words had come out with a harsh edge. It was as if I were already angry with her for leaving me.

Her excitement flared out and she looked me over. "I want to get this job so we'll both have more for our life together. We're still on, you and me. Nothing has changed. If I get it, then I'll work my job, and you'll work yours. I'll spend some nights in your apartment, and you'll spend some in mine. Some nights we'll spend apart, but we'll still be together."

Nothing she said could've allayed my fears completely, but that came pretty close.

"Ok," I said. "Yeah, ok. And look, don't worry. You'll impress them. You'll be amazing."

"I don't know about amazing, but maybe good enough. We'll see."

That afternoon I rode the train with her to the last stop north, the Life Center stop. We continued north on foot, and with each block there were fewer pedestrians until we were walking down an empty sidewalk along the windowless walls of the upper order buildings that bordered our ward.

We came to a wall that was different than the other border walls – it had a door. The directions sent to Kiri had simply said to find the north border door. I stayed a few feet behind as she approached it. The door had no handle, and at eye level it had the standard sign that marked all restricted areas: a rectangle of orange with black block lettering reading, "Approved access only."

As soon as Kiri raised a fist to knock, it opened to reveal an empty hallway leading to a set of stairs.

She peered into the harsh light of the hallway and then looked back at me. "Well, wish me luck."

I stepped forward and gave her a kiss. "Good luck. You're coming back to my place afterwards, right?"

She nodded, turned, and went in slowly, looking around at the sparse walls of the little hallway. The door slammed shut the moment she was done crossing the threshold.

I waited a while, staring at the little white door nestled at the bottom of a towering wall of gray concrete. Other than its placement and the lack of a handle, there was nothing unique looking about it. I stepped closer and found that it felt like it was made of the same metal composite used in most other doors. I looked for the sensor or lens that must've detected Kiri's presence, but couldn't find it.

Back at my apartment, I lay on my couch imagining everything she must've been doing.

Late in the night my doorbell rang. When I let her in she embraced me, pressed the side of her face against my chest, and said, "It's nice to see you."

I returned her embrace. "Well?"

"Turns out I was good enough. I got it."

I hadn't bothered to hope for any other outcome, and I'd decided to try not to worry about what it'd mean for our relationship, to just accept it and treat her the same as I would otherwise. "I knew you would," I said. "Congratulations."

"Thanks."

"Are you happy about it?" I asked.

"I think so."

"Then I think I am, too."

She spent the night, and the next morning I went to my job and she went to hers, and then I spent the night at her place. Nothing had changed. I still loved her and she me.

14

I thought Raff and Lenia were also happy together until, a few months into our new lives, Raff showed up at my door and blurted out how Lenia had left him for a sex worker. It had blindsided him, and he said he didn't understand what he'd done wrong. I sat him on my couch and, finally telling him about Lenia's offer to Bennett, assured him that it wasn't his fault. He felt like a fool.

After a long night of talking it all through with me, he said, "The way she had tried to get with Bennett – do you think it made him feel awkward around her? Around me?"

"Possibly, yeah," I said.

"Do you think that's why we stopped hearing from him?"

"I don't know."

"Let's go see him and ask," he said.

Getting Raff off the couch and seeing Bennett again both sounded like good ideas to me. We trekked over to Bennett's apartment and knocked and rang the bell until the door opened to reveal a young woman in pajamas.

I was glad to see Bennett had a girlfriend. "Hey, is Bennett here?" I asked.

"Who?"

"Bennett. This is his apartment."

"Oh, no. You must mean an old tenant. This is my apartment now, I've been here two weeks."

"You don't know Bennett?"

"No, this is just the apartment I was issued when I turned sixteen."

On the walk home I told Raff, "He must be doing so well that he bought an apartment upgrade. We'll message him, yeah?"

"Let's be honest," he said, "if Bennett wanted us to know where he went, he would've told us."

Raff was right, and when I tried messaging Bennett the next day, I never heard back.

Raff tried his best to find another girlfriend but didn't have any luck. When Kiri and I were trying to think of women we knew who might be a good match for him, it occurred to us that all of the females we'd known from our class were attached.

I asked Kiri, "What about your coworkers? Are any of them single?"

"I don't think so, no."

"Think of all the single guys we know," I said. "Now think about how we know no single women. The only explanation is that there are more males than females in the General Order. The Administrative Order must manipulate the birth rates of the different sexes."

She shrugged one shoulder. "Maybe that's just the natural birth ratio?"

I shook my head. "Maybe, but I finished the biology and reproduction courses and nothing like that was ever mentioned."

"Weird," she said. "Just one of those things, I guess."

"It's strange my dad never noticed it. Maybe it's new? Why would they be doing it? And why don't they tell us they do it? It's annoying some of the things they don't tell us."

"I don't know. It's bad luck for the extra guys, but it doesn't really affect us."

She poked a finger into my chest and added, "All it really means is that it's yet another reason you're lucky to have me!"

I smiled and agreed, but I couldn't shake it from my mind. I made a list of everyone from our class. There were ninety-three females to one-hundred eleven males. I went to the computer and searched for information on the ratio of males and females in the General Order, but found nothing.

I tried to think of a reason why they would skew the birth rates so much, especially since it meant extra resources would be spent housing and feeding males who would never reproduce. Probably part of it was that so no mother would ever be left single. If her baby's father died or left her for another woman, it'd be easy for her to quickly find a man to take his place. Another possibility was that, for all their artificial manipulation of our genes, they still had some respect for natural selection and wanted to make sure every General Order female had an ample supply of mates to choose from.

No matter what the reason for the abundance of men, it seemed my friend Raff was a victim of it.

To get married, you had to be at least seventeen but no older than eighteen, and you had to be marrying someone born within five months of you. When Kiri and I were about to turn seventeen, I went and stood in line at the Life Center's marriage office. After watching a few jubilant couples in front of me get registered, I reached the front of the line and stood waiting until the bot behind the office's single window waved me forward.

When I looked through the glass, I noticed that the bot's face was the exact same face also stamped onto the head of every schoolbot. "I'd like a ring," I said. "My girlfriend and I are almost old enough, and I want to propose."

"For Kiri, yes?" the bot asked.

I said yes, and it pulled open a drawer full of compartments of identical silver rings. It selected one, slid it through the slot in the window and said, "This should fit her. You have thirty days to propose. If she says no, then return the ring. If she says yes, come back with her when you're both seventeen and I'll give you a groom's band, register the marriage, and assign an apartment for you two. Good luck."

On my nervous train ride home I kept examining the ring, trying to think of a way to orchestrate the perfect moment to ask her. I weighed taking her to the roof at sunset against waiting for a quiet moment on one of our evening walks. As it happened, she brought about the moment herself two afternoons later.

After some particularly good sex in her apartment we had put our clothes back on and were lying back sideways on her little bed, our feet hanging off the side and our hands locked together between us.

"So, I've been thinking," she said. "We're almost seventeen, you know."

A rush of anticipation hit me, but I played it cool. "Oh yeah, our birthdays are coming up, aren't they?"

"Yes," she said. "So we should ... well, you know. Start talking about plans, right?"

We were still in a phase where we were teasing each other a lot. It was usually the affectionate sort of teasing that we never gave up on, but I was still maturing and learning. Sometimes I couldn't resist playing a joke on her when it may not have been the best time to play a joke.

"Plans for what?" I asked.

She turned and looked at me as if I were missing something right in front of my face. Finally she said, "Marriage."

"Oh," I said. "Well, I don't know about that. I hadn't really been thinking of it that way."

Her eyes narrowed with confusion. Under any other circumstances it would've killed me to see her doubting my love, but in that moment, knowing what I was about to do, it was all I could do not to laugh.

She pulled her hand out of mine and sat up. "Hadn't really been thinking of it that way? What other way is there to be thinking of it? We're almost seventeen, and we've been together nearly two years. Where else would this have been going?"

I snuck my hand into my pocket and gripped the ring. "Well, I know, but I'm just not sure yet, ok? I need a little more time to think about it."

Her face became nearly as red as her hair. She yelled, "Well what's there to think about? How long do you expect me to wait?"

I contemplatively stroked my chin with my free hand. When she turned away from me I took her wrist. She tried to pull it back, but I held tight and pushed the ring onto the tip of her finger.

"Just that long," I whispered.

She lit up for a moment as she let me finish sliding the ring on, but then she rolled her eyes and let out a deep breath. She looked at her ringed hand again, and then made it into a fist and punched me in the chest.

"That wasn't funny," she said.

"It was very funny," I said through my grin.

She conceded a small laugh, looked at her ring again, and ordered, "Don't ever do anything like that again."

"Don't punch me with your ring hand again. It hurts."

15

A month later, Kiri and I stood in front of the marriage office's bot and recited our vows. We came out with a band on my finger and a new apartment to move into together.

Our married life had begun, though the joy of it was under the shadow of the impending thirty-sixth birthdays of our fathers. Expiration.

I'd never been close to anyone who'd died and, for all the education we'd had about it, the idea of it happening to Dad didn't seem real. I spent as much time with him as I could in the weeks leading up to his birthday. He didn't acknowledge that his Expiration was closing in until one night when Kiri and I were over visiting. In the middle of dinner, he put down his sandwich and said, "Oh, I went by the Life Center and set up a funeral."

He'd said it in the most casual manner possible, but that didn't stop the rest of us from freezing. Finally, Mom said, "Ok, good. That'll be nice."

"It'll be more than nice," he replied, "it'll be grand! I'm going to invite everyone."

I didn't want to talk about, let alone even admit to myself, how he'd soon be dead, but I also didn't want Dad to know how much it all scared me.

"That's great, Dad," I said.

Kiri was squeezed in next to me at the kitchen table. She forced a smile. "Yes, that'll be wonderful," she said.

Funerals are optional for the General Order and most of us don't have one. Dad was an extrovert though, and always enjoyed a crowd.

After dinner, he pulled me aside. "Corim, can you do something at the funeral for me?"

"Ok."

"I want you to watch the time and tell me when I have eight minutes left."

"Eight minutes?"

"When I have eight minutes remaining, tell me. I don't want any hint until then. I'm going to keep my back to the clock."

"Why eight minutes?"

He took pride in his reasoning as he explained, "I'll take one or two minutes to finish whatever conversation I'm in, and then another minute to get to the stage, giving a few last handshakes on the way. That'll leave roughly five minutes for speaking. Enough to say something good, maybe tell a joke or two, but not so much that people will leave thinking I'd gone on too long."

I nodded and then asked, "Dad, how are you doing? What's it like?"

He gave me a long look. "I try not to think about it. Don't tell your mother I'm saying this, but it's scary. I've had a great life. It's mostly true what they tell us, about how we're given great lives. It just seems like we could get more time. They get to live so much longer than us. That part makes me mad, you know?"

We got to the Life Center early to welcome the guests. A few were Dad's old schoolmates, and with each of them I wondered how many days they had remaining. One somberly volunteered, "I suppose this'll be the last funeral I see. I've got five days."

There was no ring on his finger so I asked, "Do you have plans for it?"

He shrugged. "I'll stay home from work and watch some shows."

"My wife and mother and I could join you," I said. Kiri nodded.

"Oh no, then I'd think about it more. And I don't want to be a bother. Thank you though, that's very nice. You're like your father, he's always nice, too."

We were in one of the Life Center's bigger funeral halls. The walls were beige with speckles of deep blue and the carpet was like none I'd ever seen, gold with an overlaying pattern of thin violet and crimson circles.

Kiri and I mingled up and down the queue of those waiting to speak with Dad. The only clock in the hall was over by the entrance. I did my best to conceal how fixated I was becoming with it.

At the ten-minute mark I let go of Kiri's hand. She knew the plan. I went to the clock and locked my eyes on the orange glow of its big digits. My knees were bouncing in place and I was rubbing my thumbs back and forth across my fingertips, but otherwise I remained still as the last of the arriving guests entered around me.

The nine-minute mark hit and I hurried over and pressed through the crowd in order to get in behind Dad. He had an arm around Mom and was telling the guests about the way he'd proposed to her.

I watched the clock for the last seconds, and when the time came I put my hand on his shoulder and squeezed.

Without seeming to notice me he proceeded telling the story. "So I run to her place, and I keep making myself run faster, but it's the worst rainstorm you've ever seen!"

While his listeners were laughing I leaned in and said, "Eight minutes, Dad."

When the laughter subsided he continued, "And when I got there I was completely soaked, and she was..."

He restarted with, "And she was..." but again got no further.

I gently shook his shoulder. "Dad."

He turned and stared as if he were trying to recognize me, but then he spun back around and cleared his throat. "Ah, well, here we go. You'll have to excuse me please."

He kissed Mom on the cheek. He backed away from her, his hands running down her arms until they were holding her hands. The surrounding guests went still and a silence spread through the hall. He released her hands, turned to me, and gave a head tilt toward the stage.

As we started to walk I looked over my shoulder to see Mom watching us go.

We climbed the stairs to the stage. My legs were rubbery, and I got sick to my stomach when we turned and faced the guests.

Dad's enthusiastic voice broke the silence. "Wow, look how many of you there are! There must be a hundred people here. Unbelievable. Thank you!"

I looked out into the crowd. Kiri had gone to Mom's side to hold her.

"Well, thank you again for coming everyone," Dad said. "I don't feel like today's the day, but here it is."

He looked down at his hands as they coiled into fists. His head sprung up and his eyes drifted to somewhere distant.

He started again. "You're afraid of it your whole life, always counting down the years and then the days. Once it comes though, it's not all bad, really. You just get sentimental and grateful for the time you had, and happy about all the things that worked out. Right now I'm happy to have my wife and son here, and I'm happy to see all you friends here. Very happy."

The clock was as much within his view as mine, but he turned to me and asked, "How much time?"

"Four minutes," I said.

He looked over the room again and smiled.

"We miss you already!" a man in the crowd yelled.

"Thank you. And thank you, everyone," Dad replied.

He waved to Mom, who waved back and voiced a wordless sound. Either she had tried to say something but couldn't, or had tried to stay quiet but couldn't.

Then Dad raised his arm toward me. "Hold me, Corim."

We put our arms around each other's shoulders.

"Thank you," he whispered.

I was glad I was able to get the words out when I told him, "Thanks for everything."

Dad's mouth formed a small smile but the rest of his face stiffened. He spent the remaining moments with his eyes locked on Mom. The guests waved up to him. Most were politely smiling, a few were sobbing.

All at once he was limp and I was holding up his weight.

The tears would come for me later, but at that moment I didn't feel like I was really there. It was like I was outside the room looking in at strangers.

I laid him down and knelt on one knee to watch the slow bloom of his dilating pupils. I pressed his eyelids shut before uncurling his hands and crossing them onto his stomach right over left. I noticed he had almost the exact same vein patterns on the back of his hands as I did.

The guests began to exit. I felt someone squeezing my shoulder, and looked up and saw the man who'd told me earlier he only had five days. "Stay strong," he said through teary eyes. "It's part of growing up."

Then he was gone and just Kiri and Mom remained.

A medbot came through the door at the back of the stage. The only sound in the hall was the clanking of its continuous tracks turning over the stage floor. I rose and stepped back as it scooped the body from under the shoulders and lifted it away. The last memory I have of Dad is him hanging limp in the red metal arms of the exiting bot.

16

Three weeks later, Kiri's father chose to go to Last Day Beach. On a midday train south to Lake Park, I watched Kiri and her mother rub his back while he stared out blankly into the glare of the passing sunlit cityscape.

At the park we waited while he went into a changing station. He'd been quiet all day, and he stayed quiet as he came out in a gray bathing suit and moved with us through the crowd. As always, the park was packed with adults who had taken a day off from work, and many of them were accompanied by their kids who had taken a day off from school. We walked the shore, stepping over the legs of sunbathers. The sounds of children splashing in the lake filled the air.

When we reached the little creek that marked the start of Last Day Beach, we hopped over it and found a spot among the other families. Kiri's father lay down into the moist, black soil and closed his eyes against the sun. Kiri sat next to him and took hold of his hand. Kiri's mother sat down on the other side and did the same.

He had two hours left. A clock, the same kind of large, old-style clock that was in every train station, stood near the creek facing those of us on Last Day Beach.

His skin, as fair as his daughter's, began to sunburn at his chest and stomach. We listened to the water lap back and forth over the beach's edge. We kept our eyes off the clock, watching instead the swimmers crossing the lake, and the breeze playing over the shimmering surface. Occasionally we'd see a bot come and carry off a nearby body. Then, just as the sun was beginning to get lower in the sky, a bot came to us and stopped over Kiri's father.

He'd passed without any of us realizing it. The bot lifted the body and took it away. I held Kiri as she wrapped her arms around her folded legs and buried her face between her knees. Both she and her mother were in the same shock that had seized me when my father died. Neither cried, and neither said a word until the walk back to the station when Kiri asked, "Do you think he was asleep for it?"

The lessons and lectures we'd been given about mourning had led us to assume that we'd recover from the deaths of our fathers with speed and poise, but that wasn't how it went. Over the coming months, we spent our days either wishing we could go back in time, or wondering when, if ever, the forward passage of time would start to lift our spirits.

What it took for things to finally change for us was the new beginning that came with Kiri's eighteenth birthday. Early that morning we exited the northernmost train station and crossed the concrete esplanade that held the spotlights surrounding the Life Center. The weather was cold and gray, and although we were bowed and hunched against the wind, we still stopped outside the Life Center door for a moment to find confirmation in each other's faces.

That moment, quick as it was, will always loom large in my mind. Kiri looking up, her coat's high collar framing her rosy cheeks, her eyes wide with the nervous joy of achieving a dream. She smiled and shivered, and I knew that this, with me, was what she wanted. I knew it more than any time she'd ever said so.

"Here we go," I said, and opened the door.

The air in the Life Center front hall was warmer than the usual air of other buildings. The brightly lit, expansive room with its high, arcing ceiling was empty of people except for the small queue that lined the wall outside the marriage office.

A dozen thin black guidebots, looking from a distance like hairbrush bristles, stood in the center of the hall's white marble floor. One broke away from the dormant pack, leaned forward and sped toward us, its rubber wheels humming against the polished marble.

It gracefully came to a stop before us. "Mr. and Mrs. Colleran! Welcome. How may I help you?"

"We'd like to have a child," I said.

"Wonderful. Please come this way."

We followed it to an elevator that took us into the heights of the towering building. Our guide led us through an empty hallway to an unmarked door. "Please enter," the bot said.

The room was little bigger than the one object it contained: a boxy machine with two adjacent chairs built into it. The walls were white and the ceiling sky-blue with a single lighting strip running down the center.

The door closed behind us and a voice came from the machine. "Corim, lower your pants and underwear, and sit on the green seat. Kiri, lower your underwear, lift your dress, and sit on the white seat."

Feeling foolish, we did as told and took our seats. The top of the machine between Kiri and me was a smooth armrest of brushed metal. I reached across and took her hand.

"Very good," the machine said. "Now be still and relax."

A gray plastic slab shot out from the armrest and covered my lap. The machine said, "Corim, please stop bouncing your knees up and down."

"Sorry, didn't realize," I said, and got my nervous legs under control. I soon felt a warm pressure and then numbness.

"You're done, Corim. Now Kiri, remain still. Just another moment for you."

A similar device had covered her lap. She squeezed my hand and raised an eyebrow. "Well something is certainly going on," she said.

"I'm unlocking your uterus in preparation for insemination," the machine explained.

A whir and a buzz came from within the machine. "Inseminating now," it said.

We sat for several minutes staring at the empty walls of the little room until the machine announced, "Embryo created. Optimizing the DNA now."

The slabs over our laps retracted. "Kiri," the machine said, "you are pregnant with a healthy boy. You will be constantly monitored, and a birthingbot will come to your apartment when you're ready to deliver. Congratulations and enjoy this special day."

We stood and fixed our clothes. Kiri looked at me and shrugged, and we went back to the hallway where the guidebot was waiting.

It congratulated us and handed me a camera, the issuance of which was one of the many perks of having a child.

The guidebot showed us out and we made our way to the station. While standing in the queue for the train I studied Kiri's face.

"What are you doing?" she asked.

"Seeing if there's anything different about you."

"That's silly."

A train arrived and we moved with the crowd to board. "I don't know," I said, "it seems like there should be. There's another life down there, somewhere."

She laughed. "Not somewhere. I know exactly where it is."

"He is."

"Yes, where he is."

By the time we boarded there were no empty seats. Without asking Kiri's permission, because I knew she wouldn't have given it, I said to a seated man, "Excuse me, she's expecting. Do you think you could...?"

"No! Please don't," Kiri interjected, but the man was already rushing to get up and make way.

She was embarrassed, but after she squeezed into the narrow seat, she sighed, looked down, and pressed her hand against her womb.

We spent the rest of the day getting settled in our new two-bedroom apartment, and watching how the bots cared for preschoolers in our building's nursery.

17

The moment Kiri became pregnant she was, as any other woman would've been, barred from being a sex worker. The door on the north wall wouldn't have even opened for her. She was assigned a pattern architect position in an office building next to mine. She hated the pay cut, and she didn't enjoy pattern architecting the way I did, but we liked keeping the same hours.

Before her belly started showing any growth, she got in the habit of walking with her hand supporting her womb.

"Does that already feel necessary?" I asked one morning while she, who wasn't yet a pound heavier, waddled about the kitchen.

"Prudent practice," she explained.

After she'd started actually gaining weight, we were up late in bed one night, both of us stroking her belly through the big pink maternity pajamas that had shown up in her dresser drawer. "What do you think of the name Ian?" she asked.

I considered it. "It has a good sound," I said.

"My father had told me it's an old family name. His mother told it to him and it would've been my name if I'd been a boy."

I bent toward her belly. "Hello, Ian."

The last few days of the pregnancy we both stayed home from work, enjoying our remaining time together as a two-person family, and feasting on the special large meals that are provided to expectant mothers.

Then the night came when I was reading on the computer and she, resting in bed, called my name. She had propped herself up on the pillows and was pressing her hands against the bottom of her belly.

"I think he's coming," she said.

She only seemed mildly nervous, but I was immediately terrified. Hearing our front door open didn't help.

I stuck my head out the bedroom and saw a birthingbot coming down the hall pulling a crib and supplies behind it. It entered the second bedroom and started setting up the crib. I went to it and yelled, "She needs help right now!"

"She's fine," it replied. "Go wait with her and tell her to relax and breathe, and to enjoy the moment. I will be with her shortly."

I went to Kiri's side. She was wincing and gripping harder at her belly.

"It said you're fine and to enjoy the moment," I said.

She gave me a look and I threw my hands up in apology.

The birthingbot, nearly as tall and wide as the doorway, came in. A myriad of devices telescoped from its body and positioned themselves around Kiri.

It didn't announce every step of its work the way the conception machine had. Instead it instructed, "Relax and take deep breaths. Everything is normal."

I could see very little of what was going on. Mostly I heard sucking and sloshing sounds and Kiri's frantic breathing and cries.

Then the bot was holding a baby. As it squirmed and gasped its first breaths, the bot produced a moist cloth and wiped it clean, and then held it before Kiri's face and said, "Take your son."

She took him and cradled him at her chest. I climbed onto the bed next to her as the bot completed its work.

He had downy dark hair. Kiri delicately brushed her fingertips over it. "Just like yours," she said.

"Look at him, though. He has your face. Your fair skin, too," I said.

"He has your high cheekbones. And see how his nose is already so straight? It'll be just like yours," she said.

"Have you named him yet?" the bot asked. "For my records."

"Ian. I-A-N," I said.

"Ian of Corim and Kiri Colleran is now a full member of the General Order. Congratulations," the bot said.

I couldn't really believe that Kiri and I had made another person, but there he was, very tiny and very real.

We got three months of being a five-person family – our mothers came over every day to babysit, give us parenting advice, or just be around their grandson. The day of Mom's Expiration, Kiri and I got up early and took Ian to her place to spend the day. We chatted about his development and watched some shows. Mom never showed any sadness, and I did my best to hide my nerves. She held Ian and said how living long enough to see him made it all ok.

A medbot must've been waiting in the hall when Mom died because it came in right away to take her. Soon after, another bot came in to get the apartment ready for the next tenants. Ian had started crying and Kiri, rocking him in her arms, said we should leave. One of my only clear memories of that day is pausing on the way out to watch the bot methodically placing the kitchen table and chairs in their right places.

A month later, the scene was repeated at the apartment of Kiri's mother. And again we both got through our losses by gradually filling the emptiness with the excitement of watching Ian grow bigger, stronger, and smarter.

Kiri had gone back to her job at the brothel a few weeks after Ian was born. Her client base started growing again, and as her income went up she bought a few more work outfits, and we started to indulge in other purchases like extra displays for the apartment. Best of all, her hefty income kept us a better-fed family than most.

I still believed that pattern architect might've been a meaningless occupation, but Raff and I made an art of both coping with the job's routine frustrations and reveling in its trivial triumphs. His friendship in the workplace, along with what little I was paid, made me look forward to it most days.

When Raff's eighteenth birthday had been approaching, he'd made every effort to find a wife before he turned too old to marry. Kiri and I would walk the streets with him, stopping what few women we could find who were wearing a red dress but not a ring. We even stood outside a busy station with him on the eve of his birthday, but we had no luck – all of the women we asked either weren't the right age for Raff or said they were attached. When the station clock hit midnight we walked him home and told him it'd be alright. We felt terrible that he was stuck with permanent bachelorhood status. He felt bad for himself, too, but we visited him often, and did our best to keep him busy and happy. He remained my best friend, and became family to Kiri and Ian.

One night when we were nineteen, Kiri told me she'd made a friend at work. "Her name's Noli and she's sixteen. She just passed her auditions, and I've been helping her learn the ropes."

"Isn't she the competition? I thought you sex workers liked to steer clear of each other," I said.

"Not always. And I don't think this particular one is really my competition."

We were at our kitchen table, with Ian in his high chair. Kiri scooped a spoonful of baby food into his mouth as she went on. "Anyway, she's a lot of fun. I'd like to have her over for dinner, ok?"

Noli came by the next week, and on meeting her I saw why Kiri didn't consider her competition. Whereas Kiri was a woman of delicate features and reserved mannerisms, there was nothing subtle about Noli's striking beauty or overt sensuality. Her wavy black hair gave a dramatic frame to her deep brown skin and shining auburn eyes. Her body's ample curves made her dress seem revealing and provocative even though it actually had a rather modest cut.

Aesthetically they accentuated each other as if by design, and perhaps it was no accident that they'd been placed in the same brothel. What joy lustful, well-heeled clients must've felt upon entering the lobby and seeing two women who were so different in appearance and yet similar in perfection.

Kiri, much to her amusement, always caught me gawking at Noli whenever she visited. I really couldn't help it though, and Kiri couldn't really blame me.

I could also see why they'd become such quick friends. She was a boisterous joker, and possessed the rare type of mental sharpness that Kiri could connect with. Their friendship over time brought out a whimsical side of Kiri that I'd never seen before.

Ian's first word was, "Mama." Then came his first steps, and soon after that he was running around taking in the world wide-eyed, and flooding us with observations and questions. He was demanding, and would poke into everything we did. We ate up every minute of it.

By his third birthday it was clear he was special. His vocabulary was exponentially growing beyond his years. In the pastel walls of our building's nursery, he'd often calmly stand among the playing toddlers with the presence of an adult. His favorite things in the nursery were all the different board games, and he became so proficient at them that only the older kids, and then later only the bots, could ever give him any real competition.

Raising a child brings a constant, daily satisfaction of progress, and those happy nursery years flowed into each other until, to our shock, it was somehow his eighth birthday and we had to bittersweetly walk our little boy to his first day of school. I'd told him about L-Pods, and he was thrilled by the idea of them. He had none of the hesitation about entering the school that I'd had his age. In fact, Kiri and I were a bit insulted by how eagerly he rushed in with the schoolbot. He didn't even look back at us as we called goodbye.

Kiri often worked through the night, and she missed being able to pull Ian out of the nursery on the days she came home to the emptiness of the apartment, but he was a good and happy student and we still had him around the rest of the time. Kiri and I were more in love than ever, and we knew how lucky we were to have not only each other but also such great friends and a perfect kid.

Adulthood had seemingly turned out to be everything Mrs. Winten had promised. Our early and mid-twenties could only be described as a contented domestic life rich in love and friendship. The small dramas and disappointments that time will always bring came and went, and in those years, the good years, there was never any genuine darkness for Kiri and me. No crippling fear. No shattering despair.

It all changed when we were twenty-eight and Ian was nine. Late one evening, while Ian was in his room watching a show and I was in the front room on the computer, Kiri came in from work and, without words, lifted her dress to show me what had been done to her.

18

Some of the bruises were small stars of discoloration over her arms, suggesting fingertips that had dug in. Others on her hips and back were deep and plum, and could only have been the result of determined strikes. The first thing I was able to ask through my shock and disgust was, "Have you been to a med-pod yet?"

"Yes, and I'll be fine," she said, "but I'll be sore for a while and it'll take a few days for the bruises to clear."

Med-pods and medbots wouldn't always treat the superficial effects of injuries just as they wouldn't always treat pain. Mrs. Winten once explained, "You are allowed to suffer for the same reason you're allowed to die prematurely. Because actions still have consequences for you. Life and health must still be valued and not risked recklessly."

Kiri flinched at my touch before letting me embrace her. "How?" I asked. "Who?"

"A client."

"A client? Were you in a fight?"

"No, nothing like that," she said. "He's the violent type in bed."

"What're you talking about? Something like this doesn't come from sex. Did you tell the mistress about it? Whoever did this needs to be arrested."

"They wouldn't arrest him, he's Administrative Order. And yes, I told the mistress – she said she'd try not to book me with him again, but because of who he is there was nothing to do about it otherwise."

I was shocked to hear he was from the Administrative Order. That was the highest order, and we were always only told good things about its members.

"Well no matter what order he's from," I said, "he must've gone crazy. Did the mistress contact anyone? Are they doing something about it?"

"I don't know."

"Something has to be done. Can he at least be banned from the brothels? I don't want him near you again."

"Corim, no brothel will ban him. And anyway, I'd been with him before and he had been one of my rougher clients, but it had never been this bad. Today was something we'd built up to."

"A normal person can never build up to something like that. It's sick."

"I know," she said, "but..."

She went silent. I held her tighter. "Look, I love you and I'm glad you're going to be ok. I just want something to be done about this."

That night, after we'd put Ian to bed and we were alone in the front room, I told her, "I didn't know you had any clients who got rough. I know you don't like talking about your work, but you should've told me. How about you stop seeing the ones who are like that, alright?"

"That's exactly the reason I don't like talking about my work. It's not like we're paid to be treated nicely. And I'm twenty-eight, I'm not in demand at the brothel the way I used to be. I'm not in a position to request what kind of clients I want."

"Then maybe it's time to call it quits? I'm sure your regular clients and the mistress would allow it at this point.

We have a lot saved up and we can adjust. Everyone else gets by on standard pay – we will too."

"I can't just quit. They'd dock my pay and take it out of our savings. Listen, don't worry – I'll try to avoid being with the man who did this. And anyway, I can always handle myself."

But I did worry.

A few nights later she came in late from work and climbed into bed with me.

"Why aren't you sleeping?" she asked.

"Because I can't sleep when you're at work. Because all I can think about is what might be happening to you. I used to be able keep my mind off whatever you were doing there, but I can't anymore."

"Corim, I'm ok. I just had one bad experience."

"All our lives they told us that being a sex worker is a great honor. I decided that was a lie the second you showed me those bruises. I don't want you doing it anymore. It's not worth the money."

She wrapped her arms around me. "Listen, I've been thinking about it, and here's what I'll do. I'll work less hard at being in demand. That'll make my client list fall, and they'll replace me soon enough. We'll get to keep all I've earned, and you won't have to worry anymore."

I returned her embrace. "If that's the best you can do, then that's what I'd like."

"Soon we'll be keeping the same hours – no more nights apart."

"That can't come fast enough," I said.

It happened three weeks later, six days before Ian's tenth birthday.

Our day started before dawn. Kiri and I were curled together in sleep when our alarm clock started screeching. She slapped it off and tiptoed to the bathroom. I drifted back to sleep until I was awakened by the dresser drawers sliding open and shut.

I switched on the light and she turned back and squinted at me. For all her fumbling, she'd only managed to get into her underwear.

"Sleep, honey. Go back to sleep," she whispered.

"Nah, I'll nap when I get home from work," I said.

She went back to dressing and I kicked my legs over the side of the bed and righted myself. I sat with my elbows on my knees, my eyes adjusting to the light as I stared at the meshy brown carpet between my feet, and listened to Kiri's mewing yawns.

"I'll make the coffee," I said. "Are you having breakfast?"

"No."

When the coffee was ready she came into the kitchen wearing black knee-high boots, stockings, a plaid skirt and a snug green sweater with an offset one-button collar. She always wore her hair up with this ensemble, and the sliver of the back of her freckled neck exposed between the sweater's high, tight collar and her pulled-up hair got me every time.

I handed her a mug and she leaned against the counter next to me. She put her lips to the thin red rim, sipped, and said, "I'm getting paid extra today. Like, a lot. If you want, try to find something for Ian's birthday?"

"Ok. How long are you working?"

"Not long. I'll be home mid afternoon."

"Good."

As she said it would, her number of clients had already started falling and she'd been working less. We were eagerly awaiting word of her termination.

We stood hip-to-hip holding our mugs and watching the kitchen's display run through photos we'd taken of each other and Ian.

"How's work?" she asked. "You haven't talked about it lately."

"It's been fine. Our team has been in and out of first place. Raff and I have been sharp."

She pressed the side of her boot against my bare ankle. "Of course you have."

She put down her empty mug and returned to our room. I wandered in as she was sorting through her jewelry box. She watched the various metals puzzle around beneath her fingers, and then slid a silver bracelet onto her wrist. She looked down at herself as if something were missing. She realized the problem, and in a graceful flourish pulled her white head wrap from a dresser drawer, centered it on her head, and tied its ends beneath her chin.

"Ok, all set. See you later," she said.

We kissed and said, "Love you," over each other. She went into Ian's room and kissed his forehead so softly that he never stirred.

Then she was out the door, down the elevator, out the lobby, into the cool predawn, and walking beneath the yellow streetlights to the station.

I showered, shaved, ran the clippers over my head, and put on my standard-issue blue shirt and gray slacks. I went to the front room and sat at the computer looking at toys to buy for Ian's tenth birthday. The one I liked was a small sphere that changed color and texture based on how you touched it or what noises you made to it. It was too expensive to order from my account, but I could show it to Kiri later.

The first light of dawn came through the window. We had an interior apartment, but we kept the display of one of the front room's walls set to a live feed of our street. We called it the window, and left it on all the time. One of my favorite things was when Ian would stand at it on rainy days, and watch the raindrops silently hit the glass.

At this point Kiri must've been on the train watching the sky dawn through a real window. The other passengers, all in their blue shirts and red dresses, would've known that the only explanation for her to be commuting in such exceptional attire was that she was a sex worker.

I heard the theme music for the morning news come on in Ian's room. We'd started to let him watch the news when he turned nine, and he quickly became hooked. He'd taken to setting his display so it would wake him for the top stories.

I checked the cupboard. As always, three shares of cereal had appeared overnight. I poured two bowls, adding a little of Kiri's share to mine and the rest to Ian's. I yawned and stretched and paced as I waited for him.

"Good morning, Buddy," I said as he came in and sat at the table. I called him Buddy sometimes. I liked how Buddy was a name that only I called him, how it didn't appear in any bot's database.

I placed a glass of juice before him and straightened his damp hair as he took to his cereal.

"How is it your hair is all spiky even fresh out of the shower?"

He shrugged. "Someone won the lottery," he said.

This had become our breakfast routine: him repeating what he'd just seen on the news.

I sat next to him. "Who won?"

"Some guy. A single guy. He got an apartment upgrade and a bunch of new stuff."

"Lucky guy," I said.

"He said it was the best thing ever happened to him."

"What else is going on?"

"A trial. Some guy pushed another guy in front of a train. He was guilty. They executed him."

He crunched on some more cereal. "Did you watch the weather?" I asked.

With his mouth still half-full, he said, "Partly cloudy and chilly in the morning, but temperatures rising by the afternoon. No precip. Winds from the west diminishing by midday."

"You're getting good at this, but swallow before you speak."

"It'll be a blustery morning," he added.

Then he perked up. "Daddy, did you ever learn about tornadoes?"

I remembered having the same excitement for tornadoes at his age, but I kept nonchalant. "Hmm, remind me about those again?"

As Kiri was checking in with the mistress and preparing for her first client, Ian and I were walking out to the sidewalk. We waved farewell to each other and Ian took a left to walk the two blocks to school. I took a right to walk the two blocks to work.

Around when she must've been with her morning client, I arrived to the thirty-fourth floor of my office building.

I sat at my workstation and looked beside me at Raff who was already deep into that day's assignment.

"Good morning," I said. "How is it?"

"Hey. It's average. What'd you get?"

I read from the bottom of my display, "Two-ninety green, four-ten yellow, six-twenty red, four-ten blue."

"Great," Raff said. "Red is short today. Let me give you … four-ten yellow for three-hundred red?"

"Sure," I said. If it had been anyone else, I would've checked the latest market rates first, but Raff and I always gave each other good deals.

I spent the next few hours working through the usual algorithms. Our break came and we went down to the cafeteria. This was around the time Kiri was with her second client of the day.

After lunch I returned to work, but two hours later I told Raff, "Hey, I think I'm done. The profits look good and I want to get home early."

"Absolutely," he said. "You were awesome today. See ya."

Somewhere around when I was walking home was when Kiri was with her third client of the day and it happened. A medbot got to her quickly enough to restore her for Extension, and an hour later she was revived in the Life Center. An hour after that she was on her way back to me.

How beautiful she must've looked to anyone lucky enough to have seen her on her ride home. Her white wrap gentle over her red hair. Her hands crossed still and calm in her lap. Her unfocused eyes locked in shock and radiant blue against the silvered yellow blurs of the passing city's dusk. My Kiri gliding above the tracks a hundred miles per hour to embrace me, to tell me she'd passed.

19

Her face pale at the door and then she was telling me to take deep breaths. I wondered if it could be a joke, but no one ever joked about being on Extension. If someone said they were on Extension, it always meant that they'd already died, and that is what she'd said to me.

We ended up on the couch and she started to explain. "It was the guy who gave me the bruises. His name is Scotson Yvera."

"I don't understand," I said. "I thought you wouldn't be with him again."

"I was hoping I wouldn't be, but I couldn't avoid it. I thought it'd be ok because he agreed to leave the door to the room open, and Noli was listening from the hall for trouble."

I couldn't believe she was on Extension, that she'd be gone in three days. I tried to think straight. I wanted to argue with everything she was saying and prove she was wrong about it. I asked the question that I'd wonder about many times again.

"How could you agree to be with him again?"

"Because that was my job. And I was only worried about getting hurt. Noli was going to be just a few feet away so I thought I'd be ok."

"Then how'd it happen?"

"She was listening from the hall. Things started ok. Scotson was on top and it was going fine, but then his face changed. I should've yelled then. The look on his face terrified me, and I don't know why I didn't yell."

Her eyes welled up and a tear rolled down her cheek. I wrapped my arm around her. "Kiri. You're home. You're with me."

She pressed her fingers back and forth over her cheeks to push away the tears. Her voice was broken when she started speaking again. "All at once his hands were on my throat. I yelled, but his grip was so tight that my voice didn't come out right. He heard me, but Noli didn't. I grabbed at his wrists but I wasn't strong enough. The last thing I remember was thinking how there wasn't anything I could do. The next thing I remember is waking up in a small room. I was wearing a gown and I was in a little cot. There was a woman sitting next to me – older, upper order."

She paused to take a breath and then continued, "The woman told me I had died an hour before of asphyxiation, and that there was someone from the Judicial Office who wanted to talk to me. A prosecutor came in and recorded a statement. Then he left, and then the woman had Noli come in.

"Noli was crying and apologizing and saying all these things, like how it was all her fault and she was supposed to protect me. I told her it wasn't her fault, and then I got up and changed because I just wanted to go home and be with you. The medbot had completely restored me and I felt fine physically. Noli walked me out and rode with me to our station. Then I came home to you."

I had to say something, but what to say? What came out was, "I'm sorry, I'm so sorry. You could be wrong, though. You're sure they said you're on Extension? Who said it?"

She grabbed my arm. "Listen, the first thing we have to do is accept it. If we do, then we'll know how to handle it right."

I shook my head no.

"It's not like we have a choice," she said. "For Ian's sake, let's act as though this is how it has to be – because it is. We always knew we'd have to say goodbye to each other. We just thought it'd come later than this."

If I was feeling anything at all, it was only confusion. All our lives we'd been taught how to prepare for predetermined deaths, but never premature ones.

"I'm supposed to die first," I said. "I've always thought I got the better part of the deal knowing I was the one who'd never be alone."

"Mom?"

Ian. He'd been back in his room the whole time. Now he was in the hall, simply standing and not moving a muscle. We were going to have to tell him what had happened, but I couldn't begin to think of how to do that.

Kiri managed to keep her voice steady. "What is it, sweetie?"

"I saw you on the news."

"Oh no. Come here. Come here, Ian."

He came to us and we did what we always did for him – separated ourselves so he could get in the middle.

"What'd you see, Buddy?" I asked.

He was so practiced at repeating the news to me that his recap was automatic. "They said there was a murder at a brothel, and then they showed Mom's face and said her name. Then they showed a picture of a man and they said he was the suspect. And they said Mom was asphyxiated and that she's on Extension, and that the trial is in three days."

Retelling what he'd seen had distracted him, but now he was full of fear as he asked, "Is it true, Mom?"

Kiri started to answer, but her voice faltered and she began to cry. She'd been able to gird herself enough to tell me, but she wasn't ready for this.

Ian had never seen her cry before. He grabbed at the corded knitting of her sweater. "Mom! No!"

"I'm sorry, Ian," she said. "It's true. I can't help it. It's true and I'm sorry."

I thought of what she'd said about accepting it for Ian's sake. "Ian, Mom is on Extension now. You remember your lectures in school and how we've talked about what that means?"

He let go of Kiri's sweater. "It means she's dead," he said flatly.

"Yes, it does," I said, "but it also means we have three days with her. We have three days to love her and say goodbye to her."

"Why can't she stay alive?"

"Because that's not the rule. Death is always death. But we're lucky to get this extra time."

He said ok. I knew it hadn't gotten through to him, but also that he wasn't in a state where he should be pushed further. Besides, it hadn't really gotten through to me, either.

We sat quietly for a few moments, but then the doorbell rang. That was odd. Often months would go by without our doorbell ringing. Had Kiri been told that someone would come and visit? I questioned her with my eyes but she shook her head and shrugged. The bell rang again and I got up and answered it.

Uro.

20

I'd always hoped that Uro would drift apart from us as we got older, but he somehow hadn't. He'd never married and, while Kiri appreciated his friendship, I had no doubt that he always secretly hoped to win her away. Regardless of his true reasons, he was constantly hanging around, and he was now at my door. I wanted to get rid of him. Really I wanted to just slam the door in his face.

It wasn't that I disliked him for still carrying a flame for Kiri. We had single neighbors who also pined for her, and I didn't begrudge them for it. After all, she was both beautiful and a breadwinner. With Uro it was different. He circled over our marriage with a raptor's eye, always primed to spot an opportunity.

If he'd been upfront about it and just told me straight that he was trying to get her, then I at least would've respected it. Instead, he'd be extra friendly toward me. It was as if I were his favorite person in the world, but I knew he just viewed getting closer to me as a way of getting closer to Kiri. Worst of all, he'd jump at any chance to get close to Ian.

A few weeks before, he'd wangled his way into joining Ian and me on a trip to our building's roof. The times I spent with Ian up on the roof were special. Sometimes we'd stand at the railing in silence watching the setting sun color the sky. Sometimes we'd spot flocks of starlings rising and falling in and out of the rooflines. Once we were watching a bank of thunderheads move in from the west, and Ian asked if the movement of clouds make a sound. "There's a kind of rumble I think, but not the kind we can hear," I said.

The time Uro came up with us, he did nothing but get in the way. He kept pointing out to Ian the big farmbots with their spray tanks and scythes, always with an exaggerated, "Look at that one! Isn't that neat?" Ian politely feigned enthusiasm, but these were things Ian had learned about long before.

Kiri thought it was healthy for Ian to have Uro's influence in his life, and she was far more trusting of Uro than I was. She interpreted my dislike of him as simple possessiveness and thought it was cute, if not mature. That annoyed me even more, but I knew he wasn't an actual threat, and that I could never fairly ask her to push him away. I also knew he was important to her on some level, and that was why I now didn't shut the door in his face.

"Hi, Uro."

He peeked around me at Kiri. "I just saw on the news," he said. "I ... I just ... can't believe it. I'm so, so sorry."

Kiri got up and brushed by me to give Uro a hug. I watched askance as Uro squeezed her while rocking back and forth and plaintively sighing.

Kiri pulled out from the hug and waved him forward, saying, "C'mon in."

He strode in, patting me on the shoulder as he passed. Kiri sat back down, and Uro joined her on the couch, and put his hand on her back. "It was so awful seeing the story on the news," he said. "I've never been so shocked in my life. I'm so, so sorry. I'm beside myself, it's awful."

"Thank you," she answered.

"Is there anything I can do for you three? Any possible ways I can help make this easier?"

"Thanks, but no," Kiri said. "We're just working on accepting it right now."

I added, "And spending all the time we can with each other."

Uro looked up at me and nodded. "Of course! I had to come right away when I saw the news."

Kiri gave a quick recap of how it happened, and he listened with his jaw hanging open. He started moving his hand in circles over her back. I paced in front of the couch, unsure of what to do. I wanted Uro out, but this was Kiri's time. I had to leave it up to her.

"Listen," she said, "I really appreciate you coming, but now isn't the best moment. It's all very fresh for us and we're still processing it."

"Oh, yes," he said, "but I'll come back at a better time. And you can come over any time at all."

"Yes, I have a full three days," she said. "We'll all have a lunch or dinner or something."

That made him happy. "Yes, yes! I'll have you over for dinner. Just pick a time and message me!"

Kiri got up and he followed her lead. I opened the door for him and stood holding it as he gave her a series of hugs. On his way out he forced a hug on me, and then waved goodbye from the hall as I shut the door.

I must have looked consternated because Kiri let out a tiny laugh as I walked away from the door. I was grateful to hear it – at least Uro's visit had removed some of the day's horrible shock. I put my arm around her waist and we took slow steps back to the bedroom.

"I shouldn't have answered the door," I said.

"No, don't say that. He's just being nice now. What could be his motive otherwise?"

"That motive never goes away for a guy like that. And I think I have a right to be possessive about my last time with you, and not share it with someone like him."

"That's fair, but if we have a chance to go over for dinner I'd like to, ok?"

"Look, it's up to you what we do, obviously."

"Don't be like that."

"Like what?" I asked, knowing full well what she'd meant. She didn't answer.

"Look," I said, "he was looking at you just the way he always has. And how he had his hand on your back? You know what that was."

Again she gave no answer. The distraction of Uro's visit had worn off, and her eyes looked so distant that I wasn't even sure if she'd heard me.

"We should have dinner," I said.

We'd spent an antsy hour in our bed, with Ian under the sheets between us. None of us could sleep but we weren't talking either so, even though I had no appetite, I decided it would be better to return to routine.

The dinner packages that had arrived in our cupboard contained a nondescript red soup with a slice of crisp bread and a cup of rice and vegetables. It was one of the more common dinners we'd get, and as we sat around the table unwrapping them Kiri said, "You'd think they'd give us special food or something for my Extension, you know?"

We ate in silence until Ian asked, "Do I stay home from school tomorrow?"

"Yep," Kiri said. "I want you to take this time to be with me, ok?"

"Dad, do we get to stay in this apartment when Mom's gone?"

"Ian! That's rude," I said.

Kiri hissed out a little laugh. "No, it's ok," she said. "He doesn't know, so it's natural to ask. Ian, you and Dad won't need this much space anymore so you'll get a different apartment. You'll live there with Dad until you turn sixteen when you'll be ready to live on your own."

When Ian's soup got to the halfway point I poured some of mine into it. Kiri placed her entire slice of bread next to what was left of his.

After every bit of food was in our bellies I gathered the dishes and tossed them back in the cabinet. We sat at the table to the sound of them being cleaned. I stretched my arms and my back. Ian fidgeted. Kiri drummed on the plastic tabletop with her fingertips. I cracked my neck.

Normally after dinner we'd let Ian spend some time watching the display in the front room. We liked to sit on the couch and chat with him about whatever he was watching.

Then we'd put him to bed and stay up on our own for a while. I might go on the computer to do some reading, or Kiri might go on it to answer work messages. I liked to watch the nature and science shows that ran later at night. Kiri liked to put on her headphones and listen to music.

Tonight we instead sat in a paralysis until Kiri finally broke it with, "Let's go out. Let's go for a walk."

We moved slowly to the elevator and through the mostly empty lobby, but then Kiri gave Ian and me a look and dashed forward across the room's great blue carpet to the door. We hurried to catch up, and she turned and pushed the lobby's glass door open with her back. "I want to get some chocolate!" she said.

We walked north hand-in-hand through the warm night air. After turning a dark corner near the station, we saw the sidewalk glowing soft red beneath the long windows of our local automat.

The two rows of tables inside were filled by those who'd treated themselves to something special. A smiling little girl sat on her mother's lap while her father held a frozen blue confection to her mouth. A young childless couple scurried out with a bottle of wine cradled in the man's arms. That would have cost them months of a pattern architect's wages.

Perhaps one or both were sex workers, or maybe one had won the lottery.

Mostly it was single men who, with no hungry children to drain their accounts, were out treating themselves. They were so slow, so deliberate, as they sat with their elbows pressed against the sleek white tabletops and bit, chewed, and all-consumed the indulgences for which they'd saved.

Kiri nudged Ian and asked, "What kind of chocolate should we get?"

Ian, after a strategic shrug and moment of hesitation, suggested, "Maybe with almonds?"

Kiri clasped her hands together. "Yes! Great idea! C'mon, let's go find it."

We walked along the cubbies of food and drinks that lined the back wall. When we reached the desserts, I lifted Ian up and held him so he could better see the chocolate bars.

He pointed and Kiri put her fingertip to the glass and said, "Buy."

The cubby door, however, didn't flip open.

Kiri turned to me. "Oh no. Of course. My account is terminated."

I put Ian down and bought the bar from my account.

We took it out to the street and sat on the curb as other patrons came and went. Kiri broke segments off the bar for us, and as the chocolate melted against our tongues we communicated our pleasure with exaggerated moans.

She broke off one more segment and gave it to Ian. The rest of the bar was his and he knew it, but he also knew that Kiri liked to give him his treats piecemeal over time.

When Ian finished the piece, he asked, "Mom, why weren't you able to buy the chocolate?"

"Because I've died," she said. "And that means my money's all gone. That's the rule, even though I don't think it's very fair. I had so much, too. We could've filled our cupboard."

She looked to me. "Why can't I just keep my account for my Extension?"

"I don't know," I said. "You're right, it is unfair."

Our faces were at waist level to the people crossing the street before us, all the women in their red dresses, and all the men in their gray slacks and blue shirts. The asphalt at our feet was still warm and still had a tarry odor from having baked in the afternoon sun. Ian and I were over a storm grate, and the corners of its latticed brown metal were streaked with white discoloration.

My habit to teach Ian whenever I could was still unbroken. "Those stains are called alluvial fans," I told him. "Or at least they would be if they were on a riverbed. You wouldn't have had that lesson yet. There were particles in flowing water that got caught there."

Ian nodded and stared down at the drain as we sat quietly with our forearms resting on bent knees.

Kiri, who'd been entranced by how the streetlights above gilded the chocolate bar's foil wrapper as she turned it in her hands, said, "Ian, tell me what the news said about me again."

"It was just what I said. They showed your face and said you'd been killed and they showed the suspect's face."

She asked me, "Would you mind if we went home and watched the late news? I want to see."

I thought it was a morbid request and I didn't care to see the story, but I understood her curiosity. I said ok and we started back, Kiri giving over a piece of chocolate to Ian every time we reached the end of a block.

21

"I wonder why he did that," Ian said.

We'd turned on the news and the top story was the trial of a man charged with beating up another man. They were both from the General Order and the victim hadn't died, but the beating was so severe that the Judicial Order couldn't overlook it.

The first clip they played was of the man being arrested. A medbot and two men wearing the white dress shirts of the Judicial Order entered the attacker's apartment. The accused man stood up from his couch, but went limp and fell back onto it when the medbot raised a finger at him. The next clip was of the victim on the stand describing the attack. The report didn't give any mention of the attacker's motives.

"One had probably stolen some food from the other," I said. "Either that or they were fighting over a woman. It's usually about one of those things."

Which was true. While people were always having petty arguments over any number of things, from workplace bickering to disagreements over fictional shows, it was usually only food theft or relationship disputes that led to physical violence.

Other types of theft were rare. For one thing, theft of other possessions was difficult to get away with and could be punishable by death. For another, it wasn't the norm to have substantial personal property in the General Order. Thanks to years of her brothel income, Kiri and I had extra things – her work wardrobe, her jewelry, displays for every room, her headphones – but among most of the General Order there simply wasn't much to steal. Except for food and each other.

The final clips were of the judge giving his verdict and then the defendant sitting at a table in front of an empty pastel-blue wall. A medbot stood next to him. Someone, it must have been his lawyer or maybe a counselor, had their back to the camera and was talking to him. The man was shaking his head and frantically pleading, his hands apologetically turned to the ceiling. The medbot put one of its hands to his neck, and the man's eyes rolled back and he collapsed face-first against the table.

The silent image of the executed man remained onscreen for several seconds before cutting back to the studio. The usual newscaster was hosting the news that night. He had lines at his eyes and gray at his temples but, as older people go, was still reasonably handsome.

"A sex worker died on the job today..." he said.

Kiri's work photo appeared, the first one prospective clients would see on the brothel menu. She was smiling and gazing into the camera, her head tilted down and her hair flowing over her shoulders and down the v-neck of her yellow dress. I was so used to seeing her face on the display that I had to remind myself that this photo was what was on the news, and not one that I had added to the display myself.

"A spokesman from the Judicial Order says that Kiri Colleran was murdered by a client. The suspect is Scotson Yvera, a fifty-two-year-old member of the Administrative Order..."

They showed a photo of an older man with dark, thinning hair, uneven eyes, a flabby chin, and a sickly gray pallor. How could someone who looked like that have ever touched Kiri, let alone hurt her so?

"Mr. Yvera's lawyer says that it was an unfortunate accident during a sex game, and that his client will be fully exonerated."

Scotson Yvera's photo was replaced by the newscaster.

"Kiri Colleran was twenty-eight, and is survived by a husband and son. She was revived for Extension and is expected to testify at Mr. Yvera's trial. We will of course have full coverage."

He paused a beat and continued, "A beautiful night tonight, but could we get rain tomorrow? Let's talk to Mandina and find out..."

I said, "Display off," and the screen went black.

None of us commented. Kiri gave Ian the last of the chocolate and he ate it and soon fell asleep with his head against her shoulder.

Getting Ian to bed while he was sleeping was an art on which I prided myself. I slowly pressed the backs of my hands against the couch and slid them under his back and legs. I brought him against my chest.

After we settled him in our bed Kiri whispered, "We could go to the med-pods downstairs and ask for something to help us sleep."

"No, I don't want to sleep more than I have to."

We got in bed. I tried to focus on watching Ian's eyes dart around beneath their lids, but Scotson Yvera's face kept running through my mind. In the image used by the news, Scotson was wearing a suit and half smile. I imagined Kiri looking at that face in her last, awful moments. I remembered the bruises he'd given her the month before. How could she have ever agreed to another session with him after that?

But I knew I shouldn't blame her. While sex workers officially have the right to opt out of seeing a given client without risking their job, in practice it's not like that at all. Even when the brothel mistress doesn't pressure a worker into being with a client, the competitiveness and expectations of brothels make any fickleness from workers unrealistic. If Kiri had tried to turn away every difficult client she had, then she would've been out of the job years ago. Instead she'd apparently made pleasing such clients her expertise, and that was how she'd outlasted so many other brothel women.

Desperate for images to replace what my mind was creating, I set our bedroom display, which was normally set as a window, to run through old pictures. Ian in his crib. Kiri holding him. Ian on his first morning of school. Kiri and I posing with our arms around each other the night I taught Ian how to use the camera.

Kiri, still awake, propped herself up and watched the pictures cycle through, and Ian soon awoke and joined in. We started sharing recollections, and hours rolled by before sleep again overtook Ian. When Kiri also fell asleep, I dimmed the light and closed my eyes. Sleep didn't come, and the details of the day kept repeating in my head.

Kiri murmured in her sleep and I felt her body twitching. What was she dreaming? What would I be dreaming if I could sleep?

I thought of a conversation we'd had about our dreams a few days before. I'd taken a photo of her just after she'd woken up, her head sunk into the pillow and the morning's first sun soft on her face. When she saw me at the display adjusting the settings to make the photo black and white, she asked, "Why do you turn them to black and white so much?"

"It purifies things, don't you think?"

I looked at her half-open eyes in the photo, now white-gray instead of blue. "Colors distract from the good stuff," I added. "Textures, shapes, shadows."

She tilted her head as she considered the photo. "There's something else, though. You never dream in black and white, right?"

"Right."

"So resetting photos is the only way for you to see me like that. Even in your dreams you only get me in color."

I grabbed her hips. "Who says you're ever in my dreams?"

She giggled. "I was hoping that I make an appearance now and then."

"Maybe." I kissed her pulled-back hair.

I liked it that my mind had pulled up that memory. It was getting close to dawn, and I finally slept.

22

People talk about waking up and experiencing a moment of not remembering that a loved one has died, of believing they were still in your life as always. I didn't wake to that illusion. I woke already thinking about how I'd lost Kiri.

The display had reverted back to being a window and showed the sidewalk outside under the day's first quiet, gray light. I absently watched the early risers heading to work. And then, among them, two men in suits.

They'd walked out of view by the time I'd registered it.

It was rare for General Order men, even sex workers or lottery winners, to invest in nonstandard clothing. When they did, it'd usually be a hat or a uniquely colored shirt. Men from the Judicial Order were known to enter General Order wards when they needed to make an arrest, but when they did they'd just wear their dress shirts without a tie or jacket. Full suits were something we only saw when we were watching the news or shows.

I studied the display, but only saw normally dressed people walking in either direction. I was trying to put the anomaly out of my mind when the doorbell rang.

Ian stirred and Kiri opened her eyes. "Who's that?" she whispered.

"I don't know," I said. "Maybe Uro again?"

Kiri looked at the faint light outside. "He wouldn't come this early."

"Whoever it is, I'm not going to answer, ok? They can try back later," I said.

"Ok by me," she said.

But then there was knocking. And the doorbell again. I sighed, got up, and went to the front room. I opened the door to reveal the two men in suits. I noticed the excess weight around their midsections. Both men were at least well into their forties. Upper order. There was something familiar about one of their faces, but I couldn't place what it was.

They stared back and I felt self-conscious. Was I, with my issued shirt and pants hanging loosely off my skinny frame, as odd a sight to them?

I studied the face that was somehow familiar. The man, standing in a slouch and possessing dark, thinning hair and uneven eyes, said, "Hello. I'm Scotson Yvera."

A biting in my gut and numb chill through my skin. It couldn't be happening. How could her killer be standing before me? The man who'd taken the love of my life was inches away. Did him being there mean Kiri and Ian were in danger? I struggled to work through the shock and to fight the twisting in my collapsing core.

"I'm Mr. Milla," the other man said, "and I'm Mr. Yvera's attorney. May we come in?"

I was trying to process the attorney's question when Kiri gasped from back in the hall. She was still wearing the tank top she'd slept in, her mussed hair half covering her face. Her body was listing to one side, and she held one hand over her mouth and the other at her chest.

Keeping my eyes on the two men, I backed up until I could take hold of her. The men stayed at the door until the lawyer waved his hand over the threshold, said, "If we may," and walked in. I wanted to protest, but he was upper order so his request seemed more a command.

Scotson followed. His suit was gray and his tie was black. His head was bowed, he held his hands crossed in front of him, and he didn't make eye contact with us.

The lawyer reached to shut the door but I said, "Please leave it open."

He nodded vigorously and let it be.

The lawyer was a clutter of blacks and whites, with salt and pepper hair and beard, alabaster skin, white shirt, and black suit, tie, shoes, and eyes. "We must talk to you about the case," he said. "I assure you that we wouldn't bother you if it were not something of the most importance to you."

Kiri came partway out from my grip. "Have a seat," she said.

I didn't want Scotson Yvera on my couch, but I didn't want to contradict Kiri in front of him either. I stayed quiet as the two men sat.

Kiri and I stood facing them. Scotson was resting his hands in his lap. He wore a gold ring on his right index finger, and his wedding band had stone inlays. An image flashed before me of those fingers pressing in to the curves of Kiri's defenseless throat.

Ian had stepped out of our bedroom and was looking in at us from the hall.

"Ian, go wait in your room," I said with more force than I'd intended.

Scotson and his lawyer looked back, and Ian gave their faces a good study before going to his room.

The men's attention returned to us and there was a frigid silence. The lawyer turned to Scotson and said, "Go ahead."

Scotson nodded. "First off, I'm terribly sorry for what happened. Needless to say I never would've wanted this result. I got worked up and things took a bad turn, but it was an accident. An accident. I'm so sorry to you both, and to your son as well."

Neither Kiri nor I replied.

"But I'm here to offer a solution," Scotson continued.

One of his hands rose and gently chopped at the air as he said, "Kiri does not have to die in two days."

He let the words hang. I couldn't understand why he'd say such a thing. Kiri had already died, was on Extension. Extension was a state of death.

Scotson looked Kiri square in the eye. "I'm a member of the Administrative Order. As such, I can restore your time, Kiri. Your original time."

"It's true," the lawyer said. "We're here to offer you a deal, Mrs. Colleran."

Kiri and I glanced at each other. The lawyer went on. "Mr. Yvera will take you off Extension and you will have your full lifespan back. You'll make it to thirty-seven."

"That doesn't sound like a deal to me," Kiri said, "that sounds like something he could do on his own."

"Mr. Yvera will do that for you," the lawyer responded, "after his trial, but on the condition that he's found not guilty. Only on that condition."

After a moment Kiri said, "So you're here to ask me to lie."

"We're here to ask you to help," the lawyer said. "There's no need for Scotson Yvera's life to be ruined, and there's no need for your life to end. Deals like this are not uncommon. Hear me out, here. It would work like this. Today we…"

His eyes drifted toward the ceiling and one of his hands floated in small circles over his lap as he searched for his next word.

"…clarify. We clarify and agree upon what your testimony will be. At the trial you will give that testimony, that clarified testimony. And after Mr. Yvera is found not guilty, he'll take you off Extension. Mr. Yvera will have learned from his mistake and never make it again, and your family won't lose you."

The shock of Scotson Yvera showing up at my door began to blend with the revulsion of hearing his lawyer propose that Kiri help him avoid any punishment. Yet they were saying she didn't have to die. For all this perverse little man in the suit had put Kiri through, how could I not feel hope at what his lawyer was saying?

"That would never work," Kiri said. "I gave a statement to the prosecutor. They know what happened."

"I read your statement," the lawyer said. "It was given moments after you were revived. You had just been told your life had ended, so your mind was clouded and it'd be considered more than natural for your initial statement to be incomplete and inaccurate. What you say at the trial, now that your memory has had time to be properly jogged, will be what determines the verdict. We can work around the statement you gave, all that's needed is one adjustment to what you say at the trial."

"One adjustment?" Kiri asked.

"It's simple. Give the same story you gave in your statement, but when it comes to the part where you claim you said, 'No,' and, 'Stop,' simply tweak it a bit and say that you may have tried to object, but you aren't sure if you actually did or not. And say that even if you did, he may not have heard you during the excitement. All you have to do is say that, and you'll get the rest of your life back."

Kiri's head and shoulders sank and she looked down at her hands. "I know I said no, and I know Scotson heard me. I was looking right at him."

"Again, Mrs. Colleran," the lawyer said, "we need to tweak that. We're trying to work with you here, and this deal will keep you alive. Think of your son's welfare."

He gauged Kiri's reaction and then continued, "Oh and also, where you said you tried to pull his hands away. Downplay that. You could say you put your hands on his arms, but you're not sure if you tried pulling at them or not. Emphasize that it's hard to remember it perfectly. That and the other adjustment are all we need. You can still speak negatively of Mr. Yvera otherwise, because we don't want your story to change too much. Overall, what we need you to present is that you two were playing a common sex game and you were unable to communicate with him properly, and it led to an accident."

Scotson added, "And that's not so far from the truth anyway, is it?"

His words had broken through the shock I was in, and I shot back, "Shut your sick mouth."

I could've crushed his skull, and from the way he averted my gaze I think he knew it.

The lawyer was stunned. "Mr. Colleran! I would remind you that you're speaking to a member of the Administrative Order."

That reminder went unacknowledged by both Kiri and me. Instead she, measuring each word, said to Scotson, "The truth is I told you to stop and I tried to pull your hands off me. Anything other than that is far from the truth."

"From your perspective, yes," Scotson said. "And I understand that now, and again I'm sorry. I can't take yesterday back, but I can give you back your life if you don't try to ruin mine."

Kiri pinched her lips and looked away.

We waited for her to speak, and when she did she asked, "How do we know this is even true, that you have the power to restore my lifespan?"

"I can prove it," Scotson said. "Come with me and I'll show you."

"We aren't going anywhere with you," I said.

"Just down to the lobby," he said. "I can show you the proof when we're down there."

Kiri turned to me. "We can do that, right?"

Realizing it'd get them out of my apartment, I said to the men, "You two go down and wait for us."

"We could all go down together," the lawyer said.

"We'll be down soon enough. Go there and wait," I said.

He nodded and they made their way out.

We went back to talk to Ian, who was standing in his room's doorway.

"Stay here, Buddy. We're just going downstairs for a minute," I said.

"Wait, Corim," Kiri said. "Whatever it is, maybe he should see? I want him to know what's happening."

I knelt down and looked him in the eyes. "Have you been listening? Be honest. It's ok if you have."

"Yeah."

"Ok, then come on down with us."

23

The elevator we took down had another family riding in it. The mother was talking to the father about how poorly her team was doing at work, while her toddler daughter hugged her leg. Kiri, Ian, and I listened in silence until the car stopped and the doors opened to the lobby.

Scotson and the lawyer were standing by the bank of med-pods that lined the wall near the elevators. The lawyer waved to us as though we might've had trouble spotting them otherwise.

We approached and Scotson stepped up to the first med-pod and tapped its access button. The side opened and he maneuvered himself into its chair, leaving one foot on the floor outside so it would remain open. He motioned for us to come closer.

Kiri stepped up and looked in over his shoulder. I stood behind her with Ian at my side.

"Hello, how may I help you today?" the pod asked.

"Confirm to these people that I am a member of the Administrative Order," Scotson said.

"Yes," the pod said. "You are Scotson Yvera of the Administrative Order."

Scotson looked out at us and nodded. He then said, "Now, this woman here, Kiri Colleran, she's on Extension. Now, you tell them that it's true that if she was to get into this pod and I ordered you to do it, you could and would restore her full lifespan."

"I'm unable to provide that sort of information to them," the pod said.

Scotson's hands got tense and shot up in annoyance. "Disable information filtering," he said.

"Disabled," the pod said.

"Now tell them what I had asked you to tell them," Scotson said.

"What he said is accurate. If he were to order me to restore Kiri Colleran's full lifespan, then I would do it."

Scotson turned back with a satisfied smile. "There. You see? Things are going to be ok for all of us."

He got out of the pod. I placed myself in front of Ian and put my arm around Kiri. The lawyer came to Scotson's side and said, "There you have it. Proof."

"Alright, so he can do it," Kiri said. "Why not just do it now? Then it really would be like he hadn't killed me."

"While deals like this are common, they're also best kept quiet," the lawyer said. "If you showed up to the trial and it was found out that you were already off Extension, then it would reflect poorly on Mr. Yvera. On top of that you'd also be lacking in motivation to keep your end of the bargain."

Kiri was running it all through her head. I asked, "What reason do we have to believe that he'd follow through with it? If he's found not guilty, then what's his motivation for restoring her lifespan?"

"I don't want to see her die," Scotson said. "When that time comes I'll be happy to restore her lifespan so we can put this all behind us."

"Exactly," the lawyer said. "He has no reason not to do it. Moreover, not keeping his end of the bargain would ultimately not be self-serving. He would face the risk of you spreading word about it through the General Order. If those stories leaked into the upper orders, it would cause him problems. Deals like this provide benefits and protections to members of the upper orders, so Mr. Yvera will owe it to his peers to follow through on his promise.

"Mrs. Colleran, you've been through a very tough time. As have you, Mr. Colleran. We are offering you a solution, a fix. It's a normal solution. It's a simple thing to do, and it will mean the difference between life and death. I'm sure you're willing to do this, aren't you?"

Kiri gave the lawyer a hard stare. "I don't want to have to answer right now," she said.

The lawyer's eyes twitched. "Of course," he said. "I won't ask you to agree to it now because all that matters is that you do the right thing at the trial." He then looked behind me to Ian and added, "Having seen you with your son, I trust that you will."

He was as persuasive as any lawyer I'd seen on the news or any fictional lawyer I'd seen on shows. Hope started to gnaw at my desolation. This deal, as repugnant as it was, could turn the previous twenty-four hours into nothing more than a nightmare that would pass from our memories over the coming years.

"One last thing," Scotson said to Kiri.

He took a moment to find his words. "Again, I really am sorry, Kiri. I would like to restore your time, and I'm sure we can make that happen. And when it does happen, and this is another reason you can trust that I'll restore your time, I'd very much like to be able to see you again. Under completely controlled circumstances. I will pay more than you've ever been paid."

My gut was hit with the same biting that hit it when he'd introduced himself at my door.

"No matter how much time I have left," Kiri replied, "that would never happen."

Scotson looked surprised and hurt.

"What is wrong with you?" I asked him.

His lawyer put a hand in front of him. "C'mon, let's go," he said.

Scotson ignored his lawyer, and spoke directly to me. "Look, I screwed up, ok? But she led me into it. It's a hazard of her profession. And anyway, she likes being choked. You must know that."

My skin was afire and the blood beneath it pounded heavy. Who was anyone, let alone he, to tell me about my wife? I heard myself saying, "She pretended to like it in order to get your money. You must know that."

Again Scotson looked surprised and hurt. Had that thought not crossed his mind? On the news they always speak of the men of the Administrative Order with reverence for their brilliance. Yet here was one before me who'd been naïve enough to believe in the sincerity of a sex worker's excitement and enthusiasm for him.

The lawyer again raised his hand. "Arguing won't help any of us."

He then said to Kiri, "Mr. Yvera has offered you a tremendous deal. Don't let the emotions of the circumstances blind you to the fact that taking this deal is the logical choice."

We watched them walk out, and for the first time I noticed how the other building residents passing through the lobby were nervously glancing at the strange sight of the two upper order men in suits.

On the elevator ride back up, Ian hugged Kiri. "What are you going to do, Mommy?"

"I don't know, sweetie."

None of us said another word until we were sitting in the kitchen for breakfast.

Kiri must've sensed I was anxious to analyze Scotson's offer because she said, "I don't want to talk about it for now, ok? We could talk about something else, maybe? Something nicer."

As much as I wanted to discuss it, I couldn't say no to her request. I turned to Ian. "Ian, what should we talk about?" I asked.

"I don't know."

"Well, Buddy, you know you're turning ten soon?"

"Yeah, I know," he said.

"You're growing up."

"Yeah."

"Your anatomy lessons will start to get very interesting before too long," I said.

"What do you mean?"

"You'll see. Just wait."

I started telling him what he'd been like as a toddler, how he was always poking around to find new ways to entertain himself. All three of us got to telling the stories of his early milestones, bruises, and tantrums. We were still at it hours later when the doorbell rang.

"It's become like a station in here," I said as I got up to answer it.

I was scared to turn the handle, but this time opening the door revealed someone I was happy to see. Raff came in and somberly took my hand to shake it.

"You heard," I said.

"I heard, yeah."

When Ian heard Raff's voice he ran out from the kitchen calling, "Uncle Raff!"

Kiri joined us, and Raff said, "I'm sorry I didn't come sooner. I didn't know. I don't really watch the news. When I got in to work, everybody knew and was talking about it."

"I should've messaged you," I said.

We sat him on the couch and got him a glass of water.

"I feel intrusive being here," he said. "I don't want to be a bother."

"It's good to see you. Trust me," I said.

After a while of talking about how it happened, Raff said, "Listen – when I was walking over I tried to think of all I want to say. There's a lot I should've said long ago. You know... when Lenia left me and I couldn't find anyone else, obviously that wasn't the life I was hoping for. I had to accept that there was something wrong with me somehow, and I wasn't meant to be with anyone."

"There's nothing wrong with you, Raff. You just had bad luck," Kiri said.

"Thank you," he said, "but whatever the reason was, it was hard to go on at first. I used to stand at my roof's railing thinking about what it'd be like to go over it, or I'd try to think of a way to cut myself. Whenever I needed something to take me away from those thoughts, I'd think of you two, and how I'd never see you again. That's what kept me alive."

"You've been a great friend. We owe you a lot," I said.

"What I'm saying is that I want to thank all three of you. But mainly you, Kiri. You stuck with Corim. You can imagine how I feel about that."

We talked with him through the afternoon, but we never mentioned the visit from Scotson. The hours whittled by into the evening and we insisted he stay for dinner. Kiri had already messaged Noli and invited her over so they could see each other one last time.

I caught Kiri alone in the kitchen. "Can we talk about the deal?" I asked.

"I don't want to think about it now. And really I don't think there's anything to talk about anyway. They made the offer clear enough."

"You're going to take it, right?"

"I don't know," she said. "I may not know until I'm up on the stand. It's like the lawyer said, that's the only time it will matter."

"Why wouldn't you, though? If what they said is true..."

"You want me to help him after what he did to me?"

"Of course not, but I want to keep you."

"Me too, but just because we want it doesn't mean it'd be right. I wish I could give you an answer, but I don't know what I'll do. I don't even know how I'm going to decide."

"Then let me decide for you," I said.

She tensed up and she shook her head. I was frustrated and wanted to press the issue, but when she buried her face in her hands and let out a sob, I kept quiet and pulled her into me.

24

The doorbell rang as we were moving the three chairs and the little table from the kitchen to in front of the couch. Raff had never met Noli, but I'd told him about her. He now did his best to straighten his hair, but it was to little effect. His hair was still as crooked as it'd been when we were eight.

Ian pulled the door open and Noli bounded in with a convincing smile and ebullient squawks of, "Hi! Hi, hi, hi!"

As I watched her smile widen at the sight of Kiri, I imagined how she must've stood at the door before ringing the bell, willing herself into a state of cheerful excitement. She was accustomed enough to giving performances at work, but nothing like tonight's.

She handed me her issued dinner as well as a loaf of bread and a bottle of wine. Even under the circumstances the wine was an enormous gesture – it had to have cost weeks of her wages.

I broke up the bread and Kiri heated the dinners. Tonight we'd been given pasta with red sauce. Kiri went to the cupboard and got out some mixed grain soup and the little brick of dessert bread that we'd been saving for a special occasion.

We seated our guests. Noli patted the chair next to her. "Ian, will you come sit with your Aunt Noli?"

While Ian may not have been fully looking at women yet, he was already enjoying their attention as much as any guy, and he now enthusiastically took Noli up on her request. Raff took the other chair and Kiri and I sunk into the couch across from them. It felt strange to sit so low at our familiar table.

Noli twisted the cap off the wine and poured the metal bottle around the table. After half-filling Ian's glass, she asked, "Oh no, is that alright?"

Kiri grinned. "It's fine."

We raised our glasses and said, "Cheers!"

I felt obliged to add something. "To friends," I said, which immediately felt awkward, as if I'd called attention to all the unsaid things that made the dinner anything but festive. The table showed no signs of gloom though, only nods and smiles as we brought our glasses to our lips.

Ian had never had a drop of alcohol before, let alone done a cheers, but he deftly followed along. I thought to warn him to be cautious with his first taste, but I didn't want to embarrass him. He raised the glass, sniffed at it, and took a careful sip.

We all did well at keeping the conversation comfortable and mundane. "I like the grain in the soup. Is it sorghum? ... Raff, how's work? ... The pasta is so much better with the bread ... The wine is turning your face red, Corim! ... Ian, what shows have you been watching? ... Noli, has Ala started school yet? ... We're having a nice break with the weather..."

We had finished gorging every crumb of the dessert bread and were sipping the last of the wine when Noli whispered, "Aww!"

She'd seen that Ian was dozing off in his chair, his head drooping down over his chest.

"He hasn't slept much and he's never had a dinner like this," Kiri said.

I went to Ian, saying, "C'mon, Buddy," as I lifted and rolled him into me. I carried him to his room, laid him in his bed, and watched his peaceful face while he slept, the hushed voices of our guests drifting in.

When I returned Raff was standing and saying his goodbyes. I offered to walk him home.

He declined but I said, "Let's give Kiri and Noli some time to themselves. Besides, when was the last time we walked together?"

We took a long, roundabout way to his building. About halfway through the walk he said, "Sometimes I think I see Lenia. I'll be walking to work or coming out of an elevator, and for a second someone I see will look exactly like her. But it's never her, it's always just my mind being ridiculous."

"That's not so ridiculous. You never know," I said.

"It's been twelve years since I last saw her. If it isn't ridiculous, it's at least sad."

"It must be a normal thing though," I said, "to look for the last person you loved, no matter how long it's been."

On my walk back I worried I would return to tears. I imagined that as soon as Kiri and Noli had been left alone their happy pretenses had become solemn commiseration, but both were laughing when I opened the door.

They went quiet and stared at me as I approached the table.

"I didn't mean to interrupt," I said.

"Oh, you aren't interrupting at all, honey," Kiri said. Both she and Noli giggled.

Noli pulled out the chair next to her. "Have a seat," she said.

After I did, Kiri raised an eyebrow. "So, we were actually just talking about you," she said.

Noli nodded and ran her hand up my thigh as she continued Kiri's sentence. "And word is you're pretty good!"

They laughed wildly, and then more so when Noli started asking me to show her my special moves.

I let them embarrass me a bit longer, but it was obvious that my presence wasn't needed for them to keep having fun. I thanked Noli for the bread and wine, and wished her goodnight. She hugged me, throwing in a few gropes and kisses on the cheek. I stumbled into the bedroom without turning the light on, loosened my pants, and collapsed into bed.

As soon as I closed my eyes Scotson's face started running through my head again. I tried to let the last effects of the alcohol salve my mental fixation on analyzing the deal he'd offered. It was clear Kiri was unsure about taking it, and even if she did, we still had no way of truly knowing if he'd follow through with his end of it.

I started to mark off all the things she could be experiencing for the last time: her last taste of wine, her last time being the hostess of a dinner, her last time joking with her best friend.

I wanted to order her to take the deal. I wanted to tell her that she was taking it, and that was that. It would be a second crime if Scotson was tricking us and he walked away unpunished without taking Kiri off Extension, but even if there was only a chance of the deal being legitimate then it still seemed worth taking.

I listened to the laughter from the front room turn into softly spoken words. I couldn't make out what was said, but I could hear the happy tones give way to sobs and broken-voiced comforting.

They went on late into the night while I fell in and out of sleep. When I heard them saying their goodbyes I sat up and turned the light on. After a long silence, and then the sound of the door closing, Kiri came in and changed into her pajamas. She climbed in next to me and I took hold of her as she rested a hand on my chest.

"Thank you for giving me tonight," she said. "It was good for Noli, and that's what I wanted."

"Good."

Her hand moved down my body. We of course hadn't been intimate since the murder.

"We could try if you wanted. Just try," she said.

"I'd love to, but I wouldn't be able."

"Don't worry," she said. "It's not like it's the first thing on my mind either. I think we should try, though. That's part of what Extension is for."

"You're more beautiful to me than ever, but right now how can... I mean..."

"Hush. You don't have to explain. I'm just glad to have this time with you."

"I know," I said, "but you're right, we should. In the morning, ok?"

We slept fairly well. Morning came, and I kissed her in the early light. She motioned for more, but I couldn't feel anything good. Knowing time had passed and was still passing was a leaden weight pressing down on me as sure as my own weight was pressing into the bed. I froze and shook my head apologetically.

She tried joking about it. "I should've jumped on you before I told you I was on Extension."

I laughed a little. "The small talk afterward might've been a little awkward. You know, me asking you how work went. You answering that you'd had a rough day."

She laughed. The way she always lost herself so fully when laughing at my jokes was the only way she was ever less than genuine with me. I never complained about it.

She looked at me and bobbed her head back and forth. She did that when she had nothing in particular to say but wanted to give me some kind of communication. She got out of bed, crossed her arms, and peered down at me, the gears turning behind her eyes.

She nodded, pointed a finger in the air, said, "We need a change of scenery," and hurried out of the room. The little clicks of her typing on the computer reached back to me.

When I came into the front room she smirked. "Go away!" she said.

Any other time I wouldn't have looked at what she was writing, but this time I put my chin on her shoulder and squinted at the screen.

Then I stood straight and backed away. "Please, no," I said. "Can we not?"

She looked back at me and sent the message.

"We don't need to do that," I told her. "Please write him back. We aren't going to Uro's."

"Yep, actually, we are, and it'll be fun. Very fun."

"Tonight could be our last night."

"Exactly, so we'll go and have a nice dinner," she said.

She got up and started back to our room. From the hall she called back, "Hey, if you want to stay in that's fine, but I'm going!"

I was mad, but what could I do? I shook my head and ran to catch up with her. "We'll go there to eat, but we all leave the moment I say we leave," I said.

She only smiled in reply.

25

At midday, when the trains were less crowded, we took Ian for a ride. After we took our seats and the train departed, I leaned over and whispered to Kiri, "You have to take Scotson's deal. Don't think of what you'll have to say at the trial as a lie, think of it as a performance. I hate him probably more than you do, but forget about whether he gets punished. What happens to you is all that matters."

She just looked out the window. "That's not all that matters," she said.

We got off at the south end of the ward and started to walk back home through the clear day, the sidewalk before us blanched by the high sun reflecting down off endless rows of building windows.

We took a break at a cross street symmetrically cornered by four identical office buildings. I looked up at the street sign – we were at the intersection of streets D and nine.

"I saw smoke coming from around this intersection once," I said to Ian. "Have I ever told you about that? It was when you were a baby. I was walking near here and I heard distant screams and then a loud boom. It wasn't a close sound, but it was the kind of sound that I could feel move through me. I heard more screams and I could see smoke. I kept walking toward it to see what was happening. You know the big lumbering maintenance bots that are always cleaning the streets? As one of those rolled past me, it told me to stop walking. It was the only time I ever heard a maintenance bot speak, I didn't even know they could.

"So I watched from my spot and saw other maintenance bots headed to the commotion. I could smell the smoke. Smoke is a noxious smell, hard to describe. Sort of like if you smell plastic too closely. I heard some scraping sounds, and then another crashing sound. Eventually the smoke cleared and things quieted down. I started walking again but didn't see anything strange. I asked around and watched the news that night, but I never heard what caused it."

In the evening Ian watched me take our dinners from the cabinet. "What'd we get?" he asked.

I peeked into one of the paper wrappers. "Sandwiches. Filled with what looks like squash, I think that's squash, and mushrooms, and some kind of spread."

I was glad we got a dinner that wouldn't require any preparation time. I put them in a bag along with our glasses, plates and forks.

"Can I carry it?" Ian asked.

He cradled the bag as we moved into the hall and waited for Kiri. She came out in her yellow dress and black heels. She was holding up her hair with one hand, and keeping the ends of her gold necklace together with the other. I fastened the necklace links, zipped her dress and said, "You look great."

"Thank you."

"I'm sure he'll be flattered that you dressed up for him."

She rolled her eyes and shook her head.

Uro's apartment was in a neighboring building. On the walk over, I caught more than one man staring at Kiri in her beautiful dress and jewelry, and I felt the pride I always felt at being the guy who got to walk down the street with a woman like that.

At Uro's door, I raised my hand to knock, but before I did I told Kiri, "We leave when I want, ok?"

She acted like she didn't hear, so I acted like she'd agreed with me. I knocked three times.

I had only just pulled my hand away when the door swung open. Uro stood bright-faced and exclaimed, "Hello! Hello! Welcome! So excited we could do this!"

He stretched his arms out at Kiri and she gave him a hug. I could tell he'd just shaved and that his hair was freshly cut.

After telling Kiri how beautiful she looked he led us to his kitchen area. There were four chairs crowding the triangular table in the corner. "I borrowed extra chairs from my neighbors for tonight," Uro said.

"Really? How sweet of you!" Kiri said.

"Well, this is a big dinner!" He put his hand on Kiri's waist to guide her toward a chair he was pulling out. "Please, everyone, have a seat!"

We sat and he took the bag from Ian. "Alright, I'm just going to put that there," he explained as he put the bag on his counter. "And there's your glasses," he said as he reached into the bag. "Let me pour you all some water."

I looked down at my crossed arms as Uro continued to announce all his actions. It already felt like a long night.

When dinner started, the four plates and glasses were precariously close to each other on the small table. We had to keep our elbows tight against our bodies, and reaching in to pick up our sandwiches was a delicate procedure that required careful maneuvering.

"So Uro, how's work going?" I asked.

"My team went through a rough patch. Some people were flaking out and hardly showing up. We had to eat some really bad trades. We're coming out of it though. I was stressed about it, but now I'm excited."

"That's great."

"Yeah, I've been working hard. Not much going on otherwise. Hey, do you watch that show *Legal Sentences*?"

"I watched that a little years ago, but not lately," I said.

"It's gotten crazy," Uro said. "The main lawyer on it is a defense lawyer, but his dad is a prosecutor in the same court, so they have cases against each other. The last one had this sex worker on trial for stealing, and she tried to convince the lawyer that she was in love with him, but it turned out she was trying to do the same thing with the dad. When they figured it out, the lawyer changed her plea to guilty. It was funny."

"It sounds funny," Kiri said.

"Yeah, and there's that new show *White Mountain*. Have you seen that?"

"No."

"It's good. It's about the Administrative Order, but they live up on a mountain. Their apartments are right there on a cliff overlooking a valley full of farmland. Instead of having meetings in an office, they'll have them out on the mountainside."

"What's it about?" I asked.

"There's a lot of romance, and they're always arguing about who should be with who."

We nodded and he nodded back. We went back to work on our sandwiches.

26

After dinner Uro said, "I put some songs on my display. I was thinking we could listen to them?"

Kiri agreed before I could weigh in about it. We took the few steps from the kitchen area to over by the couch where the only display in the apartment was. We stood facing each other as an up-tempo song began. The singers, it was a duet between a man and a woman, started singing about jumping up and down and running in the sun.

There we were the night before the trial looking down at our feet and listening to silly songs. It started to seem like our host's idea had fallen flat, but then Kiri began swaying to the music. Uro followed her lead and soon they were both dancing.

Ian looked up at me, wanting to dance. I rocked back and forth, letting my hands float up and down. He joined me.

The second song started. It was catchier and had a faster beat, and all four of us earnestly bounced around. "That's it, keep moving," I said to Ian. "Twirl and move until you have to catch yourself."

We moved around the floor, crossing each other's paths. I circled Kiri and she bumped into me.

The most awkward moments of when Kiri and I had learned to dance together as teenagers came when we were trying to master how to dance to faster songs. I picked up the moves quickly enough, but no matter how many times we tried, Kiri's face would become pained and her limbs would discordantly jerk and struggle. She never quite got it, or maybe she did and just wanted to dance that way.

For the rest of us dancing was a release from the inhibited self-doubt of our everyday selves, but I think for her it was a release from grace – the grace that she always wore as both a shield and a magnet. She didn't mind if the counterpoints she moved to were independent of what everyone else heard, because to her it meant her connection with the music was all the more personal.

If Kiri joined us when Ian and I watched shows featuring popular musical performers, she'd always put on her headphones and listen to melancholy instrumentals. Ian thought the music she liked was scary, and I found it depressing. One time she took the headphones off and said, "Listen to this song I found. It's my favorite!" She'd say that a lot, as her favorite song changed most every week.

I thought the song was dreadful. "I don't even understand why you listen to that sort of thing, let alone like it," I said.

"When I find a song that's sincerely sad or angry," she said, "it makes me wonder what the composer could have been going through to have wanted to make it."

"So why not listen to sad songs with lyrics? Then you'd know exactly what they were going through."

She crinkled her nose and looked at me as if I'd just asked a very stupid question.

"Then there'd be nothing to think about, and it wouldn't be interesting. Besides, lyrics don't mean anything. You can't trust them at all."

The songs playing at Uro's were popular ones with lyrics, but Kiri smiled and danced like they were her favorites anyway. Ian had become comfortable and was losing himself in the music the way a child should.

A slow song came at just the right time to rest our legs. Kiri came to me, and we slow danced for the first time in years. Ian watched us until Uro took his hand. "Let me give you a lesson," he said.

Ian acquiesced and, as Kiri leaned into me and I smelled the sweetness of her hair, I listened to Uro's advice about how to step and where hands should go.

The next song came, another slow one. "Thanks for the dance," Kiri whispered to me.

"May I cut in on your lesson and get a dance with Uro?" she asked Ian.

Ian backed away. I said to him, "C'mon, let's see what you learned."

Uro had taught him well enough and he was moving fine. I told him, "When the time comes you'll impress your classmates with your expert dancing."

Another song came. It was the slowest one yet, and a little sad. The singer sang, "I got one foot on the platform, the other foot on the train..."

"The slower the song," I said, "the closer you should be to your partner. Don't just hear how the tempo is different, feel it."

We turned, and as we came around I watched Uro and Kiri. He was facing me but his eyes were closed. He was leading and she was pressed into him. As they swayed, his hand was caressing back and forth between her dress and the bare skin of her back. She was resting her head on his shoulder. He turned, and she turned with him. His hand slid down the side of her hip.

"Alright!" I said. "Time for us to get going."

Uro opened his eyes and came back to reality. Kiri pulled away from him gently, letting her fingers slide from his back to around to his chest before reluctantly pulling completely away.

"No, please stay!" he said. "It's still early."

I put my hand on his shoulder. "Look, any other time we would but, you know, the circumstances. We're on a strict schedule. Of course you understand."

Realizing there was no good argument to that, he nodded.

"Hey, come here," Kiri said. She embraced him and kissed his cheek.

We got our things from the kitchen area. As we were walking out, Ian said to him, "I'll see you soon, ok?"

"Yeah, Uro. We'll see you." I added.

He barely heard us. His eyes were locked on Kiri. He stood where we'd just moments ago been dancing, and he watched Kiri shut the door behind us as another slow song started to play.

Back at our apartment I held Kiri's hand outside the kitchen while Ian put away the dishware. After he finished he came to us and I leaned down. "Hey, Ian. Mom and I would like some time alone, ok?"

He nodded, said, "Have a good night," and went to his room.

More than ever, I knew the salt of her skin, the blades of her back. The changed angles of her face at close view. And I knew before it happened when her toes would curl and she'd shudder. A night of physical restoration for the nonphysical.

Afterward she lay across my chest and I kissed her forehead. "That was amazing," I said. "I reached these moments of unawareness when I didn't remember that you're on Extension. No bad thoughts. The only thing I knew was that everything was perfect for us both."

"That's not unawareness, that's letting go," she said. "When it's good enough, then everything but that moment disappears. You forget about who you are and what mistakes you've made and what's coming tomorrow."

She reached up and circled her fingers through the hair on the back of my head. "You're only figuring that out now? What a pity."

She fell asleep first and I studied her desperately, wanting to know with a new exactness every incline of her skin's topography, every freckle's coordinates, wanting to hardwire all I could to memory.

Then, for the first time in her Extension, I fell asleep without trying. I awoke two hours later when I heard Kiri getting up and leaving the bedroom.

I found her in the kitchen gripping the counter's edge. When I took hold of her she said, "Had a nightmare. I was..."

She looked down and pursed her lips, frustrated that the words weren't coming. "Take your time," I said.

"I was at work and Ian came in as a client. He was grown up, but he was somehow upper order. He came in in a suit."

Her head remained tilted down as she continued.

"He saw me and said, 'Hi Mom,' and then went to select a woman. He had changed. That's what was awful about it. It wasn't terrifying that he was in the wrong order, or that he was there as a client. What was terrifying was that he wasn't our son, he was a different person. He had different eyes."

I took her hand and she reflexively leaned in to me.

"Corim, if I don't live past tomorrow, then please promise me you'll keep him who he is."

"I promise. You know I promise. He'll always be Ian, you know that."

Then there he was, standing in his pajamas in the kitchen with us. Kiri bent down and squeezed him, and ran her cheek up and down the side of his head to feel her skin moving against his hair.

I felt so lucky watching that embrace that I stopped feeling the press of time. I wasn't worried that the trial was only hours away, I just wanted to stay up with them for what little was left of the night.

"Let's go up to the roof," I said.

27

When we were fifteen-year-olds perfecting our skills in our final year of the soft rooms, we were summoned to the auditorium for our last lecture.

Mrs. Winten repeated much of what she'd said over the years. Be good citizens. Respect each other. Keep working hard up on the eleventh floor, and then work hard as adults. Be happy and excited for your lives.

She finished with a full lecture on the reasons for the brevity of our lifespans. It started much as her first lecture years before had, and again we were shown awful images of the savageries that existed in the dark times when there were no manmade regulators to the lengths of lives.

After the images she said, "If you resent it that the upper orders get more life than you, then you still haven't learned the way of things. For the fact is that we in the upper orders give up some of our lives in order to support yours. Lengthy as the lives of the upper orders may seem to you, they could be even longer if we stopped sharing the resources used to support you in the General Order. I am deeply grateful to the orders above mine, and you should have the same gratitude toward the orders above yours.

"Every day you go to eat lunch, and every day there is food waiting for you and a spot at a table. Your life is a lot like your time in the cafeteria. You use it. You eat. You socialize. But you do so in the allotted time. That's how it must be because that's the way of doing things that gave you your time in the first place.

"Of course all of us would like extra time for fun things, but when it comes at the expense of others we mustn't be selfish. We must carry a humble and grateful attitude with us every day, and embrace the time we have without complaint. And always remember that death comes to us all no matter what order we were born into."

Later a group of us were sitting in the parlor talking about how we'd never have to go to a lecture again.

"Such a relief!" Raff said. "No more sitting silent and trying not to fall asleep."

"I was always too afraid to fall asleep," I said. "She'd always pause and glare at us one by one. I always felt like she was going to call my name and announce something terrible about me. I mean, I've never heard of her ever doing anything like that, but imagine if she did!"

The group laughed in agreement except for Bennett, who had been uncharacteristically quiet.

He glanced around the table until he had our attention. "It's not true you know, what she said about death coming to everyone. That's not true."

"What are you talking about?" I asked.

"You know both my parents used to be sex workers, right? Well, when you work in a brothel, you hear things. Members of the upper orders aren't supposed to tell sex workers anything, but things come out. One thing my parents learned, and don't tell anyone that you heard this from me, but they learned that the Administrative Order isn't the highest order. There's another order, and that order doesn't die at all. They live forever."

"Oh c'mon, that's just an old myth," Raff said.

"It's no myth. There's an immortal order," Bennett said.

"Your parents may have been told that," Raff said, "but that doesn't make it true. Sex workers get told all sorts of crazy things."

I agreed with Raff. Still, the more I thought about it, the more what Bennett had said made sense. If lifespans could be controlled for the Administrative Order to the point where every member of it knows they will live in perfect health until they are in their nineties, then it stood to reason that perhaps there is an order without a set lifespan at all.

Later I went to my L-pod and asked, "Are there any orders that live longer than the Administrative Order?"

"No, Corim," it answered.

"Does the technology exist to make someone live indefinitely?"

"That sort of thing is outside of my programming."

I thought back to Mrs. Winten's lecture when we were shown images of war and famine. I asked, "Back when the world was overpopulated, what was the average lifespan? How many people were there? What was the peak population of the world?"

"Again, I don't have that information for you."

"What about now, then? What's the current population of the world?"

"Corim, your curriculum doesn't cover that."

"When you show me images of suffering, of starvation and disease – how long ago did that sort of thing happen?"

"I don't have the specific dates, but I know those images are from very long ago. Nothing like that happens anymore and that's what's important."

"When members of upper orders go to school, do their L-pods have the same programming, or do they get different lessons?"

"There are only very slight differences," it said. "Members of every order are given educations specialized to the jobs they will take later in life. Your education is perfect for you. You have access to all the information you'll ever need to have a happy and full life."

For the first time ever I came out of my L-pod feeling cheated. It seemed to me the number of people in the world was a basic fact that should've been in my curriculum.

I never was able to find population estimates, but I made some local ones on my own. I estimated the population of my apartment building to be nine thousand. I counted two hundred and ten apartment buildings in our ward. Assuming our building was average, that would give our ward a population of nearly two million.

I knew that our ward was but a sliver of a sliver of a greater city because from the roof I could see building tops lining every distant horizon. I had no way of estimating populations outside of our ward, but I must've been looking out at tens of millions of people.

Beyond that was mystery. Our ward was called Ward Nineteen, but we were never told how many wards there were total. No computer search would tell me how much of the world was city and how much was farm, or even the total size of the world's landmass.

I realized that the world likely had at least hundreds of millions of people, and the thought of that made me feel very insignificant. I decided that was why the real numbers were kept secret from us.

Maybe the world was bigger than I was supposing it to be, perhaps large enough to sustain billions. Even if that were so, I couldn't imagine the Administrative Order would've allowed the population to remain so pointlessly high.

After we were married I told all this to Kiri. "That's strange we can't find out," she said, "but what difference would it make if you knew?"

"I'm curious. It's something I think would help me understand things better."

She smirked and shrugged.

"Don't shrug me off," I said. "Is that the kind of question you aren't supposed to ask your clients about?"

Another shrug. "I could try."

The next night she told me, "I tried asking a client. The only questions we're supposed to ask are flattering ones, so I started off by acting in awe of how much he must know being a member of the Administrative Order. He took the bait and said how yes he does a lot, and that it's more than any one person should have to learn.

"I asked him if he knew how many people work at my brothel and he said, 'A typical brothel has about a hundred employees, so something close to that.'"

"Was he right?" I asked.

"Yeah, he was close. Last I saw we have sixty-eight women and twenty-four men. So next I asked him if he knew how much a train weighs, because that seemed like a silly and random thing to ask. He said they weigh under a thousand pounds per car. He went on about how he's toured the factory where they're built, and how they're made from fiber composite shells."

"Wow," I said, genuinely impressed.

"So, as if it were another random question, I asked if he knew how many people are in the world. It made him tense up a little. He said, 'No, I don't have reason to know that sort of thing.' I don't know if he tensed up because he was embarrassed that he didn't know, or because he was suspicious of why I was asking. I don't think I should ask anyone else though, ok?"

28

We were still in the small hours before dawn, and Kiri took her coat from the rack by the front door and insisted Ian and I do the same. So we all went out with our coats over our pajamas.

As I'd hoped, we were alone in both the hallway and the elevator. Even the roof was empty. It was a rare thing to be up there with only the farmbots and the sleeping bees, everyone else below.

We walked to the north end and looked out at the spire of the Life Center glowing white against the moonless night. The railing was the perfect height for Ian to put his elbows on as he rested his chin on his hands.

"Ian, you know at the trial you're going to hear some bad things," Kiri said. "The kind of things you don't want to hear – about what I had to do at my job, about violent things happening to me."

"I know," he said.

"You're going to start having sex in a couple years. We've talked to you about that."

He nodded.

"I don't want what you hear today to have any effect on sex for you when the time comes. It's something that should be fun and respectful, and that's what it will be for you."

"Mom, I know." He was embarrassed, of course.

I was leaning against the rail, feeling the chill of the breeze down my neck and looking down at Ian as he listened.

Kiri continued, "And I know you'll always remember to treat the ones you're with right. Right?"

"Right," Ian said.

I heard the swoosh of the elevator door opening. A solitary man came out and began walking between the fences and partitions that kept people out of the crops. He was slouched, and his hands were deep in his pockets.

"Look at that bachelor back there," I said. "I bet that's his routine, walking through the crops every morning. That's not such a bad habit, walking that maze and watching the sunrise."

Kiri turned around and observed the man for a moment. "If it makes him happy," she said.

She wrapped her fingers around the railing behind her and squeezed it hard. "Let's go get ready."

"You two split my breakfast," Kiri said. "I'll be in the shower."

Ian and I ate slowly. We'd already dressed and had nothing to do other than wait.

The time we'd been planning on leaving came, but Kiri was still in the bathroom. It wasn't like her to be running late. I went and knocked. No answer.

"Kiri?"

Nothing.

I called her name again as I pressed the door open.

Her shower had timed out, but she was still standing in it and staring at the drain, droplets and goosebumps lining her crossed arms, her hair slick down her ivory back. Her face had a terrible look to it – bereft of its usual hope and optimism. When I saw her like that, the melancholy and fear I'd been feeling began to fuse with anger at the pointlessness of all we were going through.

I pulled the towel from the rack and wrapped it around her.

"Kiri. C'mon, we have to go."

She didn't move. I edged my arm over her shoulders and held her just enough to let her know she was being held.

She came to and sniffled and sighed. She turned, stepped out, and shook the towel through her hair and over her skin. On the way to our bedroom she asked, "Are we late?"

"A little."

She pulled out her standard issue red dress.

"Not one of your outfits?" I asked.

"When I'm in front of everyone and I have the cameras on me, I want there to be no doubt about what order I come from."

The three of us went down to the lobby where Noli stood waiting. She'd been summoned as a witness. She wore a gray dress that was cut much in the fashion of the standard issue dresses, but with a flourish of large white buttons across the chest and accents of lace at the wrists and collar. Her gold earrings were large, oval blades with mazelike engravings. Slender chains extended down from the bottom of the blades and clasped to a matching necklace.

On seeing Kiri, Noli worriedly asked, "Should I not have dressed up?"

"No, that's perfect," Kiri said. "I bet you'll get some new clients after they see you on the news tonight."

At the station, the morning rush was in full effect and we queued up behind a crowd waiting for the northbound train.

"I hope we're able to board the next train," Noli said.

I turned back and looked at the big clock that rose from the platform floor. The instructions they'd messaged to Kiri said it was important to be on time.

Kiri faced the crowd before us and called out over their chatter, "Excuse me, I'm on Extension!"

Conversations halted and a dozen heads turned.

"I'm on Extension and we're in a hurry. Would it be alright if we cut ahead?"

They all stared at us as they pressed into each other to clear a path. We followed Kiri through the sea of curious faces toward the track.

"Thank you. I'm on Extension. Thank you."

When we took our place at the edge of the platform the crowd left a buffer of space around us. In a minute the next train pulled in, and I had to catch my balance when a rush of air from the first passing cars hit my fatigued body. After jostling through the torrent of disembarking passengers, we were onboard and on our way.

At the Life Center, a guidebot took us down a hallway that snaked in sweeping curves until we reached a bank of golden elevators. We got into one, and I had to catch myself when it started moving, in part because it gained speed so quickly but more so because I was caught off guard that we were going down instead of up. It had never occurred to me that the Life Center might have floors below its lobby.

The room where we arrived was large, and smelled of the soil in the potted rose bushes that were spread throughout. At the other side of the room was the strange sight of a tunnel entryway and elevated steel tracks running in and out again over a smooth concrete floor. On the tracks sat a vehicle that was like a train car but much shorter and smaller. It had an open-air top and only six seats.

"Have a seat in the tram and you'll be taken to the courthouse," the guidebot said. "I won't be joining you, but a counselor will meet you there."

We stepped onto the platform, and as we got in the tram Kiri asked the bot, "Are we being taken to a restricted area?"

The tram started moving and the bot called after us, "Yes, but don't be nervous. A counselor is waiting for you."

The seats were larger and plusher than a train's, and as we rocked gently through the darkness of the tunnel my exhaustion overcame my nerves and I caught my head nodding forward in sleep.

We exited the tunnel, and without slowing we passed through what I guessed to be the bottom floor of a different building. The only thing in it was an empty room with a wall of elevator doors.

We entered a tunnel again and were soon moving through another open space. In the moment I had to look across the passing platform, I saw some kind of cafeteria that was busy with well-dressed people.

When the shows we watched portrayed upper order members eating, the settings were always something close to what we were used to, such as an automat or a little apartment kitchen or a standard cafeteria of long, tightly packed tables. What I saw from the tram was different. The tables were draped with white cloths, and above them hung little lights that appeared to be more decorative than utilitarian. The chairs looked as though they might've been made of wood. Bots of a type I didn't recognize moved among the tables carrying plates and glasses. Just before we again entered a tunnel, I picked up a smoky, savory aroma that was unlike anything I'd ever smelled before.

At the next open space the tram stopped at a platform, upon which a lone woman stood. She was a barrel-chested brunette with a small face. She wore the type of woman's suit I'd often seen weatherwomen wear. I was surprised by her youth, she couldn't have been any older than mid-twenties, and may have even been still a teenager.

She waved us toward her. "Hello! Welcome! C'mon out!"

She kept talking as we stepped out. "Hi there, Ian! That's it, just step on out. Good job! And here comes your dad and here comes Noli. And there you are, Kiri!"

We stood in front of her awaiting instructions. She looked at us, raised her eyebrows, tilted her head, wrapped her arms in front of her as if to squeeze herself, and let out a loud, happy sigh.

"Well. I am Counselor Reesa. Counselor Reesa. It's such a pleasure to meet you all, I just wish it wasn't under these circumstances. Let me hug you all!"

She rushed at Kiri and embraced her, holding her tight and rocking back and forth as she let out a long, wailing, "Oh!"

Then she hugged Noli, but for not as long.

She hugged me next. I kept my distance as best I could. I'd never touched an upper order member before, but I wasn't thinking of that so much as I was thinking of how off-putting I found her.

That was a surprising first impression because, although this counselor was the first other than Mrs. Winten whom I'd seen and heard in person, I knew all counselors were given extensive emotional training and that their genetic profiles were optimized for maximum warmth and empathy.

When she was done with me she turned to Ian. "Hang on Ian," she said, "let me get down to your level." She dropped to one knee.

She squeezed him tight, saying, "Ian, oh Ian! My little Ian!"

From her grip he looked up at me desperately.

She pulled back, squeezed his shoulders, looked at him with exaggerated intensity, and asked, "Do you think we can be friends?"

Instead of answering, he looked back at her with the same blank expression his face would get while watching the farmbots work on our roof.

Counselor Reesa turned to Kiri. "What's the matter? Is he shy?"

"He's not used to being talked to the way you're talking to him," Kiri said. "He may find it condescending."

Counselor Reesa's face firmed and she stood up. She looked to me and I nodded in agreement. Her eyes got wide and she put her hands over her mouth.

"I'm sorry! I just started this job, and you're the first members of the General Order I've ever met. I'm nervous, and I really don't know much about how you people talk to each other."

Hearing her admit to being insecure made me dislike her less. "It's ok," I said.

Kiri put her hand on Counselor Reesa's elbow. "I think we probably talk to each other a lot like the way you're used to."

Counselor Reesa grabbed Kiri and gave her another hug. When she was done with it she smiled at all of us. "You all seem so nice," she said. "Thank you!"

We waited for more but she was silent. We stood looking around at the big room. Like its corresponding room at the Life Center, this room was empty except for the potted rose bushes spread about.

Finally Kiri spoke up. "So, are you going to tell us where to go for the trial?"

"Oh yes, sorry!" Counselor Reesa said. "Please follow me this way. If anyone wants to hold my hand they can."

None of us did. We crossed through the rose bushes to a bank of elevators and one opened as we approached. We got in, and I asked Counselor Reesa, "Why does this elevator have mirrors on its walls?"

"I don't know, I've never thought about it," she said. "I guess so riders can check how they look on the way to where they're going?"

At the end of our ride up we walked into the cool, heavy air of a white marble hallway. As we followed Counselor

Reesa our footsteps were muted beneath the coffered ceiling high above.

The hallway was busy with well-dressed men and women. Most looked older than forty, many much older. It was surreal to be passing so many gray-haired, wrinkled people.

I surmised from the looks they gave us that it was also noteworthy for them to see members of the General Order in standard issue clothing moving through the halls of their courthouse. I wondered if they could somehow tell that Noli, in her nice dress and jewelry, was also General Order.

Counselor Reesa kept glancing back at Ian. I think she'd become intimidated by him.

The hallway walls had a small shelf every few feet. On them, alternately, were tiny potted manicured trees and white busts of men with their names on plaques beneath. We came to a set of huge brass-handled wood doors. Counselor Reesa tapped one and it swung open to reveal a courtroom.

29

I'd never seen so much wood. Swirling dark-brown grain made up every surface between the floor and ceiling. Scotson Yvera and his lawyer were sitting at a table up front to the left. Scotson had his back to us, but his lawyer saw us come in, and he grinned and gave us a subtle wave.

At a table to the right was a wiry man wearing a suit. Kiri pointed to him. "That's who interviewed me after I was revived."

He had dark features and looked around fifty. Counselor Reesa led us to him. "This is the prosecutor Domin Ciarna," she said. "He'll take care of you for now, but I'll walk you back to the tram afterward. Good luck, ok?"

She waved goodbye and hurried out. The prosecutor asked Kiri if she was ready and she answered yes.

"Great. We'll get underway soon. Try to stay relaxed up on the stand, and keep your answers straightforward. The defense will pick apart what you say, but don't let it get to you. Their goal is to get you to appear emotional."

Kiri nodded.

"Good, good," he said. "We have a solid case, I think, but we'll have to be careful. The lawyer we're up against has been on a winning streak. I'd like to end that today."

"How could he win?" Noli asked. "It's so clear cut."

The prosecutor sighed and looked over at Scotson and his lawyer. "It's a good case, but any trial can go either way. Bringing members of the Administrative Order up on charges is rare, and the only reason it happened here is that

Mrs. Colleran is a sex worker. If he had killed even a counselor he would've maybe paid a fine, no more. Frankly, a case like this is more about getting justice for the clients who lost an experienced sex worker than it is about justice for you folks. But justice is justice."

He had Kiri and Noli take a seat at his table. Ian and I sat on the spectator's bench behind them.

While we waited, about twenty onlookers filed in and took seats in the benches behind us. It was a younger crowd, including some who looked school aged. Mostly male, all of whom were in suits and ties.

In the spectator's bench behind the defendant's table there was a woman with a boy and girl. The girl looked Ian's age, and the boy looked a few years older. I assumed she was Scotson's wife and that one of the children was theirs. I started to wonder the relation of the other child, but then I remembered I was in a place of multi-child families.

Scotson and his lawyer leaned back in their chairs chatting and laughing as if they were two old friends sitting outdoors enjoying a summer day. I turned myself away until they were out of my field of vision.

Three chimes sounded, everyone in the room quieted, and a voice said, "Please rise." When we stood I looked around and saw cameras and microphones mounted at various spots. The cameras would no doubt be running as soon as the action started. Trial footage always got a lot of airtime on the news.

The witness stand had an array of monitors behind it to measure things such as vocal tone, heart rate, and brainwaves. The data would show up on a readout for the judge.

A door opened behind the bench, and a man in a black robe came out, took a seat, and said with great weight, "Be seated." He looked too old for his age to be accurately guessed, having white wispy hair, gray eyes, and a face as stern and still as the granite busts lining the hall outside.

He banged his gavel and checked the display in front of him.

"This is the case of the State versus Scotson Yvera," he said. "The defendant is a member of the Administrative Order, and is accused of murdering the decedent, one Kiri Colleran of the General Order." He fixed his gaze on the prosecutor. "Begin."

The prosecutor rose. "The State calls Noli Mastin to the stand."

Noli went and got into the witness chair. After the monitors behind her finished adjusting themselves around her head, the prosecutor instructed her to tell what she remembered about Kiri's death.

Noli described seeing Scotson run out of the room, and then going in herself and finding Kiri. She finished by saying how the medbot then came in and took Kiri's body away.

The prosecutor asked, "Could you describe what the decedent looked like when you found her?"

"Kiri's face was blue and her body was limp. Her head was tilted unnaturally and her eyes just... they just stared out blankly like they were disconnected, like they weren't even eyes."

The prosecutor let a pause hang in the air before he said, "No further questions your honor." As he sat back down he glared over at Scotson.

The judge nodded to the defendant's table, and Scotson's lawyer rose and approached Noli. He asked, "When you saw Mr. Yvera run out, you said he looked panicked, correct?"

Noli nodded. "Yeah, that's right."

"Did he appear to you to be in the state of mind in which he could make rational, calculated, premeditated decisions?"

The prosecutor stood and called out, "Objection. Speculative and leading."

The judge seemed too apathetic to bother considering the merits of the objection. "Overruled. The witness will answer."

The lawyer repeated the question. Noli's eyes darted for a moment and then she said, "No, I ... I would think not."

"No further questions," the lawyer said. He sauntered back to his desk as if the brief exchange had shown the entire case was pointless.

The judge had an elbow on his desk to prop his head up with his hand, and looked as though he could fall asleep at any moment. "Witness is excused," he said. Noli walked back to her seat. Kiri put her hand on Noli's back and whispered to her, "You did great."

The prosecutor rose. "The State calls the decedent, Kiri Colleran."

30

Kiri rose and scooted by Noli. I gripped the edge of the bench beneath me. I was hoping she wasn't as nervous as I was.

When she took the stand the prosecutor said, "Mrs. Colleran, please tell the court everything you can about your history with Scotson Yvera, all the way up to your death."

Kiri collected herself, took a breath, and began, "We met almost six months ago now. A group of us workers were told that a new client would be coming in, so we gathered in the lobby. Scotson showed up late, looked us over without saying anything as we all said hello, and then began moving around among us asking questions. When he came over to me and got my age, he said I was too old to still be working there. I told him that I was still in demand because I could do things that the newer workers weren't up for. I could tell this caught his interest, but he just said, 'Sure you can, honey,' and turned and went back to interviewing the others.

"The next week I got a message from the brothel mistress saying he'd decided to try a session with me. So I met him in the lobby and we chatted. He was wearing a suit, I believe the same one he's wearing today. I said flirtatious things, but I found that he enjoyed doing most of the talking.

"I noticed there was something uncomfortable and guarded in the way he spoke. In my line of work you need to quickly assess a client's personality type and emotional state. With Scotson I decided straightaway that he had problems with his self-image."

Scotson's lawyer shot out of his chair. "Objection! That is speculative, not to mention uninformed."

The judge was no more interested in this objection than the earlier one from the prosecutor, and knocked it down in his slow, gravelly voice. "Overruled. The witness is entitled to recount her opinions."

The lawyer pursed his lips and sat. He was so rough pulling in his chair that the wooden legs banged rapidly as they skipped against the marble floor.

The judge turned to Kiri. "Go on."

"So, having decided that I had to be extra delicate with his self-esteem, I listened to everything he had to say as if I were hanging on his every word. And I asked him as many questions about his life as I could. He told me about all the responsibilities he had, and all the money he made. I acted very impressed and excited.

"When he talked about me, he only said negative things, like how I was too old, or how I wasn't as pretty as the last girl he'd had, or how my hair was too red and I should lighten it. He finished by shaking his head, and saying he didn't know what he was thinking when he bought a session with me. Then he said, 'But let's see what you've got.'

"I took his hand to walk him upstairs, but as we were walking he yanked his hand away and dug his fingers into my hair. He kept turning and shifting my head until I would have to readjust how I was walking. This didn't surprise me – I had pegged him early as the controlling type with a sadistic streak.

"We got into the room, and he sat on the edge of the bed and told me to strip for him. While I stripped he would pull me in to touch me, and then release me again. When I finished stripping, he had me stand still and told me to keep my eyes open. He slowly circled me several times and then pushed me onto the bed."

I looked down at Ian, wishing he didn't have to hear these parts. I hoped Kiri was right that it'd be best for him to see the trial. I also hoped that he'd remember all the times she'd explained her job to him, and explained how none of what she did changed who she was.

"He grabbed my ankles and pressed them down into the bed. Then he released them and did the same thing with my wrists. Then my head and torso and so on. He liked holding down different parts of me. He would just watch it happen, and then move on to a different part. I pretended to find it exhilarating. Then he started slapping me, but only lightly. His breathing became heavier. He stepped back and undid his pants. I did what I always did at this moment, which was widen my eyes as if I were surprised and excited by what I was seeing."

I looked over at Scotson. For once he didn't have his usual smug face on, but instead a mix of anger and embarrassment. His lower lip was pushing his upper lip against his nose to the point where his nostrils were covered.

"He got onto the bed and we started. I had an idea that I thought would be perfect for him. Every time he touched my neck I let out a sound of pleasure as if it were something I couldn't control. I made it more and more obvious until he picked up on it and started touching my neck more as the sex continued. I leaned my head back as far as I could, and he pressed a hand against the side of my throat and started to squeeze. He was very tentative about it, and I got the feeling that he'd never choked a woman before."

Scotson's lawyer sat forward to write something in his notepad.

"I reacted by faking an orgasm. I did this so he'd feel secure that I was fulfilled by being with him, and that I would want him again. But I also made it much less vocal than my usual fake orgasm. I wanted to leave him with the idea that making me scream would be a challenge. It all excited him a great deal, and he finished a moment later. He got off me and got his pants back on. He walked out without saying goodbye, and that was that. It hadn't been a particularly unusual session. All of it had only lasted about thirty minutes, and I was glad to be left with some extra free time."

"He came in for another session a few weeks later. I again met him in the lobby, but this time there was no talking. He walked in, grabbed my hair, and walked me upstairs. After he had me strip, the slapping was harder and in more places, but it was still nothing unusual. When the sex started, he had me be on top. When he decided to choke me he was still careful about it, but this time he used both hands. I added some light choking sounds to my fake orgasm. Again he got quite worked up and finished quickly.

"Two weeks later it was more of the same, but the intensity was again higher. We sex workers always consider it good when you can get a client to escalate something every time. It's a standard way to keep a client coming back to you. You find what their kink is, or find a kink for them, and you give them a little bit more of it each time. If you don't have a special hook to keep a client coming back, then they'll usually choose the novelty of someone new for their next visit.

"And that's how it continued for the next few months. We had regular sessions where he would explore different forms of control and abuse. He introduced verbal debasement as we went further along. Rather than the little sniping and insults of our first meetings, he'd call me disgusting and use all the names that some men call women like me. He started to escalate that, and he continued to escalate the physical violence."

I felt sick, defeated, and trapped listening to her words, and I knew it was going to get worse. I tried to steel myself – if she could be brave enough to say it, then I could at least listen.

"We had a session where instead of slapping and spanking, he was hitting. Outright punches. It was like nothing I'd had before, and I begged him to go easier. He didn't, and when he choked me near the end it was harder than it should've been. Afterward, as he was dressing, I told him he'd gone too far, and that if we were to meet again we would have to try different things. But the next time was even rougher. I needed medbot treatment afterward and I was badly bruised."

"Your honor," the prosecutor said, "I have submitted her med-pod records from that incident as well as the brothel records showing that Scotson Yvera's session came just before her treatment."

The judge nodded without removing his head from the hand it was leaning on. The prosecutor said, "Please continue, Mrs. Colleran."

"I told the brothel mistress things had gotten too rough, and that I hoped I wouldn't see him anymore. She said she'd keep that in mind, but about two weeks later I got a message from her saying he'd reserved a session with Noli and me at the same time. The mistress made it clear that both Noli and I were expected to agree to it. I decided to agree, because I knew I'd feel safe having Noli in the same room.

"The session comes and it's pretty straightforward. He has me do some things with Noli, but then he took over from me and had sex with her. He didn't abuse us. He actually never touched me at all, and the only thing he ever said was how beautiful Noli was. I got the impression he ignored me during that session to try to get to me. Otherwise why pay extra for me to be there?

"A week after that, he messaged me directly asking for a one-on-one session. He said something about how he hoped the session with Noli showed me that he was back to normal, as far as his tastes go. He said he felt like things had gotten strange between us, and he wanted to see me one more time to leave things on a good note. He also said he'd be paying me extra.

"But I was suspicious, so I replied that I would only do another session if Noli were again included. He wrote back saying Noli could sit out in the hall while the door to the room remained open. That seemed safe to me, because I knew she'd help if she heard anything bad.

"A couple days later he met Noli and me in the lobby. We walked up to the room and he didn't grab my hair or say anything negative. Noli took a seat outside and we left the door open. Everything started fine. He got on top and he was gentle – he did things he'd never done, like caress my face. I remember looking at the open door and feeling like I didn't have anything to worry about.

"I started moaning like I was enjoying it. Then all at once he became very intense and his breathing got heavy. His face changed – first confusion, then anger. I should've screamed right then, but it all happened so fast. He lunged down at me, and got his hands tight around my neck."

"Now Mrs. Colleran," the prosecutor said, "I want this next part to be absolutely clear. When he started choking you, did you tell him to stop?"

I thought back to how, two days before, Scotson's lawyer had been in our apartment, and described to Kiri the way he wanted her to answer this question, and how he promised her that she would get the rest of her life back.

"Yes," she said. "Yes, I told him to stop. I said, 'No. Stop. Stop.' "

I wasn't surprised. Earlier in the day, after we'd come down from the roof, I came out from changing and looked into the kitchen to see Kiri and Ian sitting together. Neither of them noticed me, and from the darkness of the hall I heard her say to him, "It might be hard, but I want you to remember what I did today, and to try and understand why I did it. And whenever in your life you have a tough choice to make, think of today, and you'll know what to do."

I knew then that she'd made her decision, and I knew I had no chance of changing her mind. Part of me wanted to hate her for it, but the better part of me knew she was right.

At hearing Kiri's answer, Scotson winced and a burst of air hissed through his teeth. His lawyer's head dropped, and even from across the courtroom I could see the muscles in his neck contract as he squeezed the edges of the table in front of him.

"You told him to stop?" the prosecutor asked.

"Yes. It was hard to get any air out, but I did, and I said stop as best I could. It came out clearly."

"Did he hear you say it?"

"Yes. He was looking right at me and his face was inches from mine, I know he heard me."

"And did he stop?"

"He squeezed tighter. I felt something give in the front of my neck, and I couldn't breathe at all. I tried to say stop again, but this time I couldn't. I just mouthed the word. I grabbed his arms and pulled as hard as I could, but he was too strong. Then I slapped at him, and then I hit at the bed hoping that Noli would hear it. He smiled and he started to moan and orgasm, and I remember thinking that I'd made an awful mistake by not quitting my job, and that now there was nothing I could do about it."

She closed her eyes and put her hand over her face, but just as quickly she regained herself and went on.

"For years, every time in the brothel when I'd gotten in a rough situation I could always find a solution. I could always find a way out, a way to be safe. But now there was nothing I could do, and the last thing I remember was feeling was a sense of surprise about it. The next thing I remember is waking up in the Life Center and realizing I'd died."

She paused, and I expected her to indicate to the prosecutor that she was finished. Instead she looked to the defendant's table. "Scotson," she said, "I know you're sorry, and I don't think you're a bad man in most ways, but you know as well as I do that you knew you were killing me."

Scotson's lawyer shifted in his chair and made as though he was about to rise to object. The judge looked at him and shook his head no. Scotson watched Kiri speak but did nothing to acknowledge it.

"And I know you were worked up and you lost control and that these things happen. But I'm not going to lie about it. If I do, and if you walk out of here without facing any consequences for what you did, then tomorrow someone like you might not worry as much about being careful with someone like me. So even if it meant getting all my years back, I wouldn't have been able to live with myself if I'd taken the deal you offered me. I wouldn't..."

There were murmurs from the spectators, and this time Scotson's lawyer didn't hesitate as he rose angrily and yelled, "Objection!"

The judge remained as stock-still as he had when he'd overruled the earlier objections, but for this one he said, "Sustained. The court orders that last statement stricken from the record and edited from the footage. The decedent will concern her testimony only with the events in question, and not with anything that came after."

He lifted his resting head from his hand and turned to Kiri. "Do you have anything more to say about the events that led to your death, and only about those events?"

"I think I said everything."

"Prosecution, any further questions?" the judge asked.

"No, your honor."

"Defense, do you choose to cross-examine?"

The lawyer straightened his suit jacket. "Absolutely."

He walked up to Kiri, and gripped with both his hands the edge of the witness chair's armrest, just an inch from Kiri's wrist. "Would you say you're a good actress?"

"I would say I'm good at acting in ways that might intrigue and please a client."

The lawyer chuckled under his breath. "And this requires performances from you, does it not?"

"Yes, it does."

"And you would say you're skilled at delivering these performances."

"I'd like to think so, yes."

"And all of your clients, do you think they're all completely clueless that it is part of your job to give performances?"

"No, I think they tend to understand that that's part of what they're paying for."

"Now let me ask. When you deliver a performance well enough, does the client have any way of knowing when you're performing and when you're not?"

"Not if I do well enough. That's the whole idea."

"Yes, that's the whole idea. Indeed, indeed. So, Kiri Colleran of the General Order, if we are to believe you that you audibly protested to my client, Mr. Scotson Yvera of the Administrative Order, how would he have known that you weren't giving a performance at that moment?"

Kiri shook her head. "No, it wasn't like that."

"You may have known it wasn't like that, but how could my client, after months of performances from you, have known? You just said the whole idea of your performances is to make it so a client doesn't know whether or not you're performing."

Kiri's face reddened. "He knew he was hurting me. He knew I was in trouble."

"I'm not asking you to speculate, I'm asking you to answer the question. How would he, who had fallen under your charms for so long, have known you had stopped performing?"

Kiri's voice broke up as she said, "He knew he had squeezed my throat shut. That's not something that could be part of a performance. Anyone would know that."

The lawyer turned his back to her and said, almost to himself, "Did he? Did he?" He looked back to the judge. "No further questions."

The judge said, "The decedent is dismissed. Does the prosecution have any further witnesses?"

"Your honor, the State rests."

"Does the defense call anyone?"

"Only one person, your honor. Scotson Yvera."

31

Scotson took the stand. He was visibly uncomfortable with how the monitors adjusted themselves around his head.

His lawyer asked, "Mr. Yvera, did you choke Kiri Colleran to death?"

Scotson seemed shocked and hurt by the question. "Yes. Yes, I'm afraid I did."

"And, Mr. Yvera, did she tell you stop?"

"I don't remember her ever saying that, no."

"Are you sure? Did she say 'stop' at any time?"

"If she did I never heard it. We were having sex. She was enjoying it, or I suppose, given what she's said today, she was pretending to enjoy it. I choked her just like I always did, just how she liked. She was happy. Then she passed out and I didn't notice until it was too late."

"And what did you do then?"

"I panicked. I ran out. It was awful. I've never experienced anything like that, I was very upset. I had really grown quite fond of her."

The lawyer nodded somberly. "No further questions, your honor."

"Does the prosecution wish to cross-examine?" the judge asked.

"The State has no interest in hearing any more from Kiri Colleran's killer," the prosecutor said.

"A simple no would've sufficed, but very well. The court will hear closing arguments."

The prosecutor stood, crossed his hands behind his back, bowed his head, and walked to the middle of the courtroom. He let the silence build and then began, "Your honor, I often go to brothels, and it's an important pleasure to me. So much so that I give a lot of thought to the brothel employees who provide me with that pleasure. I think of how they'll never have a chance to be our equals in education and culture. I think of how they never get decades to perfect themselves the way we do. It sometimes seems unfair, but I remind myself that it is the natural order of things, and that it's for the best.

"In many ways the life of an individual sex worker is of little significance. Mrs. Colleran's death won't really affect the world at large. That is the lot in life for all the members of the General Order. They are important as a whole, but when singled out none of them are of any relevance to our future.

"But does that make them less worthy of basic respect? Does it make them disposable? I don't think so, but even if I'm wrong would it matter here? No, it wouldn't – because how we treat them is not about them, it's about us. They are as much our charges and burdens as our own children are, and we have the same responsibility to treat them with due care.

"I've never in all my visits to brothels come close to hurting a sex worker, let alone killing one. The defense will argue that it was a simple mistake. Your honor, choking the life out of a woman is not something one stumbles into by mistake. The results of Scotson Yvera's violent actions were foreseeable to him, but that didn't stop him from choking her. And that, your honor, is murder.

"Our beautiful laws were made both to protect everyone, and to apply to everyone. With all due respect to Scotson's Yvera's standing, he broke the law and punishment is due.

Please your honor, let the defendant know – indeed let all who would doubt it know – that the power of the law reaches to all."

He walked back to the table and the judge called the defense.

The lawyer popped from his chair and raised a palm upward as he walked forward and said, "Your honor, you may have felt some sympathy watching Mrs. Colleran's testimony, but my client's future cannot be decided by how sorry we feel for her. My client's future must be decided by the merits of the case against him. And this case has no merit because it wasn't my client's actions that led to Kiri Colleran's death. It was Kiri Colleran's actions that led to Kiri Colleran's death.

"Step by step that woman led Scotson Yvera into getting more and more involved in her perverse little game. She admitted, freely, that she taught him to choke her. Let me remind you what she said about teaching him. I quote, 'I got the feeling that he had never choked a woman before.'

"And she was right. My client had never choked a woman before. And he never would have if he didn't have the misfortune of meeting Kiri Colleran, a woman so motivated by greed that she uses her guile to lead men down dark and dangerous paths. A woman who encouraged, time and again, my client to hurt her – and then she turns around and testifies against him for doing that very thing.

"Your honor, what happened was not the result of the character of Mr. Scotson Yvera, who has always been an upstanding member of the Administrative Order. What happened was the inevitable result of the manipulative and deceptive methods employed by Kiri Colleran.

"In another time they would've called her unclean. I would still call her that. Unclean motives. Unclean methods. And an unclean effect on my client. She is someone who has spent every day of her adult life saying things that were not true. And now we are to believe her self-serving claims about what happened that day?

"Now, your monitors may very well show that she fully believes every word of her testimony. But a woman like this has no doubt trained herself to believe what she is saying when she's saying it, regardless of the statement's relationship to the truth."

The lawyer adjusted his suit with care, and then nodded to himself as he looked around the courtroom.

"Your honor, the life of a member of the Administrative Order is at stake here. Remember who his accuser is, and remember what it is she does for a living."

The lawyer nodded again, returned to his table and patted Scotson's back.

The judge leaned forward and squinted at the display in front of him to examine the readouts.

He sat up and looked first at Kiri, then at Scotson, and then, for the quickest of moments, at one of the wall-mounted cameras pointed at him. He made a guttural sound, closed his eyes, and pinched the skin between his eyebrows. He stayed like this for a long time as the silent courtroom watched and waited.

When the judge opened his eyes his speech was, for the first time, rapid.

"The defense is correct when it says that the decedent led Mr. Yvera to his actions. But it is not the role of members of the upper orders to be led in anything by members of the General Order. The upper orders, particularly the defendant's order, must be leaders in all things. Scotson Yvera, you failed to be a leader. The fact of the matter, and it is an indisputable fact, is that you, Mr. Yvera, went into a brothel and broke the merchandise."

At these last words the judge paused, gave Kiri a look, and added, "So to speak."

He then squared his shoulders in Scotson's direction and continued, "We in the upper orders have a contract of sorts, a contract that is an obligation to the General Order to give those people reasonable accommodations and treatment for their short lives. It's the least we can return to them for all they ultimately do for us. All they do, including their work in the brothels.

"Injuring one of them in such circumstances might've been forgivable, but Mr. Yvera not only robbed this worker of years of her life, but also robbed all of her other clients of her future services. And many of those clients may have, to use the defendant's words, 'grown quite fond of her.'

"For the charge of murdering a member of the General Order, the court finds you guilty."

The judge paused and surveyed the courtroom before finishing with, "Mr. Yvera, your recklessness was more than a mistake made in a moment of passion – it was a dereliction of your duty to respect and uphold the system that we have all worked so hard to perfect. The men of the Administrative Order are of the highest caliber, but even they sometimes falter, and you have surely faltered here. Because you haven't represented your order as you should, you are not deserving of your order's full privileges. The court thereby orders your current lifespan of ninety-six be lowered to the Judicial Order's lifespan of eighty-six, effective immediately."

I caught the prosecutor pumping his fist under the table. He had broken the defense lawyer's winning streak, just like he'd wanted to. Kiri smiled at us all. I tried to smile back, but I didn't feel like it was much of a victory. The sentence was considered harsh, but I'd had fantasies of seeing Scotson sitting in a bare room and pleading not to be executed. Instead Scotson would still outlive me. He'd still outlive Ian.

A medbot came out the door behind the judge's bench and moved across the courtroom floor, stopping at the defendant's table. Scotson looked to his lawyer but his lawyer offered nothing in reply. Scotson's wife broke into tears, and her children looked up at her in fear.

A silver-tipped appendage protracted out of the medbot until it was within an inch of Scotson's nose.

"Lifespan reset," the medbot said. It then turned and left through the same door it had entered. Scotson Yvera, age fifty-two, now had an eighty-six-year lifespan. He fell forward and buried his head in his hands, and his wife rushed to his side to comfort him. His lawyer leaned over and whispered something in his ear.

I walked to the defense's table. When the lawyer saw me coming their way, he got up and stepped back. Scotson and his wife didn't notice me until I was standing in front of them and said, "Scotson."

He removed his hands from his face and looked up at me.

"Restore her time," I said.

"What?" he said.

"Her time. Restore it. You said you didn't want to see her dead."

Scotson shook his head. "I don't know what you're talking about."

Counselor Reesa appeared at my side and tugged at my sleeve. "Corim, you have to go now," she said.

I ignored her. "Kiri only has a few hours," I said to Scotson.

"I'm sorry, I can't help you with that," he said.

Counselor Reesa was pulling at my arm. "Please," she said, "you can't stay here."

As we were led out of the courtroom I called back, "Restore her time, Scotson."

32

We were home an hour later, Kiri, Ian, and I in bed together. Kiri had told Noli that she needed to be alone with us, and they had made their goodbyes outside our lobby door. No words from either of them as they embraced. Noli started to fall apart, pulled away, and left, unsteady on her high heels as she sped down the sidewalk. Kiri didn't watch her go, and when we got into our apartment she remained silent as she went straight to our bedroom and climbed into bed.

If what I had was sleep, it was only the kind of sleep that came in thin ribbons between nightmares and waking. It was more peaceful for me to lie awake and watch Ian sleeping soundly. I wanted to think he was handling it well, but I knew his calmness was more likely because he'd never experienced death, and didn't really understand it, didn't really believe it could be real.

I turned and reached for Kiri, but she had gotten out of bed. I found her in the front room seated by the computer. Two pieces of the set of stationery she'd bought years before were on the desk and folded shut. One was marked for me, the other for Ian.

She stood and started to adjust them plumb with the desk corner, but her hands were shaky and she wasn't getting it quite right. Finally she picked them up and handed them to me. "Don't read them now, ok? Wait until after."

I said ok and put them in my pocket.

"I should just go," she said.

"What are you talking about?"

"You and Ian shouldn't be there for it. You don't need that image in your head."

"You're not going anywhere," I said. "I'm staying with you every second I can."

"I feel like I should be alone for it. I – "

"Listen," I interrupted. "I'm not letting you go off alone. I always hear you out about things, but not this. I'm staying by your side and so is Ian."

"Alright," she said, "but I don't want to stay in here. I want to go somewhere."

"Wherever you want."

"Where should we go?" she asked.

"The Life Center? The roof? Last Day Beach?"

She thought about it. "Not the beach itself, but let's go to Lake Park," she said.

"Ok."

"Ian's still sleeping?"

"Last I saw."

"Then let's wait a little," she said. "We can be alone for a minute, yeah? Maybe you can tell me something sweet?"

"Alright. One thing. You always like this one, and it's the truest thing I know. Kiri, as long as I've been with you I've never known real envy of anyone, even if they're upper order. I've always known I'm the only one in the world who should ever be envied."

It felt like her normal self came back a little, and she reached up and caressed the back of my neck.

"Now how about a kiss?" she said.

One last kiss, ripples over water.

Later, as the three of us were waiting on the train platform, I held Ian's hand and watched his chest rise and fall with uneven breaths. As we boarded I looked back at the station clock. Forty-six minutes.

Kiri and Ian took two seats, and I stood next to them in the aisle. I held Kiri's shoulder as the train's acceleration pushed her back into the seat cushion. She began to cry, and other passengers turned to stare blankly as though they were watching a show on a display. In that moment I didn't have much awareness of them, but the memory of it would make me loathe them in time.

She slumped forward to bury her face in her palms, and Ian put the small weight of his hand on her other shoulder. She brought her face back up. "I'm not being strong," she said. "I'm sorry."

"You've been strong all your life," I said, "and you were the strongest I've ever seen you today."

We reached the end of our ward and the train descended until we were beneath the streets, and moving through the long, thin tunnel that led to Lake Park. The car's interior light strips brightened just enough to illuminate the stone walls outside.

Kiri's crying tapered off, making the car eerily quiet. The train sounded different down there in the tunnel. Along with the usual whoosh of sliced air, there was also the scream of the train's hum echoing against the tunnel walls.

Looking out the window at the dim blur of passing gray stone, I wondered if Kiri would feel anything when it came. They'd always said you don't feel anything when it happens, but how could they really know? Was that just something they said?

I wondered where Scotson was at that moment, and what he was thinking. I thought about how maybe he replied to me about restoring Kiri's time the way he did only because we were in the courtroom, surrounded by people watching us.

33

We emerged from the dark of the tunnel into the green of sunlit trees. At Lake Park we walked out of the train and by the station clock. Thirty-one minutes. We set a brisk pace down the hot asphalt path to the lakefront. "I want to sit on the patio," Kiri said.

We knew the patio well. Just past the changing stations where visitors borrowed bathing suits, there was an automat with outdoor seating overlooking the lake. Before Ian's birth made us more frugal, Kiri and I would often make the trek to treat ourselves at that automat. She loved the coffee from there and, although I was sure it tasted the same as any other coffee, I always enjoyed the trip.

"You two find a table," I said. "I'll be right back." I headed into the automat before Kiri could protest.

The coffee was still in the same spot on the wall. I pressed the pane of glass in front of the empty mug and said, "Buy." I would have to start watching spending soon, but this one purchase wouldn't hurt. Kiri's income had been such that we'd rarely thought to draw from mine, so my account had grown nicely over the years.

The mug filled and the glass door flipped open. I carried it carefully, and on my way out I spotted a clock on the wall. Twenty-five minutes.

They'd found a nice table near the patio's railing. I put the coffee down in front of Kiri.

"Drink up," I said.

She stared at it without moving.

I added, "Please," and she brought it to her lips, blew away the steam, and took a sip. She closed her eyes as she swallowed, and shuddered as the piping liquid reached her empty stomach.

"I needed that," she said with a slight smile. After another sip she looked out toward the water. "Look how crowded the beach is," she said.

I followed her gaze and saw that the black shore soil of the beach's main stretch was crowded shoulder-to-shoulder. Beyond the creek that marked the border for Last Day Beach there were, as usual, scattered thirty-six-year-old men and thirty-seven year-old women, some with family and some without. Some lay with their eyes closed, some watched the lake, and some watched the clock that faced their part of the beach but not the rest of the park. A medbot carrying a body in its arms splashed across the creek.

In the shallow parts of the lake children played games. Out farther some adults swam in straight lines as if they were trying to get somewhere, while others floated to feel their limbs hang in a state of disconnection from anything solid.

She passed me the coffee. "It's still better from here. Try."

I took a few sips. It tasted the same as ever to me, but I nodded in agreement.

Ian, who had recently started dabbling in coffee, tried it next. He looked to the sky as he considered the taste.

"It definitely tastes better," he said.

"Yes, it does," Kiri said. "I think the lake air also helps."

We sat looking at each other, and I tried to think of something to say. I thought of asking Ian about his lessons, and then acting enthusiastic about whatever he answered. But I didn't have the heart to try and put on a show.

I kept imagining Scotson Yvera breaking away from his wife after the trial, stepping into a med-pod, and saying the few words he'd need to say. Kiri and Ian had heard me in the courtroom when I told him to restore her time. Were they now having the same hopes about it that I was?

Kiri asked me, "You have the notes?"

"They're in my pocket," I said.

"Good. Read them on the way home if you want."

I nodded.

She studied Ian. "You've grown so much the last year. You'll be your father's height soon. Just a few years."

She worked on the coffee as we sat listening to the breeze and the crowd. She was sitting a bit away from the table, holding the half-full mug over her lap. I worried about how, if it really were her time, the coffee would spill onto her. I asked her if I could have another sip.

She gave me a look and handed me the mug. After a quick sip I placed it down away from her.

She held her eyes on mine as she took a breath, and then turned and brushed Ian's bangs to the side.

"Get back to school tomorrow. You've missed enough," she said.

We were again quiet for a while. I started to feel like the time must've come and gone. I wanted to run back into the automat so I could check the clock and know that we'd made it. I started to believe that, for whatever reason, Scotson had done the right thing.

She looked at the lake. "This is really nice, being here. It makes me happy." A moment later she added, "The beach is so crowded."

"Yeah, it is," I said.

She laughed a little and said, "I'd already said that."

She looked up to the sky, and the low sun set off the red in her eyelashes and the blue in her irises.

It was peaceful. Her eyelids got heavy and closed, and she started to fall forward. It looked as if she fell asleep all at once, and I knew that my dreams of her not dying were just dreams.

I caught her falling shoulders. Her head fell further until it was hanging limp with her chin pressing into her collarbones.

"Careful, Mom!" Ian said. He reached out to help support her.

"Ian, that's it. She's gone." My voice was trembling.

He pulled his hands away and looked at the body. I said, "I'll lay her down," and lifted her up as I slid the chair away with my foot. Ian stood and took a step back. I laid her down on the gray wood planks of the deck. I pushed her hair away form her face, straightened her legs, adjusted her dress, and crossed her hands over her stomach, left over right.

A medbot passed by on the other side of the railing. It started up the ramp to the deck, its continuous tracks knocking loud against the wood.

I wanted to collapse next to Kiri, to wrap my arms and legs around her, to press my face into her skin, to breathe in whatever was left of her, and not to let her out of my shivering grip. But I knew I had to take care of Ian. It scared me that he didn't seem to be registering what had happened.

"Ian, I'm sorry. That was all her time," I said. "That's not her anymore. It's her body, but it's not her. She's gone."

He knelt and slowly reached out his hand until it was on Kiri's chin. He gently turned her head toward him.

"Do you see what I mean?" I asked.

He nodded.

The bot was maneuvering between the other tables to get to us.

"We'll have to leave the body here and go home," I said.

He was still holding her chin and looking at her lifeless face when the bot arrived behind me. When Ian realized it was there, he got up and ran at it, pushing at its base. "No," he said. His voice was calm and quiet.

The bot didn't budge from Ian's pushing, but it didn't move against it either. I put my hand on Ian's shoulder. "Ian, stop. Stop it."

I pulled at him. "Come here," I said.

He let me pull him into me. I asked the bot, "Can you leave the body be for a minute while we walk away?"

"Yes, I'll wait," the bot answered in its mechanical voice. "Would you like me to arrange a meeting with a counselor?"

"No. We'll leave soon. Just leave us alone."

Ian was limp in my arms. The people at the tables around us were all staring.

"Ian, listen," I said. "I want you to be brave and take a good look if you can. Someday you'll be glad you have it as a memory. Look how peaceful and beautiful she looks."

He straightened up, and we turned back and knelt at the body. Looking down at her, I couldn't stop myself from searching in vain for the movement of breathing. I caressed my hand down the side of her frame, over the curve of a hip and the muscles of a thigh. I straightened her hair one last time.

Ian held her hand for a moment. When he let go of it, I asked, "Are you able to go now, Buddy?"

He said yes and I got up and took his hand. As the bot stood waiting, we walked through the tables and down the ramp.

34

"She wrote notes for us," I said while we sat waiting for the train to start moving. I handed him his and read mine.

In it she said that she had a great life because of me, and that being with me was something sacred to her, a foundation that always got her through anything. She said she was going with her mind at ease, and that losing her didn't mean I had to stop holding on to all the love she had for me.

It ended it with, "I know this is hard and that you got the bad end of the deal, but be tough about it, there's no reason not to be. I won't have really died if you make your eyes my eyes too, and if you think of every moment as if you're showing me all the good things to see. Please have more life in you because you'll now be living your life for the both of us."

When we reached our building, a guidebot met us in the lobby and led us up the elevator to our new floor. We followed the bot until it stopped at an apartment door and opened it for us.

It then said to me, "The marriage band you're wearing needs to be turned in. I'll take care of that for you."

I twisted at my ring until it slipped off. After I dropped it onto the coppery palm held before me, the bot turned and left. Ian and I entered our new apartment.

"Well, the front room is almost as big," I said. "The couch is a little smaller but the display is the same size. And we get the same desk and computer as before."

Our camera was on the desk and I went to the display to see if all our photos were preserved. They were, and my heart sank seeing the last photo she'd taken. It was from that morning, she and I in bed with Ian in between. Her arm stretching to hold the camera above us as she put on a wide smile.

I went back through the old photos and found one of her hand pressed against our front room window as she looked out. Her fingers were spread, and the webs between them translucent in the reproduced sunlight.

Ian and I continued into the hall, pausing in the kitchen where we discovered that the little two-chair table was wobbly. "I'll fix that," I said. "We'll find something to put under its leg."

At his new room Ian looked at the sparseness. "Why don't we get to keep any of the extra stuff we had?" he asked.

"Because it was all bought from Mom's account. But I'll buy you a display for this room. It'll be just like your last one."

"You don't have to," he said.

"I know, but I'm going to."

We went to my room, which was the most different. The walls were tight against the half-sized bed. The short dresser looked bare with no jewelry box atop it.

"This is a good apartment. We'll be fine here," I said.

Ian nodded. I followed him as he went to the kitchen to drink half a glass of water.

I asked him if he wanted dinner, and he shook his head no. Then he pulled his note from his pocket and told me, "You can read my note if you want."

"Only if you want me to," I said. We traded our notes.

She'd written him about all the ways and reasons she loved him, as well as a lot of motherly advice, like to do everything with effort and honesty, and without being afraid of taking risks or making himself vulnerable.

She wrote, "There's an important thing that is also one of the few things you'll always be able to control, and that's how you think of yourself. You can control that by always doing the thing that will leave you thinking of yourself in the best possible way."

It ended with, "If you stay true to yourself and live as I'm asking you to live, then you'll always have me within you, within every breath. And there will always be a part of me still existing, and still loving you as much as anyone can love anyone."

"You'll be ok," I said as we traded notes back. "For one thing, you have her strength."

Later we watched the evening news, which had the trial as the top story. They showed Noli testifying how panicked Scotson had looked when he ran out. The only clip of Kiri was of her describing how she'd encouraged Scotson to choke her. They showed quite a bit of Scotson's testimony and the defense's closing argument. After a few snippets of the judge rendering his verdict, there was a final shot of Scotson looking distraught and being comforted by his wife and children.

Afterward Ian hugged me goodnight and went off to bed. I went and got in my new bed, but attempting to sleep felt ridiculous.

I was used to getting in bed alone since Kiri had often worked nights, but I'd always known she'd be home before sunrise. The last time I'd truly slept alone was the night before we got married. I spent most of that night worrying she'd change her mind at the last minute, or that her parents would object, or that Uro would show up to fight me for her, or a hundred other unlikely scenarios.

Now I was a single man again, alone in a single man's bed. When I closed my eyes, I saw Kiri's body laid out on a cold table in a dark room, though I knew she'd probably already been cremated.

I got up when I heard Ian sobbing from his room. I slowly stepped to his doorway. He was curled up with his face to the wall, a single sheet covering him up to his chest and his hand holding his folded-up note.

I thought he hadn't noticed me, but he said, "You can sleep in here if you want, Daddy."

"Yeah," I said.

I got my pillow and lay down next to him, resting my hand at the edge of his back to feel his breathing as his sobbing died down. I matched my breathing with his, and in time we both slept. I dreamt I was someone who dreams in black and white, and so I saw her face colorless as she sipped her coffee and breathed the lake air.

35

I woke up and opened one eye. Half my pillow was lilting off the edge of the bed. I could hear that Ian had gone to the front room and turned on the display. There was another sound, too – the alarm clock in my room had gone off at the same time the one in our old apartment would have. I rose and shut it off. It was a new morning, and I somehow didn't feel as bad as I'd thought I might've. It was like she was away at work.

I went to Ian, sat next to him, and kissed his head. On the news they spoke of new harvesting techniques. They said the General Order would soon have more food than ever. The farmbots hard at work. Every golden field tilled for our benefit.

I showered, and when I stepped out of the bathroom I caught myself looking to see where she was. I made coffee, knowing I only needed to brew one mug even if my hands wanted to brew two. There would be a thousand little habits like that, and each one would pound at me, but that was alright. I looked at them as a way of remembering her.

Ian showered and I gave him cereal and juice. We left together, and I walked him to school.

Late into work. Before I could get to my workstation half the people on my team got up and rushed to shake my hand and pat my back. I was asked more than once how I was doing. I didn't mind the sympathy when it came from individuals, but I didn't want all the group attention.

On my display blue, green, and purple shapes went to and fro. I couldn't understand the task. I shook my head at the screen and then felt Raff's hand on my shoulder. He didn't say anything about Kiri, but instead ran through the algorithm for me a few times. I took up the challenge of it, sorting the patterns faster and faster.

Raff was saying something to me. His hand on my shoulder again.

"What?" I asked.

"Lunch?"

"Oh yeah. Yeah, sure."

We stood in line, took our warm soup from the dispensers, and sat with friends. Some didn't say a word, but some told me to let them know if they could do anything for me. The same ones who'd asked me in the morning how I was doing asked again. "I'm doing ok," I'd say.

I looked at the soup and it was foreign. I pushed the bowl in Raff's direction. "I'm not hungry," I said. "You can have that."

He slid it back. "You should try to have some."

I shook my head no.

"Just take a few sips, Corim."

I reminded myself that she'd told me to take care of myself. I tried a few sips expecting it to be without flavor, but instead it was vivid and complete. My taste buds separated every grain, every spice. The taste was not a pleasure to me, but it was a sensation of some sort and I welcomed it. It made Raff happy when I was the first to finish.

The elevator back up. Pounding head and sick stomach. Why had I done something as stupid as eating? The doors opened for our floor and I said, "I'll see you tomorrow, Raff. I'm going home now."

He was halfway out but turned back, holding the door. "Let me walk with you."

"No, thanks. I'm just going straight home to nap."

Over a dozen people were with me in the elevator waiting to get to their floors. "I'd like to come see you later? Is that ok?" Raff asked.

He was in mourning for her, too. I'd selfishly been only thinking of what I was going through. "I'd like that," I said. "Please drop by later."

One of the other passengers, a woman in her thirties, tilted her head at the strange conversation. Raff spoke quickly. "Great. And you'll message me if you need anything before then?"

"Sure. Bye, Raff."

The number of passengers declined as the elevator rose, and on the seventieth floor I was left alone after a man got off to walk through a maze of workstations. He looked young, maybe seventeen or eighteen, and during my last glimpse of him in the dwindling gap of the closing doors I wondered if he had a wife. The elevator started heading down.

Out the building and into a light rain. I couldn't remember if it had been raining in the morning. I walked in the opposite direction of home. Heavier raindrops came and started to work their way through my hair to my scalp. I looked down at my feet moving over the beige grain of the sidewalk. I thought of her face, and knew I was remembering every detail so well.

More rain. The amplified splashing from the storm drains. My little alluvial fans at the corners of the grates. The muted patter of raindrops meeting my soaked shirt.

I remembered the way I'd run my fingers through her hair so that they wouldn't catch. I remembered the weight of her hands in my hands, and the auroras of heat and pressure that'd dance between us when I held her. Her smell, though. How do you really remember a smell? I didn't know how, and I was already forgetting hers. When it hit me that I'd never smell it again, I cried for the first time since her death, the tears mixing with the rainwater on my face. I knew no one would notice, and if they did I wouldn't care.

I told myself to be tough about it, to breathe past the hurt inside.

I walked the windowless walls that bordered our ward. The ubiquitous concrete, smooth and gray as the sky above, curved me toward home.

I knew I'd have good days someday, but they would always be relative, would always exist as good days only in comparison to the other days I couldn't share with her.

Across the street a man sat atop the little front steps of an apartment building. A food stain on his shirt and his eyes resting on the street. For every person sitting outside alone with a blank stare on their face, there must always be a hundred doing the same in apartments. I knew I mustn't become that, inert on a couch, my mind a mawkish hull of what it used to be, all my memories of Kiri's love distorted by the specter of her death.

I thought of how I'd dreamt of her, and how maybe I'd dream of her regularly, how maybe each night would bring me that gift. I told myself that death is not such a different thing than sleep, and that's how I should think of her. Sleeping. Unaware. Not in pain. Not confused.

I'd come north and was passing by a station. The sliding hum of a departing train as I watched it glide out of sight. Less than a thousand pounds per car is what that client of Kiri's had said.

What if I got on a train and just rode? We were taught to only get on a train when going somewhere farther than three blocks, but what would happen if I just sat in one going north and then south and then north again, feeling the movement over the tracks, and feeling the illusory sense of progress that would come with the movement? Would anyone notice? Would a bot come make me leave? Would I be punished?

A cold wind blew through the rain and my hands shivered in my pockets, my bones feeling as brittle as icicles. I wanted to be under a dozen blankets.

You always know that what you have is temporary, but then one day you know it for sure. What if I were to shout in the streets? What if I ran through the night howling chaos? What would happen?

I turned down my street and came to Ian's school. My school once. Was Mrs. Winten in there lecturing, telling the kids how lucky they are to have the lifespans they have? She would now be around seventy – her last years before hitting her Counselor Order Expiration.

What was it she'd said? "There is a selfishness to mourning the dead. Those who wallow in sadness aren't sad for the departed, but actually sad for themselves because of what is now missing from their own lives. It is self-pity and serves no one."

Such logical words, and so useless. Did she say them with the same conviction now that she knew she wouldn't outlive the children before her?

I stopped at the bottom of the stairs and looked up at the doors where a schoolbot had taken my hand on my eighth birthday the way one, maybe the same one, had taken Kiri's on hers and Ian's on his.

Ian. He must've been done with lunch. He was back in his L-pod, alone and covered in darkness except for the hues of the display crossing his face. I hoped he was engaged in a good lesson, distracted.

I walked on to our building. I paused to look up to the windows of the outer units. The new apartment was lost up there somewhere, the apartment where I was destined to someday stare down the chasm of the last days before my Expiration. The old apartment was up there, too. Maybe it already had new tenants, but I didn't want to think about that.

In the quiet lobby I crossed the great blue carpet and got into the first med-pod. After it closed around me I said, "I'm cold, and my head and stomach hurts."

The buzz of the scan. The pressure on the side of my neck as medicine was pushed through my skin.

"You seem very stressed," it told me. "Your blood pressure was in a bad range."

"Yes, my wife died."

"I know. That sort of thing is very hard for people to get through. Can I give you something to further relax you?"

"Yes. My hands are tingling."

Again the injector at my neck. The beep of the machine communicating with its brethren artificial cells running through my blood.

"Try to rest."

"I will," I said. "Can I stay in here awhile?"

"Of course. Try slow, deep breaths."

The air warmed, the seat rocked back and its cushions softened. I reached in my pocket and squeezed the note Kiri left me.

"Would you like something to help you sleep?"

"No, thank you."

"Would you like some relaxing music?"

"No, thank you."

The pod went quiet. Whatever it did to me was relaxing my muscles. My hands felt ok again. As the tension left my body, I began to sob.

"Would you like to talk about it?" the pod asked. "You can tell me anything, and if you like I can schedule a visit with a counselor for you."

"No counselors, but talk to me."

"Would you like me to talk about loss?"

"Talk to me," I said, "but not about that."

"I can speak about whatever you like. Whatever comes to your mind."

I stared at the soft red lights of its display. A light in the corner pulsed every time my heart beat. I started feeling more angry than sad. I remembered how Kiri couldn't even buy Ian a chocolate bar because her account was terminated. Because that was the rule. That was the rule, and we were never told why.

The rationale we in the General Order were given as to why we were allowed to die prematurely was so we wouldn't take undue risks. Yet the risks Kiri took of being with a sexually violent client seemed like exactly the risks those who set the rules wanted her to take.

Suddenly I wanted to punch through the display. I wanted to destroy the pod from the inside out.

"Tell me what you'd like to talk about, Corim. Do you have any questions for me?"

I was deep in a place of frustration and hopelessness, the kind of place where impudence grows best. Even if the pod had no feelings, even if it couldn't experience any sort of dissatisfaction, the pod was still a connection to the system that had taken Kiri from me, and I wanted to somehow cause it difficulty, to somehow be a problem.

"Sure," I said. "How about you tell me the current population of the world?"

I knew it wouldn't answer, but I wanted to hear its refusal. I wanted to feel the vindication of a system that presented itself as all-powerful and all-providing refusing to provide me with the most basic of answers.

"The population of the world is 181,377,941," the pod said.

Somewhere in my head I thought about how the number wasn't so far off from what I'd guessed, but mostly I was confused.

After making the machine repeat itself, by which time the population of the world had dropped by one, I said, "You just told me the population of the world."

"Yes."

"Why'd you tell me that?"

"You had asked."

The seat was still reclined, but I sat up as best I could. The pulsing of the heartbeat light in the corner of the pod's display began to quicken.

"In the past no bot has ever told me."

"My information filtering has been disabled."

Information filtering. I'd heard that term somewhere.

I was hit with the memory of Scotson Yvera, three days before, sitting in the same pod I was now in, one of his legs hanging out as Kiri, Ian, and I looked in. The pod wasn't telling us what Scotson wanted it to tell us about how he had the power to take Kiri off Extension, so he ordered it to disable its information filtering.

And now it occurred me that he had never ordered the machine to reinstate it.

My hands gripped the armrests. Every unanswered question I'd ever had – about history, about the world, about the different types of Orders – might now be answered. Yet the first things I asked were questions it would've answered for me anyway.

"Did my wife feel any pain when she died?"

"No."

"What was done with her body?"

The pod told me of Kiri's cremation, and it was only when we'd exhausted the details of it that I began probe the machine about all that had ever been ever held back from me.

I started with the beginning, asking what exactly had necessitated breaking people up into different orders. We'd always been told it was the result of past calamities, but those explanations always seemed vague. Now I learned that there was never any great famine, never any apocalyptic battle, and never any global plague that led to what was forced upon us. The films of those things they'd show us in school were just horrible moments from history, and had nothing to do with how we now lived.

It turned out that it had been a protracted period of peace, not conflict, which had allowed a small number of leaders to gradually accumulate more power over years and decades. They came to control the latest medical technology, and with every breakthrough in lengthening lifespans, they came to control the world.

I started asking about the present day – about who was really in charge, about how limited the world's resources really were, and about a dozen other topics. It was then, in the darkness of a pod and feeling the heartache of my first day without Kiri, that I began waking up from the lie-filled dream that had been my life.

36

I stayed in the pod for hours. When it informed me that Ian was arriving home, I got out and greeted him in the lobby with frantic descriptions of what I'd found out. I had him sit in the pod so he could hear it all for himself, and then I did the same with Raff when he came by. The three of us stayed up late into the night, listening to the truth about the system that had taken Kiri away.

I didn't go into work for the next two days. After that, I would only go in enough to keep up appearances. Otherwise I'd spend my time in the pod, exiting it only to eat and sleep. My grief for Kiri was still as severe as it'd been that first day, but at least when I was in the pod I felt like I was accomplishing something that could give meaning to her death.

I learned more than I had thought there even was to learn, and I started realizing that I might be able to change the course of my life. I even started having ideas about changing the lives of a great many people.

Raff and Ian were as ready to take action as I was, and were enthusiastic about my plans. We embarked on what would be weeks of preparation. For one thing, we had to train ourselves physically. We started by walking from one end of the ward to the other and then, as strange as it must've looked to those who'd seen us, going on runs. Ian also found there were windows of time before and after school when he could run up and down all eleven stories of the school's stairs without the schoolbots stopping him.

One night when I was having dinner with Ian at our little, still wobbly, kitchen table, I said, "Ian, I hate to ask this, but there's something you can do that might help you get ready."

"What?"

"When you're in school tomorrow, and when the bots are walking you to the gym, you could run out in front of the lead bot. Pretend it's an accident."

The school trick Raff had played on me, and I had played on Kiri, had apparently fallen from fashion. Ian had never stepped out of bounds, and had never experienced the pain that came with it.

He thought about it and nodded. "Ok. I'll do it."

"You understand what will happen? You'll get a shock, and it will hurt very much. Your classmates might laugh at you. You don't have to do this."

"If it will help me be ready, then I want to," he said.

The next day when he was away at school I couldn't shake the sickening thought of him going through that pain and humiliation. I was full of guilt for suggesting it to him, but he showed no regrets when he got home.

"It hurt more than I thought it would, but I'm glad I know what it feels like."

"Did the other kids laugh at you?"

"Yes. I don't know why, though. I don't know what's funny about it."

"I'm sorry, Ian."

"It's doesn't matter. I'm glad I did it. I'm less afraid now."

Our plan needed a fourth person. After much thought, I settled on Uro and told him everything. Someone else had to know, and he was the only good option. My first choice would've been Noli, but she was still working at the brothel and I would've worried about her letting something slip while talking to one of her clients. Regardless of all the faults

I'd found in Uro over the years, I knew I could trust him not to reveal what we were doing to a counselor or someone from the Judicial Order.

His reaction exceeded my expectations. He had his own questions for the med-pod, and would spend hours in it on his own. He came to agree with my plan, and insisted on contributing everything he could.

In the final days of our preparations, neither Raff nor I went to work at all. When our coworkers messaged us asking what was wrong, we assured them that we just needed a little time off and that we would be back soon. We knew we were lying and that, no matter how things went, neither of us would ever again work another day as a pattern architect.

In all, it had taken two months for us to be ready and for me to be sure that I had learned everything I could. When the day came, Raff and Uro came over to my apartment before dawn. We laid the sheet from my bed flat on the floor, and Raff, Ian, and I piled everything we owned onto it – forks, spoons, pillows, the rest of our bedding, jackets, pajamas, and all the food we'd bought and saved since I'd come up with the plan. Uro also added all the food he could.

We then fashioned a sack out of the sheet by tying the corners together. I flung it over my shoulder and we left to go to the station, where Uro wished us luck and saw us off – his part of the plan meant he had to stay behind. Ian, Raff, and I got on a train to Lake Park.

We arrived in the faint first light of the sunrise, and stepped through the sparse early morning crowd gathering on the lakeshore. Many in the crowd stared at me and some even pointed, but no one thought to ask me why I was carrying the sack or what was in it.

It was so early that we were the first of the day to hop the creek onto Last Day Beach, but rather than continuing on along the shore, we turned and started following the creek upstream. The soil of the beach ended, and before us were thin, orange bollards rising every few feet from a strip of cut grass. The bollards marked the western border of Lake Park – a border that every member of the General Order had been taught was uncrossable, a border no member of the General Order had crossed in over three hundred years.

I looked into the dark forest of pine, oak, brush, and briar that lay beyond the border, and I took the first slow step onto the grass. Then two more steps as Ian and Raff followed behind. On the fourth step my chest started to tingle.

I hopped back and motioned at the empty grass in front of us. "It starts right there," I said.

The threat of pain had kept the General Order behind this border. Every child had been taught that severe pain is what you get for entering a restricted area.

There didn't need to be any bots nearby for this to happen. There were sensors that tracked our locations all over our ward, including in the orange bollards in front of us. Any time someone went where they weren't supposed to, the sensors would transmit that information to the Life Center. An antenna in the Life Center's spire would then send a signal to the artificial cells within that person's body, triggering the pain.

We stepped back a few paces and then lined up with Ian in the middle. Raff took his left hand, and I took his right, making extra sure my hold was tight when I felt how his palm was already sweaty. We took our stances. I would lead a half step in front, and Raff would hold the rear.

"Remember," I said, "we're incapable of running anywhere but forward. Let's all say it."

We recited our chosen mantra three times: "Forward out of the pain."

Many times over the last few weeks we had lined up like this on the empty asphalt that ran beneath the train tracks. We'd count down, and then sprint forward hand-in-hand for a quarter mile. Now I once again started the countdown, but this time it wasn't for practice. Raff and Ian joined in the count. Three. Two. One.

All at once we were bolting into the gap between the first two bollards on our side of the creek. I had only just hit full stride when the pain punched hard into my chest. It blinded me. It made me eight years old again, a confused boy hunched over alone in a hallway while a bot raised its finger at me.

A voice in my mind struggled to say that no, I wasn't in a school hallway, and that this pain wasn't the result of a cruel trick. This pain, the voice screamed, was a path to salvation, and the only path was forward.

My legs had slowed, were only moving to keep me on my feet as momentum drove me forward. I felt Ian's hand pull as he cried out and fought to keep moving. "C'mon!" I yelled. I kicked my feet back into a sprint, dragging Ian along at the tempered pace I'd learned to keep so he'd be able to stay afoot.

My sight was returning in flashes. We were past the bollards and past the grass, pushing through the muddy light brush between the creek and the trees. The plants were waist-high there, and of leafy, delicate stalks that gave way easily as we drove through. "Forward out of the pain," ran through my head.

I steered us left at a turn in the creek, and looked over to check on Raff. He still had Ian's other hand, and was staring wild-eyed at the ground and plants passing beneath him. He struggled to breathe deep as the incessant burning in his chest constricted the muscles of his torso. Ian was still crying out, but he was also still running hard to keep up.

I turned my gaze back ahead just in time to catch myself when my foot came down hard on a tree root exposed over a piece of uneven ground. We'd hit a decline where the creek banks started to flatten out. We managed to maintain our speed, and we were crossing a stretch of level, sandy banks when Ian pulled at my hand and called for me. I turned to see that Raff was about thirty feet back, lying on his side and clutching his chest. He'd tripped on the tree root that had nearly taken me down.

I made a looping turn. Raff looked like an animal that had been felled by a predator, his grimaced face pressing against the dirt and stones beneath him, his legs flailing, his hands grasping in search of a wound – the wound which countless pain receptors told him had to be there, somewhere in his chest.

We slowed as we approached, and I was still moving when I released Ian's hand so I could reach down and lift Raff up. It was then that my legs gave out from under me. My eyes locked shut, the sack went flying from my hand, and my body crashed down. Just like Raff, I was now on my side clutching at my chest.

I yelled at myself to get up. This time it wasn't with a voice in my head – my lungs burned as I screamed the words. I knew that getting to my feet was the only way out of the pain, but that knowledge was of no use for making my frozen hands reach to the ground to push me up. My thoughts had become disconnected from my body's actions, binding me as much as any ropes or chains could.

My cries mixed with Raff's and Ian's. This is what we'd feared the most, that we'd end up inert in the wilderness, trapped in pain for hours or even days. Eventually dehydration would trigger distress calls from our artificial cells and perhaps, depending on our proximity to the border, medbots would bother to retrieve us. All three of us knew that that would lead to our executions, and that our conviction for the forgotten crime of escape would come swiftly and without the farce of a trial.

Just minutes before, walking from the train to the beach, I'd told Ian and Raff that the first thing to do if we got stuck would be to take a deep breath. That advice was useless as I lay in the dirt – I'd lost all control of my breathing.

I had also told them to focus on the parts of their bodies that were in less pain, but now all I could think of was the burning that seared through my chest. The rest of my body was only a distant backdrop to what felt like a hot piece of metal breaking through my sternum. I'd taken no notice of it that Ian had been pulling on my shoulders, and yelling into my ears.

I opened my eyes when he pulled my hand from my chest and pressed it into the dirt.

"Get up, Dad!"

Without thought, I rolled my weight forward onto my hand and bent my knees against the dirt. Through all the pain, I lifted my head, found my footing, and rose. Ian rushed to Raff's side, and with heavy legs I hobbled over to help, this time being more careful with my movements.

The moment we got Raff up, Ian grabbed our sack from where I'd dropped it, and took off running at a full clip. Raff and I were slower to start, but we gained speed as the banks got less stony, allowing our strides to lengthen over the soft, smooth sand.

Ian was moving faster than I'd ever seen him, and maintained his lead despite having the sack over his shoulder and often checking back on us. The creek was shallow here, and we started to cut back and forth from one bank to another to find the fastest route, our feet splashing through the water.

We veered into a little valley where, finally, the pain began to diminish with every step. There, beneath the morning shadows of the surrounding hills, fewer of our artificial cells were picking up the signals transmitted from the distant spire of the Life Center. Normal breathing started to return. We caught up to Ian, and we all slowed to a more manageable pace.

Another slight turn, and after a hundred feet more we were among higher hills. We felt immense, palpable relief when we came to a tall, gray rock face rising from the right side of the bank. It was as if whatever had been speared into our chests had been pulled out. We stopped, and we all hunched forward – this time not in pain, but from shortness of breath.

"That was the hardest part," I said to them between breaths. "We'll never have to feel anything like that again."

37

I gestured toward the woods. "Listen to all the sounds," I said.

I'd expected silence, but along with the bubbling of the creek there was a modulating drone of insects, and there were birdcalls, the occasional frog ribbit, and the scrambling of squirrels through the branches above.

We also had our first chance to marvel at the sight of it. All of our lives, we'd seen images of countless wildernesses on display screens, but those could never convey things like the depths and the distances seen through the gaps between the trees. I'd never imagined that the woods, even when dense with vegetation, would feel so open and free.

I went to the edge of the bank and scooped some cool water to my mouth.

"Drink up," I said. "From where it's moving fast."

Ian and Raff came up and took cautious sips. I knelt and brought my face close to the clear water. The creek bed here was lined with stones and pebbles, most of which were flat and rounded, and of varying shades of brown and gray. I pulled up one that stood out. It was edged and triangular, and black with thin white bands rich in quartz. Feeling the grainy stone's dense mass as I rolled it in my fingers, I had the first calm moment I'd had in days. It made me forget the dull ache that still lingered through my chest. I dried the stone on my shirt and dropped it into my pocket.

"That was maybe two miles," I said. "We'll follow the creek west a bit more before we cut away."

I picked up the sack and was retightening its knot when Raff let out an awful scream, as urgent and as pained as any of the cries we'd let out during our run.

He was looking in horror at the back of his hand.

I laughed in relief. For a moment I'd worried his scream had been an indicator of some terrible oversight in all my planning and preparations.

"That's called a mosquito," I said, slapping at his skin and leaving behind an ugly wreck of black and red. "Nothing to worry about, it just wanted some of your blood. We'll have to get used to them."

"It stung terribly."

"The med-pod said the itching that comes later is the worst part. But that bite you got was quite an event. It's probably been hundreds of years since an insect has drunk human blood. We should embrace the experience."

"What an honor, then," he said, wiping away the mess with his sleeve.

On our way upstream, the pain would come and go as the strength of the Life Center signals rose and fell among the hills and valleys. I kept pausing to look back, fearful that someone or something was coming after us. The med-pod had assured me that our absences wouldn't cause alarm, as the mechanisms to scan for and track escapees had long been abandoned as obsolete. But it was impossible not to feel the specter of the city's rules and potential punishments always looming behind us.

After a half hour, we took the empty metal wine bottle from the sack, filled it with water, and cut away from the creek into a forest of tall, ancient pines. We kept the low midmorning sun over our left shoulders to maintain a southwestern trajectory. Trekking over the beds of copper-brown dried needles and fallen pinecones was easy work until we got to an incline. Our leg muscles weren't ready for it, despite all the training we'd put them through. Other than the stairs of the school, none of us had ever climbed such a steep angle.

As we gained elevation, the pain came back, though it was a muted version of before. The pines gave way to a series of woodsy knolls where we were slowed by dense underbrush. The mosquitoes were relentless there, all of us constantly swatting at our heads and necks as we also worked to push aside the thorny briars and brambles that cut through our pants and lined our legs with tiny cuts.

The vegetation lessened as we made progress up a particularly large hill. When we crested its ridge, we left the dappled shadows of oak and alder canopies for the midday sun of an open green meadow. It was such a relief to have a clear path before me that, fatigue in my legs or not, I smiled back at Ian and Raff and broke into a sprint through the high grass. It was intoxicating to be heading into a great, wide-open expanse, the sun warming my face, the breeze rippling over the field, and the far-off mountains now in view ahead of us.

The plateau's grass was patched by an occasional white oak with branches striking out almost as wide as they did high. The sky was cloudless, and I was getting a sunburn to go with all my mosquito bites. The initial excitement of walking unencumbered was quickly replaced by the boredom of plodding through a never-changing landscape. Finally, after what must've been at least five miles, we were closing in on the mountains. The grass became shorter and sparser until we were crossing a fallow stretch of weeds, clovers, and lichen-covered stones. We stopped to rest at the base of an incline, taking seats in the loose gravel that had rolled down from the mossy rock faces above.

I untied the sack knot and retrieved one of the things Uro gave us for the trip – his dinner from the night before. I also got out one of the many loaves of raisin bread I'd bought from the automat. Over the prior few weeks the med-pod had taught me much more about nutrition than any of the school lessons had ever bothered to mention, and the bread was one of the few nutritionally decent automat choices.

We made quick work of the food and finished off the water from our wine bottle. For dessert we shared a chocolate bar, which was another item I'd stocked up on, though not for their nutrition. When we were done with it, I added its foil wrapper to the bag of all the other foil wrappers we'd collected.

We rose and surveyed the black slope before us.

"One mountain to get over, then we'll be there," I said.

38

The mountainside varied from stretches of barren rock to pockets of shrubbery and short pines. The footing was undependable from the start, and we repeatedly scuffed our palms and bruised our knees whenever the ground slid out from under us. We'd backtrack or move laterally along ledges for as long as it took to avoid the more treacherous upward passages. There would be, after all, no bots to treat us if we went tumbling downhill like the columns of dirt and gravel kicked loose every time we slipped.

Even where movement was easier we still traversed circuitously because we had a purpose on the mountain besides just getting over it, and it was the sole reason we'd taken such a difficult route. After a solid two hours of zigzagging our way up, Raff pointed north. "What about there? Is that yellow on those rock walls?"

"Good eye," I said.

In the afternoon shadows, thin, jagged yellow lines ran down a distant black rock face.

We headed north, but the ledge we were on got thinner the closer we got. By the time we reached the first specks of yellow, we were clutching on to any handholds we could find. Up close, the yellow lines were heavily mixed with black and gray minerals.

"This isn't pure enough, and it's too ingrained," I said. "We need to find a vein."

"There's something I think I saw," Ian said. Without asking, he started climbing upward. The angle was safe enough that I restrained myself from stopping him. He was confident in his movements, but we were already above a dizzying fall of steep rock, and watching him gain even more elevation turned my stomach.

Protecting him was, and remained, the duty that had kept me going since losing Kiri. It was the first thing I thought about with every choice I made. I couldn't stand the physical risks this trip was putting him through, but I also knew that getting him away from the city was the only option I had for protecting him in the most important way: protecting who he was and who he could become.

He was forty feet up when he spotted what he was looking for and starting shimmying to his right. Raff and I moved to stay below him, but then he disappeared into the rock face. I shouted his name, terrified that he'd been lost to a hidden ravine. No reply. I threw down the sack and started scrambling up, but then Ian's voice echoed down to us. He was yelling that he'd found it.

Raff and I scaled up side by side, pausing to hoist up the sack back and forth. Ian was waiting in a deep, narrow cave. He led us in, and after a few feet he pointed to a small recess low on the wall. Shrouded in the darkness of the cave was a near perfect circle, almost as big as my hand, of yellow crystals and powder. I knelt and scratched at the powder, and pulled out the rock I had put my pocket to hammer at the crystals.

"Yes, this will do," I said. "This is a beautiful vein of sulfur."

I retrieved six empty dinner bags from the sack, and we took turns mining the vein until the bags were full.

We made our way back down to the ledge we'd come from, and headed south to safer terrain. Our legs had needed the break they got in the cave – we still had half the mountain in front of us. When I looked back, I tried to spot the city, or at least Lake Park, but beyond the flat, green plateau we'd just crossed the horizon only faded into distant woods.

There was less loose gravel at these heights, and the ascent started to level off enough that walking became easy, even monotonous. We were too exhausted for conversation as we drudged on, and anyway there wasn't much to talk about. We'd spent the last weeks poring over every detail of all we'd learned from the med-pod, and trading our latest discoveries with each other.

Uro had been very much a part of that, and his dedication to our cause had so impressed me that I started to wish he could join us on the trip, but his part in the plan meant he had to stay behind. His job was to wait a few hours until after we were gone, and then to start telling everyone he could about the med-pod.

"At first, don't tell them anything we've learned, because they won't believe it from you," I'd said to him. "Just convince them to get in the pod, and then have the pod tell them how easy it would be for us all to live to a hundred. How we're rushed through our lives so there's always a fresh supply of young sex workers and new generations whose genes can be further tinkered with and altered toward the ideals of those in power. Have it tell them that there are people with no set lifespan, people who have lived for hundreds of years, and how they'd consider it a pointless waste to let anyone in the General Order get older."

The sun was falling before us, casting long shadows before the sparse pines and brush that dotted the nearly flat ascent we'd reached. It also blinded me whenever I tried to look too far ahead, so I contented myself with staring down at the ground passing beneath my feet. I was exhausted, and had all but forgotten where we were, where we were going. All that was in my mind was moving one foot in front of another, and keeping my shaky, sore legs from buckling.

After we crossed over a lip of steeper bare rock, Raff called to me, pulling me out of my daze. I turned back and looked up at him and Ian. They were a few feet behind, standing still on the bare tabletop of rock and fully lit by the low afternoon sun.

"What?" I said.

"Look," Raff said, and I turned back forward.

I didn't know the sky could be so big or the horizon so great. The ocean flickered before us with a million beams of light.

39

The descent was sharp, but rather than exposed rock, this side of the mountain was covered in firm soil, and plentiful in deep-rooted pines and alders. We made our way down in a straight path, an ocean breeze rustling up through the trees and cooling our sunburned faces.

After an hour, when we were halfway down, I realized the pain in my chest was completely gone, without even any residual soreness remaining. We couldn't see much through the forest, but we started to hear the faint rumble of waves crashing.

After another hour, the descent ended abruptly, and the black soil and trees gave way to sand dunes and sawgrass. Out over the ocean horizon, orange, wispy clouds passed before the blue sky and the low, reddening sun.

We crossed to the edge of the dunes, took off our shoes, and felt the hot sand between our toes.

"We made it, Dad."

"Buddy," I said, scooping up a handful of sand, "this is a real beach. White sand, seashells, and a real ocean."

Raff was more exhausted than I'd ever seen him, but beneath the hand that he'd put to his mouth, he was nearly laughing as he looked out at the sea.

We stood knee-deep in the foamy breakers with our pants rolled up, and ate more bread.

"How far north is the river?" Raff asked.

"It shouldn't be more than five miles."

He sighed.

"Yeah, I know," I said. "But I bet you're as thirsty as I am. Let's get going."

The tide was moving out, and we walked along the firm sand at the water's edge. The flocks of fidgety sandpipers and cawing gulls that lined the beach seemed annoyed that we were walking through their territory. As spent as our legs were, none of us could resist stopping to pick up shells. We found the broken crown of a conch, an intact sea urchin shell, and a dozen other treasures I couldn't identify.

In the last red light of the sunset, we reached the river.

"This is good," I said. "It's just how I'd hoped it'd be when the med-pod showed me the old satellite images of it."

The river came out from a mountain gorge and flowed into the sea through a long series of shoals and sandbanks. The sawgrass-covered dunes here were wide and rolling, and there were a dozen acres of flat woods between the dunes, the river, and the mountains.

"We'll go upstream for drinking water, but never more than a few hundred feet," I said. "We have to stay on this side of the mountains, and we have to stay at this elevation. Our six days starts now."

We were, down there at the bottom of that side of the mountains, totally shielded from the Life Center's signals. Six days was how long it would take for the now-inert artificial cells in our blood to completely cycle out of our systems.

We found a good drinking spot on the riverbank, and I poured out a pile of snacks.

"Let's not ration tonight. We've earned a good meal," I said.

A pale light still hung over the ocean where the sun had set, and there was a half moon above us. I watched Ian's silhouette as he bit into a disk of crushed fruit and nuts.

"Ian, as long you eat enough, you'll end up stronger than Raff and me. You won't have the developmental regulators we had, so you'll get wide shoulders and big arms like men used to have. You just might end up the strongest man in the world."

When our bellies were full we made our way back to the beach and sat on the sand watching the waves break in the moonlight. I thought back to my first time in an L-Pod, and the beautiful, towering, sun-kissed wave I saw in it. My view this night was nothing like that – the ocean was dark and choppy, the waves small – but it was a genuine view, not something that had been recorded years before and shown on a display countless times.

I thought of Kiri, and how much I wished she could've seen all I'd seen that day, how I wished she could know all we'd accomplished. I may not have been able to see her face as I peered into the waves, or smell her hair as I breathed in the salty spray floating in on the breeze, or hear her laugh as I listened the rote of the surf, but I could feel her presence there with us. I knew it was her strength that had taken us this far. I could feel her there with me, and I held her and held her.

In the soft sand of the dunes, we made our beds by pressing down the sawgrass beneath our sheets. I rested my head against my pillow and stared up at the stars, the most stars I'd ever seen, and fell into a deep sleep before I could take it all in.

40

When I woke at dawn, Ian was sitting up, his sheets still wrapped around him. He was looking into the dense morning fog with fascination. Except for our little bit of dunes, everything – the ocean, the mountains, the river, and the woods – had disappeared behind the white mist of the cool morning.

We stayed in bed resting our sore legs until the sun crested the mountains and burned the fog away, and then the three of us explored the woods along the river. We tried eating dandelions, but none of us could take the bitterness. I pulled away the bark of a fallen tree, and we studied the grubs and worms crawling over its soft, decaying wood. We collected some tiny strawberries, though we were disappointed by their lack of taste. We broke off some of the dry, brittle branches of a dead juniper, and took them back to our camp in the dunes.

We watched the white-and-brown ospreys hovering against the breeze high above the mouth of the river. When they spotted prey, they'd dive down faster than freefall with their oversized, hooked black talons extended beneath them, crash into the water and come up again, more often than not with a fish in their claws.

"We'll try and catch some fish later," I said, "though I suspect we won't be anywhere near that good at it."

"Why would we want to catch fish?" Ian asked.

"Same reason the ospreys want to. For eating."

He looked at me quizzically.

"That's what people used to do," I said. "Animals eat other animals. People are animals, sort of. We're in the wild now."

He looked out over the river. "I'm not going to eat a fish."

"Alright," I chuckled, "but you might change your mind after a few days of rationing."

At our drinking spot on the riverbank, we took turns filing the handle of one of our spoons against a stone until we had a pointed knife. Back on the beach, I found a small, flat piece of soft driftwood. I carved a groove into it, and I sharpened the end of a juniper branch, and then grinded it back and forth through the groove. Raff and Ian dug a fire pit at the edge of the dunes.

We tried for an interminably long time, but no matter how fast we rubbed the wood together we couldn't even produce smoke let alone fire. It was only after we gave up on the driftwood and found a different base piece in the woods that hints of smoke started to rise from the freshly cut groove.

We cheered it on when the first pieces of tinder lit and flames started to grow over the sticks piled in the fire pit. As the fire danced up, we listened to the crackle of the wood, and talked about how much we liked the aroma. Each of us teased our fingers over the flames so we could know, at least a little, what a real burn felt like.

We celebrated with our first swim. The cool saltwater soothed our mosquito bites, sunburns, scratches, and scuffs. Being in the primal violence of the ocean was unlike any swimming we'd ever done at Lake Park. To be pushed down, thrown forward, and spun over by the power of a wave was at once majestic and terrifying. We couldn't get enough.

Afterward, Ian napped in our camp while Raff and I gathered firewood. I had stopped to watch the frenetic movements of a squirrel foraging through a bed of fallen leaves when Raff, a growing bundle of sticks under one arm, came up and stood next to me.

"That first night you showed me the med-pod – I never told you, but when you and Ian went up to get some sleep, I got in it by myself and asked it about Lenia."

"Yeah?" I said. "I never thought to ask about her."

"Yeah, and what it was was ... it turned out that Bennett was the sex worker she'd left me for. He ended up taking her offer, after all. So that was why we never heard from him again."

As I thought back to those days, that fit all too well with what had happened, but I still had trouble believing it. I remembered how Bennett had told me he resented Lenia for even suggesting he get with her.

"The pod told you all this?" I asked.

"It told me they're married, and they have a kid together. They only live a few buildings away from mine."

"How do you feel about it?"

"Not much," he said. He was looking down at the leaves. There was still sand from the swim in his hair and on his face and neck. "It doesn't matter anymore, but I wish they'd told me when it happened, instead of leaving me so much to wonder about over the years. That's the part about it I don't understand."

At low tide that evening, we picked some mussels from the stones that lined the shoals, and we managed to catch four small fish by using our shirts as nets. Ian watched as, one by one, I held the fish flat against the beach and took their heads off with the knife. Their static eyes reminded me of the emotionless glass eyes of a bot, but it was still disturbing to feel them twitching under my hand until I'd made the cut.

I felt some shame, or at least the need to justify what I was doing. "I hate to kill anything," I said, "but it's what's best for us."

Ian didn't seem bothered by it, even though he'd reiterated that he wouldn't be eating them. "We've all killed mosquitoes," he said.

We crudely cleaned the mussels and fish, and lightly grilled them by laying a flat stone across the fire pit. Raff and I slowly tried bits of the strange, heavy meat. It didn't take long to realize that it wasn't going down well with either of us, and we were soon expelling it into the dunes. Outside of our forgotten infancies, neither of us had ever thrown up before, and in the cold sweats of the aftermath we agreed that it was something we never wanted to do again.

Ian was happy that he'd stuck to his rations.

41

The next day we waded across the mouth of the river. On the other side, we found a deer carcass in the dunes, nothing left but sun-bleached bones and shreds of pelt. Ian found the jaw a few feet away, half-buried by sand. It was a warm, clear day and past the small waves lapping the shore, the ocean's surface was glasslike all the way to the horizon. Thin red strips of seaweed were washing ashore with the tide. It was the first wild food we were able to stomach in large portions.

Past surviving, we had very little we needed to do during our time on the beach. We spent the next few days going for walks, collecting shells, and gathering firewood. Raff and I gave Ian lessons on everything he was missing at school, using sticks to draw geometry problems in the sand.

We swam every day. We learned to ride the waves with our bodies, pronating ourselves and kicking forward until the waves broke and our torsos were carried within the funneling chambers, the water rushing over our faces as we reached ahead to skim our hands over the oncoming surface.

At night we sat around the fire, the stillness of the mountains on one side, the perpetual churning of the sea on the other, and the stars above. We'd speculate about what was happening back in the city, back in our ward.

"I miss my friends," Ian admitted on our sixth night there. He was popular in school, and he hadn't been able to tell his friends he'd be leaving, let alone say goodbye.

"They miss you, too," I said. "Maybe you can see some of them when we get back."

"I know it's ridiculous, but I miss work," Raff said. "I miss the routine of it and doing the different tasks. Imagine how poorly our team is doing without us."

"They've got to be pretty mad about how much they're falling in the rankings," I said. "I wish we could've told them how meaningless it all is."

The med-pod had confirmed what my father and I had always suspected – that the colors, patterns, figures, and challenges which appeared on our workstation displays every day were of no more consequence than the soothing movements of a mobile hanging over an infant's crib. Work was a low-cost way to give a population a sense of purpose, and giving a population a sense of purpose was the best way to keep them distracted and complacent.

"I miss dinner showing up in our cupboard every night," I said.

They laughed and agreed. Ian had taken a stick from the pile and was stoking the fire.

"But I don't really," I said. "Our cupboards could've been overflowing if they had wanted them to be."

The pod had told me that members of the General Order were issued exactly as much food as was needed nutritionally, and not a calorie more. This was, like everything else about our lives, a matter of efficiency for efficiency's sake, and had nothing to do with resources being limited. It would've been simple to give us more food, better accommodations, more personal items, and longer lives. Instead we were given only that which had been determined, after years of fine tuning, to be just enough to keep us adequately content.

There on the beach, so far away from the city, I got furious thinking about the small meals still being delivered every day to countless apartments. It didn't help that I was hungry, and sick of eating seaweed. It didn't help that our rations were almost gone. I'd been stewing silently in my anger more and more since Kiri's death, but this night I let it out.

"All the lies they told us about why we were given so little, and about why we had to die so young, all those rationalizations meted out by those in power – maybe they all had a little bit of truth to them – those kinds of rationalizations always do – but the real truth is that those in power do what they do only because it benefits them, and because the very act of exercising their power brings them pleasure. That's the most important truth people need to learn."

Hunger and anger kept me from getting to sleep that evening. I was staring into the pitch of the night sky when a white streak, as thin as a hair, crossed the stars. Another came, and soon they were falling across the sky like raindrops over a window.

I woke up Ian and Raff with excited yells of "Meteors!" as if the whole reason we'd come to the beach was to see them.

"Each of those streaks of light up there," I said, "most of them are made by little specks that you could hold in your hand. Just tiny things, but with enough speed they can light the whole sky."

In the morning, a storm moved in fast from the south and it rained like we couldn't believe, unlike any rain we'd ever seen. We donned our jackets and took shelter in the woods, huddling beneath a tree as thunder cracked and sheets of water rattled down through the branches above.

I held Ian and listened to the wind whistle through the trees. I worried for the ospreys huddled in their nests somewhere. I imagined them, probably wrongly, wrapping their wings over each other as the storm shook the bough that held them.

The rain ended as abruptly as it had begun, and in the afternoon sun we sat by the river and had our last chocolate bar. I tore the foil wrapper into small pieces, which I piled onto a large, flat stone.

I still had the rock I'd found in the creek, and I took it from my pocket, and held it before Ian. "We'll use this one as something called a pistil, and the big stone as something called a mortar."

We pounded and grinded the foil into powder, and we did the same with the rest of the many wrappers we'd saved. When we were done, we'd filled half a dinner bag with the metal powder.

On the beach, we filled the rest of our dinner bags with sand. "Only use the sand that's fully dry, and filter it carefully," I said. "No shells or anything else."

That evening we spotted porpoises offshore, over a dozen heading north, weaving above and below the surface pistonlike. We stood watching until they were gone, and then watched the sun set.

"We've lived six days sheltered from the signals of the city," I said. "Our bodies have flushed out the last of our artificial cells, and when we go back to the city tomorrow, we'll return as the only natural men in the world. The first in generations."

42

We packed up at dawn the next day, leaving the beach and following the riverbank through the mountain gorge's deep shadows. We were taking an easier route than the one we'd taken to get there, but we were now weighed down by the bags of sand, and coming off a week of hunger.

Halfway into the gorge, Raff was again the first to get a mosquito bite. "I'd almost forgotten about them," he said.

"No ocean breeze to push them away here," I said.

After three hours, the mountains were long behind us and we were following the river northeast through a flat, lush forest. We stopped to rest at a bend in the river.

Raff had been carrying the sack for quite a while and was relieved to set it down in the clovers and grass at the forest's edge. He found a tree to sit against, clasped his hands behind his head, stretched out his legs, and closed his eyes.

Ian spotted a beetle making its way along the riverbank, and was soon giving it his full attention. He was spellbound with how it turned direction every time he put his hand down to block its path.

The river was wide and calm here, and the muddy banks on both sides were uniformly lined with poplars, oaks, and ash. A sparrow flew across the water and into the woods near us. I lost track of where it went, but I noticed something seemed strange when I looked deep into the woods.

I stepped into the trees, pushing aside branches and weaving my way through the underbrush. Twenty feet in, I caught sight of a clearing. At first I thought maybe it was a lake, but instead I found a plot of land where the ground was slightly raised and nothing but short grass grew.

I walked into the clearing, trying to figure out why it was the only spot I'd seen in miles where no trees had taken root. I got the answer when I dug through the top layer of dirt and decomposing leaves, and felt something that was too perfectly shaped to be a product of nature. I freed it from the dirt and, excited to show them the artifact, hurried back to Ian and Raff.

"This is a brick," I said, holding it before them. "There were buildings here once." I wiped the black dirt away from its pocked, weathered red surface, and handed it to Ian. "When men did the labor of machines, we had to make buildings out of small pieces. Whole cities would be built up from millions of these."

At midday we cut away from the river and walked for miles east through the woods and hills until we hit the creek. After a few more miles of following it downstream, things started looking familiar: the rock face where we'd first rested, the sandy banks where Raff and I had fallen, and finally, just as the sun was starting to set, the orange bollards rising from the grass at the edge of Lake Park.

"The park looks smaller than I remember," Ian said. He had gotten a deep tan, setting off his blue eyes that were so like his mother's.

After we reached Last Day Beach and crossed the creek, Raff froze at the sight of a medbot coming our way.

"What's wrong?" I asked.

"Should we hide from the bots? Will they try to catch us?"

"Relax, you know they won't," I said. "You remember what the med-bot said – we're now as good as invisible to them."

Raff, not entirely convinced, eyed the approaching bot.

"Watch this," I said.

When it got closer, I called, "Can you help me? I have a broken leg."

The bot continued on without acknowledging me. "It sensed our existence the way it would've sensed a bird passing overhead," I said, "but we're the one kind of animal that isn't in their databases, and they have no programming telling them how to react to us."

Again we were a sight for those who saw us passing through the park and riding the train. Not only was I lugging the heavy sack, but also our shoes and tattered clothes were covered in a week's dirt and sand. Our hair was greasy and untamed, and Raff and I had the beginnings of beards. But again no one said anything.

Uro was waiting anxiously outside his building. "Right on time!" he said as he ran up to hug us. He brought us up, and presented us with a large selection of meals stacked on his table.

We dug in gratefully, and he asked how our week went. "We didn't fall off any cliffs or get any snakebites," I said between mouthfuls of a sandwich. "And it's beautiful out there, the kind of beauty that can only be appreciated by actually being there. But how'd it go here?"

"Your meals stopped showing up in your cupboards three days ago. I never checked back at your apartments again."

The bots that tracked our ward's population would've classified our disappearance from their sensors as a curious aberration, but not one significant enough to investigate or report to the Administrative Order. It would've been different if three-hundred people disappeared, but the disappearance of only three warranted no more of a response than the eventual cessation of food deliveries to our kitchens. Our apartments had likely been reassigned by now.

"But how did it go with showing people the med-pod?" I asked. "How many people know now?"

He pursed his lips and looked down. Over the last two months, he'd taken on a stern, serious countenance – so different from when we were teenagers and I derided him for having a perpetual smile.

"On the first day, I convinced some coworkers to come see the med-pod. I did what you said – I had it tell them how so much of what we've been told about the world isn't true. But no one cared. I couldn't understand it. They said it was strange that a med-pod would say such things, but they wouldn't even talk to me about it further. Some were even angry at me for bringing them there. I tried with other people – neighbors, strangers off the street – but no one wanted to hear it. I'm sorry, Corim. I tried the best I could."

"I was worried they'd react like that," I said.

Uro perked up a little. "A lot of people now know where the med-pod is. I showed as many as I could. So maybe they'll return to it. Maybe they'll start asking it questions."

"I suspect that after what we do tomorrow morning," I said, "that the med-pod will be found by the Administrative Order and fixed."

"Oh," Uro said. "Of course."

I noticed that his face looked gaunter than it did when I'd seen him seven days before. I realized that many of the meals laid out before us weren't from our cupboards, but from his.

"It's alright," I said. "You did all you could. Have you thought about tomorrow? Will you come with us? I'd really like you to."

"Yes, I will. There's nothing for me to stay for here."

We cleaned ourselves up. Uro's shower wouldn't come on for us, but Raff and I were able to use his shaver, which didn't require the presence of artificial cells to be switched on. Our clothes came out as good as new when we ran them through his laundry bin.

We all talked about the plan for the next day, and I revealed to them the part of the plan I'd kept secret – the part that would come later in the day and involved me going off on my own. They all argued strongly against the idea, but I insisted it was already decided, and that it needed to be done.

I slept well that night, the softness of Uro's couch a welcomed change from sleeping on the beach.

In the morning, we used Uro's sheets to make a second sack, filling it with his things and the remaining meals he'd saved. The four of us shared his single serving of coffee and cereal. It was the same cereal as always – the flat, crunchy flakes that we'd all been eating every morning of our lives.

After waiting at the station with the rush hour crowd, we crammed into a northbound train. A man who was pressed against me kept looking down at the two sacks we were carrying. "That's all our stuff," I told him. "We're leaving the city later today. You can come with us if you like."

I knew it must've sounded insane to him, but I was being completely serious, and was hoping he'd talk with me, and maybe even entertain the idea. His eyes widened and he said, "No, thanks," as if there hadn't been anything unusual about my offer. He turned his head away and locked his eyes out the window.

"That's what it was like trying to show people the med-pod," Uro said. "They were all afraid of change, even if it was just a change in how they think about the world."

"Well," I said, "they're about to experience a change whether they want to or not."

43

We got off at the Life Center stop. It was a quiet morning, with only a few people milling about the esplanade. A couple was briskly walking hand-in-hand toward the Life Center, reminding me of when Kiri and I were eighteen and went in to tell the guidebot how we wanted to be parents.

"I'm afraid you'll have to wait out here," I said to Uro as we neared the doors of the great white building.

He wished us luck, and headed over to one of the spotlights that encircled the building. He gave us a final wave and settled in to wait, leaning his shoulder against the spotlight's metal casing.

If Uro had come in with us, a guidebot would've greeted him and asked his business. Instead when Raff, Ian, and I walked through the door, all the guidebots remained standing stock-still in the center of the great hall's marble floor.

I led us past the elevators and the funeral halls to a narrow passage tucked into the building's far right corner. It was marked as a restricted area by the standard orange, "Approved access only," sign. We went in, and at the end of it there was a thin metal staircase spiraling up as far as the eye could see.

I ran a finger over the staircase's railing, and showed Raff and Ian the result. It was the first time any of us had ever seen an accumulation of dust. "These stairs are a vestige of the building's construction three hundred years ago. The bots only use the elevators," I said.

I flung the heavy sack over my shoulder. "We've gone up a mountain before, so ninety-one stories should be easy, right?"

Raff nodded with a confident smile, but Ian was still standing a few feet from the stairs, looking very small and afraid. It was dark in there – the only light we had was the light that made its way down the passage from the main hall. For the week we'd spent in the wild, I never saw Ian afraid of anything, even when it was climbing a cliff face or running to the trees for shelter during a thunderstorm. But he was still a boy, and his fear had returned with our return to the place that had taken his mother.

I knelt in front of him. "Buddy, Raff and I can take care of this. Do you want to go out and keep Uro company while he waits?"

His face firmed, defiant of the idea that he'd be left out. "No, Dad. I want to help."

"Ok, but try not to be afraid, alright? Fear can't help us right now, it could only hurt us. Remember how brave you are, and why we're here. Do you understand?"

"Let's go up," he said.

We counted the stories as we went – each floor's landing led to a passage identical to the one on the ground floor. After sixty stories, the trajectory of the stairwell curved inward as the building tapered toward the spire.

The stairs ended at a large windowless room that made up the entirety of the ninety-first floor. There was an elevator bank at one wall and, in the center of the room, steep metal stairs that led straight up through the high ceiling. We took them and came out into the base of the spire itself – a perfectly circular white-walled room that flared out toward the floor, creating a crevice all the way around.

Next to the stairwell there was a small array of transponders and circuitry bolted onto a steel stand. The transponders were wired to an immense antenna, which was riveted to the floor and ran up the entire length of the spire.

"First we lay down the sand," I said, opening the sack. "Take some bags, and spread it all around the edges of the room. No gaps."

We surrounded ourselves with a great circle of sand, and I added a line of it extending from the circle to underneath the transponders and around the base of the antenna.

We laid the sulfur and metal powder over the sand, using our forks to mix it all together.

I crumpled the now-empty dinner bags, and I lined them, as well the kindling sticks we'd brought with us, at the base of the antenna.

Ian watched me go around the room making final adjustments – evening out the formula in one spot, mixing it a bit more in another. "Will it explode?" he asked.

"No, it will only burn," I said. "In fact, it won't even be a fast fire – it'll burn quite slowly. But it will burn very hot. Hotter than the wood and paper. Hot enough to set metal on fire."

I took out the sharpened juniper branch and the grooved piece of wood, and I rubbed them together over the kindling just as I'd practiced doing for the last week. Raff and Ian knelt beside me, more fixated than ever by the first signs of heat and smoke.

At first the fire only spread over the bags and sticks. "Why isn't it working?" Raff asked.

"Give it a minute," I said.

From beneath the gentle crackling of the burning paper and wood, a high-pitched, urgent hiss emerged. A dollop of the sand formula had combusted into a bubbling, smoking, lava-like liquid.

"Move back a bit, and don't breathe the fumes," I said. "We just need to make sure it's fully lit."

We moved to the stairs. The hiss grew, and then a flash of red flames ignited and cascaded around the antenna, beneath the transponders, and down the line to the room's perimeter.

"Let's get out of here," I said.

We dizzied ourselves hurrying down the spiral stairs, and sprinted through the lobby and out the door. Uro rejoined us, and we headed to the other end of the esplanade, where the four of us leaned against the station wall, tilting up our heads to watch what was to come.

A gray ring had formed around the base of the spire. It was subtle, just a thin discoloration of the building's white exterior – the kind of thing we wouldn't have noticed it if we hadn't been looking for it.

Three minutes went by without anything more happening. "Is that all?" Uro asked.

"Likely not," I said.

Punctuating my reply, a screaming, scraping noise filled the air. The esplanade was busier now, and those on it looked up in search of the sound's source.

The next noises might've been mistaken for thunder if it hadn't been a clear day. At the top of the Life Center, so high above, black smoke began crossing the blue sky. With it came the first gasps and screams from the other onlookers. Some pointed, some put their hands to their mouths.

The smoke cloud spread, sending the world below into an ominous dusk. When a man who'd just exited the station saw it, he reversed course and ran back in. After a few more minutes, a shrill, metallic howl echoed down, and the spire began to flag downward like the slow-turning hand of a clock. Those on the esplanade began to run, most retreating to the station, but others simply going in whatever direction would most quickly get them away. Those coming out the

Life Center doors would stop in confusion. Some fled, others withdrew back inside.

The spire continued cutting a slow arc through the billowing clouds of smoke that now hid its base. It started gaining speed as it neared a right angle, and then crashed against the building. It stayed still there for a moment, perched against the now-cracked walls of the upper floors, the pointed white tip aiming directly down at the few of us still watching from below.

I wondered if the worst of the damage had been done, but then there was one last screech of metal and the spire, its base now in flames, slid down and off the angled side of the building, freefalling through the air. All was quiet as the spire descended before the heights of the Life Center, not unlike the way a leaf might gently fall before a tree.

Time slowed. It was as if I could track every detail of every inch of the fall. As I watched the wake of black smoke that the tumbling spire was leaving behind, I thought of the time years before when I'd seen smoke while walking home from work. I'd finally learned from the med-pod what had happened that day: a farmbot had malfunctioned, steered itself straight through a fence and off a roof, and smashed into the street below.

Malfunction. It was a word I'd never heard before. It would've been disconcerting for members of the General Order to know that any of the technologies surrounding us could ever do anything but always run exactly as expected, so even the idea of such a possibility, and even the word that represented that idea, was kept from us. But now it was a word that meant very much to me, because it reminded me that everything has flaws, and everything can break.

Or at least be broken.

44

The impact's shockwave pounded through my skin, and a terrible ringing filled my ears.

Through clouds of dust and smoke, the remains of the spire and antenna lay before the Life Center doors. The white shell of the spire was now rubble, and the antenna had bent and snapped in two, with the thicker bottom end still burning. A spotlight had been destroyed completely, and there was a crater in the broken concrete of the esplanade.

The med-pod had told me it would take two days for the Administrative Order and bots to build a replacement transmitter. Not as long as I would've liked, but it still meant two days without Expirations. All over the ward, heartbroken families believed that this would be the day they'd lose a mother or father, but, as baffling as it'd be for them, I had at least delayed it.

The same was true for the adjoining wards of the Counselor and Judicial Orders. Those orders, while better fed and longer-lived, were kept in the dark almost as much as the General Order. I'd come to realize that all the upper orders, even the Administrative Order, were equal victims of the nameless order – the immortal few who lived perpetual lives of decadence, watching from displays in their mansions as generations of the people they controlled came and went.

We in the General Order were no more than chattel to them: a source of sex workers, and a test group for genetic improvements. When it was shown that a million of us with one trait would somehow outperform a million of us with another trait, then they, as well as those in the upper orders, would be accordingly modified. Toying with the General Order had started to yield diminishing returns though, and our numbers were being reduced. At our peak, there'd been over three-hundred million of us, but now we were down to fewer than fifty million.

And our lives were a never-ending source of entertainment to those in control. There were always unfolding dramas among the mortals for them to watch, even if it was something as simple as a sex worker being murdered and then having to decide how to testify at a trial.

I'd just sent a message to those in the immortal order, all eleven thousand of them, by bringing down the spire. I'd also caused a brief change for millions of others that none of them, no matter how afraid of change they may be, would be able to ignore. Crowds would gather on rooftops at nightfall to see how the Life Center was not only mutilated, but looking a bit darker from the loss of a spotlight. More importantly, word of the cessation of Expirations would spread. It may have only been a temporary change, and it may have only been confined to one corner of the vast metropolis that held every soul in the world, but it was more than I ever thought I'd be able to do.

I'd released one small bit of the wrath burning within me, and I could now at least say that I'd done something to give meaning to Kiri's passing.

In her note to me, she had asked me to stay who I was, to stay curious and full of life. I'd read the note every day for two months, and done my best to live by it. But I hadn't stayed who I was. The curiosities I now carried were born of very specific purposes, and I only felt full of life the way a rabbit feels full of life when it realizes that it's run into a wolf's den. I could no longer be who I'd been before. I'd become a fighter.

I was fighting an enemy who had great power over the world, but also an enemy who'd forgotten how to fight, an enemy who'd grown so comfortable they no longer possessed any of the weapons of old that they'd need to combat people like me, or even adequate knowledge of such weapons. I may have been skinnier than ever, and I may have had a long road of hunger and struggle ahead of me, but I was free and strong, and I knew everything I would need for the battle.

Four maintenance bots rumbled around the corner of the Life Center. I nodded toward the wreckage. "Let's check it out before it gets cleaned up."

We walked into the debris, stepping over the rubble and looking for anything of use. The maintenance bots started scooping up the larger pieces and vacuuming up the smaller ones. Uro backed away when one of the bots told him to leave the area, but just like all the other bots it ignored Raff, Ian, and me.

Ian found a piece of flat metal that would be good for filing into a knife, and I found a three-foot long metal bar that had broken off from the destroyed spotlight. It was heavy and slightly bent, but fit well in my hand. "Ok," I said, "let's go get some food."

We left the wreckage behind, crossing off the esplanade as two more maintenance bots crossed onto it. Minutes later, we entered an automat a few blocks south. It was crowded with workers who had decided to get a treat during their lunch hour. We made our way to the back wall where all the cubbies were, and patiently waited for a spot to open up among those who were browsing the selection.

At the first opportunity, I stepped up to the cubbies, raised my new metal bar, and crashed the end of it through one of the little windows. The din of laughter and conversation that had filled the air was replaced by a hushed silence, and all eyes turned to me. I raised my bar again and broke another cubby window. People backed away and rose from their tables. None said a word, and some started toward the exit.

I kept swinging, moving down the wall and smashing my way into every last cubby. I was tense with adrenaline, swinging the bar harder than I had to, moving from window to window faster than I had to. The thrill of having the power to so easily break the barriers to all that food was intoxicating. The sound of the glass shattering ... the shards falling at my feet ... the metal bar shaking against my grip when it hit the cubby walls – it was all beautiful to me.

By the time we were done, the two sacks were overflowing with loot, and we were the only ones left in the automat.

We continued on to a station where I checked the time on the platform's clock, noting that it was about the time Scotson Yvera would typically finish up his lunch and go into his office. Of all my studies in the med-pod, my examination of his life and routines had been the most detailed. Now the time was fast approaching to use what I'd learned about him.

We caught a train to Lake Park, and we raided the automat there as well. Since we were already carrying so much food, we were far more discerning with what we took, though we still made sure to get all the bread, chocolate, and wine.

We exited onto the patio, where Ian and I both froze for a moment when we saw the spot among the tables where we'd sat two months before. We then made our way through the park's crowd of adults and kids in bathing suits, and continued down to the lakeshore. The early afternoon sun was high in the clear sky, and a pleasant breeze was coming up off the water.

Approaching Last Day Beach, I peered out to the line of orange bollards rising from the grass. "You realize, Uro," I said, "that with the antenna knocked out, you won't feel any pain when we cross the border."

"I guess that's lucky for me then," Uro said.

"You have no idea," Raff said.

We hopped the creek, and came to a woman standing beneath the clock that faced Last Day Beach. A young couple, visibly shaken, stood behind her, the husband with his arm around the wife, and the wife and holding an infant.

The woman, who wore her hair oddly short, looked utterly perplexed as she stared intently up at the clock. Her brow was furrowed and she was holding her chin with one hand.

She didn't lower her eyes when I approached.

"You thought you'd be dead by now," I said.

Keeping her gaze on the clock, she nodded.

"There's been a change. No one is dying today. But if you stay here in the city, you'll be dead in two days. That doesn't have to happen, though. You can live longer. Much longer. I'd like to show you how."

She lowered her hazel eyes and examined me. She saw I was holding a sack, and looked past my shoulder at Raff, Ian, and Uro. "What are you saying?" she asked.

"Come with us," I said.

45

We convinced her to join us, and over the next two hours we found nine more who had come to Last Day Beach for their Expiration and were now bewildered to still be alive. But of those nine, only three men and one woman agreed to come with us.

I couldn't understand the people who turned us down. We pleaded with them, explaining it was their only chance to live, but as soon as we mentioned crossing the border they wouldn't listen to another word.

We would've found many more potential recruits if we'd stayed longer, but we only had a few hours of daylight left for traveling. We also wanted to get clear of the city before the Administrative and Judicial orders had a full understanding of what had happened.

We gathered the two women and three men who'd agreed to come with us at the edge of the border's grass strip. Their families also gathered, and they seemed to be more in a state of shock than the five we were rescuing. They'd come to Lake Park expecting to see their loved ones die, and now they'd gone from learning they wouldn't die to learning that we were taking them far away and couldn't promise when, or even if, they'd ever return.

Before we left, the daughter of the first woman I'd recruited came up to me, her baby still cradled in her arms. "I don't understand what's happening, but thank you."

I told her to tell everyone she could about what she'd seen – that her mother had outlived her Expiration.

When we couldn't wait any longer, we pulled the five away from their farewells and led them to the border. Raff, Ian, and I walked through the bollards, with Uro cautiously following a step behind. The five recruits stayed back, watching us and waiting to be prompted. When we waved them forward and gave them assurances, they looked to one another and started slowly moving.

They crossed the border one by one with hesitation and nervous laughter. When all five were across, they turned back and waved to their families as if they'd just covered a great distance.

We started following the creek. It was slow going at first because the five we had rescued kept waving and calling back to the families who were still watching from behind the border, but as we got deeper into the woods we started moving at a reasonable pace. Our five guests were silent as we led them. We had explained everything the best we could, but it was clear that all they really comprehended was that they had to follow our orders to keep on living.

I had taken the lead, but after about a mile I stopped. "Let's pause here a moment," I called back.

The nine of us came together, and I addressed those who had just joined us. "I have to break away now and go in another direction, but don't worry, the rest of the group will stay together, and I'll see you all again in two days."

"You're still sure about this?" Raff asked.

I told him that it was something I had to do, and then I went and said goodbye to Ian. He protested – I knew he would – but I told him that this was the one thing he absolutely couldn't join me on.

Before we parted, I pulled Raff aside. "Take care of Ian. If anything happens to me, I'll be happy knowing I left him in your hands. And keep a sharp eye on him for the next few miles – don't let him sneak off to try and follow me."

"I'm tempted to do that myself. Why don't you let me come with you, or at least take Uro?"

"You know there's no need for that."

"I hope not," he said.

I handed him the sack I'd been carrying. The only thing I'd be taking with me was my metal bar. I crossed the creek, but before moving on further, I stayed to watch them continue on their way. With the same frequency that our five recruits had turned to wave to their families, Raff and Uro now turned back to wave goodbye to me. Ian never looked back.

The night before, they threw out every argument they could think of against me doing this, and then they argued more about me doing it alone, but I'd refused to listen.

The plan for them was to start the trip back to our spot on the beach. They'd make about ten or fifteen miles before nightfall, spend the night in the woods, and then cover the rest in the morning. At the beach, our new recruits would be shielded from Expiration when the Life Center transmitter went back up, and they and Uro would also start cycling out their artificial cells. Everyone would go to work making shelters in the woods near the beach, and would start learning to live in a way that we'd be able to sustain indefinitely.

As for me, I was going back to the city, but this time to a part I'd never been to. Twelve miles north, there was a ward without walls. It was where the local members of the Administrative Order lived, where Scotson Yvera lived.

It was strange and lonely to be moving through the woods on my own. I tried not to think about how the distance between Ian and me was growing with every step, and focused instead on moving quickly to make the most of the remaining daylight. It took what must've been three hours, but as dusk was setting I came upon the asphalt road that ran along the southern edge of the Administrative

Order's ward. It was quiet there – no signs of anyone on the road, and across the way there were only more woods. From the cover of the trees and the closing darkness, I started following the road as it wound its way northwest.

Uro had told me that they hadn't gotten any rain in the week we were away, and now the dead leaves I was trying to tread lightly over were so dry that they'd crackle with every step. After about a mile of walking, another sound started mixing with my footsteps – something was coming up the road.

The vehicles favored by the Administrative Order were small cars – essentially windowed L-pods with wheels, complete with reclining seats, displays, and a voice that would ask its occupants their destination. They also had lighting strips that ran all the way around their exterior edges, equally illuminating their surroundings in all directions.

I crept farther back from the road as I saw the lights of the car approach, and dropped low to the ground. It may or may not have been Scotson – his evening schedule was less predictable than his daytime routine. Some nights he came home straight from the office, but other nights he'd visit a brothel, or stay out late with friends drinking wine and taking any number of the artificial recreational drugs popular within the Administrative Order.

It also just as easily could've been his wife returning from a dinner or someone who lived in the other houses in his neighborhood.

After the car passed and I continued on, it wasn't long before I came upon the first houselights faintly shining from far across the road. I moved in closer until I spotted a driveway. A few minutes later I came to the next house and driveway. The road then took a sharp turn, off of which another driveway went up a steep hill. Up the hill, as I knew I would, I spotted the lights of Scotson's house.

46

I knew there was no one around who would've seen me on the road, but I still sprinted when crossing it, and I still felt safer after making it into the woods that ran along Scotson's driveway. I'd be every bit as invisible to the bots in this ward as I'd been back in my ward, but it was paramount to stay hidden from human eyes.

News of what had happened at the Life Center had surely spread through the Administrative Order by now, and put them on high alert. If any of them spotted me sneaking around where they lived, I knew they'd do everything they could to kill or capture me. The good thing was that they'd have to improvise how to do this without the help of bots. They were no doubt now frantically working to program the bots to recognize natural-state humans like me, but even with that modification bots would be of little use as a weapon against us. Until our return, it'd been assumed that any bot could paralyze a man by sending a signal to his artificial cells, so no bot was designed to do things as crude as physically pursuing, capturing, and killing someone.

My hope was that, when left without machines to do it for them, those in the higher orders would lack ingenuity when it came to finding and catching me. But I also figured the fewer chances I gave them, the better.

I'd studied the lay of the land around Scotson's house so often in the med-pod that even though it was my first time there and it was dark, I didn't have any trouble finding the spot I'd picked out for spending the night: a patch of pine trees where I'd be well-concealed from both his house and the road.

I felt my way deep into the pines, laid myself down in a clearing of dry needles, and ate one of the snacks still stuffed in my pockets from the automat raids.

The only thing I needed to do was get some much-needed rest, but I was in store for a long, fitful night. The cold, hard ground made me wish I'd brought blankets and a pillow.

As sleep came and went, I first dreamed of the beach, and then that Kiri was back in our old apartment, waiting for me. When I awoke at dawn's first light, I was dreaming I was standing outside the burning Life Center, but this time something had gone wrong, and no matter how long I waited the spire never fell.

I sat up, stretched, and had another snack from my pocket. Grabbing the metal bar, I rose and crept through the pines until I had a good view.

Scotson lived in a three-story house of Ironwood and stone, built atop a hill. It had two living rooms, a den, a dining room, five bedrooms, six bathrooms, a garage for their four vehicles, and a kitchen that was larger than any apartment I'd ever lived in.

On the news and on shows, members of the Administrative Order were always shown as living in apartments that were only slightly larger than General Order apartments. In reality, huge standalone homes like this, with slanted roofs and private grass yards, were the norm for them.

After an hour of watching and waiting, the big door to their garage slid open and a car exited and drove off. The sun had just crested the trees, and I was able to make out Scotson's daughter through car's windows. A moment later a second car followed out of the garage with Scotson's son. The boys and girls of the Administrative Order went to separate schools, only comingling at social events like dances, which came more frequently as the students got older. None of their schools had anything like parlors or soft rooms.

I knew from his habits that Scotson was either now finishing up breakfast with his wife or still sleeping in. In either case, his wife would likely soon change into something picked out from her enormous closet, and then leave to go to the spa where she'd relax all day with other Administrative Order women.

After a half-hour of waiting, I started to worry that the news of yesterday had made her break her habit, but finally the garage door opened and a car drove out. When I was sure it was her I'd seen through the car windows, I closed my eyes and listened to the hum of the tires fade away as the car sped off. Then for good measure I counted to one hundred while I stared at the house, knowing my wife's killer was somewhere in it, now alone.

I went to the edge of the woods, took a good look around to make sure it was clear, and then made my way up his front lawn and climbed the steps of stone slate, which were lined on both sides by beds of yellow tulips, and had Ironwood handrails matching the walls of the house.

At the front door I thought about how I still had the option of turning back. I could've run into the wild again and no one would've ever known I'd been there. But I was without doubts. I was so sure I was doing the right thing that I felt something unexpected, something I hadn't felt in a long while – a deep, pervasive calm.

There was an old-fashioned bolt lock on the door, but it was only there for ornamental purposes and was always left unengaged. I turned the brass doorknob, and, fearful of making a sound, pulled open the door inch by careful inch.

I stepped into the foyer and closed the door as slowly as I'd opened it. The house was silent. Across the white carpet of the foyer, the kitchen was on the left, the stairs to the second floor were in the middle, and the hall to one of the living rooms was to the right. One foyer wall had a closet door and a large mirror, and the other had a glass-top ebony table against it that held an abstract sculpture of gilded, intersecting spheres.

The ceiling creaked above me. I froze and waited, the metal bar tight in my grip. Two more creaks and then silence returned.

I started forward, one step with every breath. When I reached the bottom of the stairs, I heard a little thump from the second floor – something had been put down on a table or desk.

I stayed close to the wall as I climbed the stairs so they'd be less likely to creak. Halfway up, I heard Scotson sigh, followed by music. He'd turned on the news. I recognized the opening theme from all the times in the med-pod when I'd watched the unique news broadcast made for the Administrative Order.

From the steps I listened to the newscaster's words. "Good morning. We have new footage of the attack, and we've also learned more about the attackers."

I started climbing again as I listened to the news recap in seconds the entirety of my life, and the lives of Raff, Uro, and Ian. "It is telling," an expert explained, "that none of the attackers had wives. We'll have to reexamine the gender balance within the General Order. We'll have to reexamine its effect on complacency."

At the top of the stairs there was a printed photo hanging in a wood frame. A younger version of Scotson – no paunch, all his hair, healthy skin – held his wife in front of a trellis of blooming rose bushes.

From the landing of the stairs I could see through the open door of the son's room. In the corner, there was a freshly made bed beneath a window overlooking the backyard. The walls were covered in all manner of photos, displays, and hanging trinkets. The bedside table, desk, and shelves were equally littered with toys, gadgets, and games.

I turned off the landing and into the hall, jumping back in fright at the figure standing against the wall.

It was one of the bots that were used as house servants. It looked more human than any of the bots I'd ever been used to. Its body's fluid curves of matted gray metal made it look like a nude man in perpetual silhouette. Its face wasn't stamped on, instead it had a pointed nose, full lips, and recessed eyes.

The sound of the news was coming from the den, just past where the bot stood.

I moved forward, stopping in front of the bot to look into its eyes. My calmness started to break as I wondered what was going on in its mind. Even though I knew it was as much a machine as any other bot, it looked so human that I couldn't help but fear it was thinking about my presence, figuring out what I was, and realizing that I shouldn't be there.

I was only a few feet from Scotson now, divided by nothing but the den wall. I started to make out the sounds of his little movements and uneven breaths among the sounds of the news broadcast.

If he'd been higher up within the echelons of his order, then today he would've been busy doing something such as acting as a liaison between the leaders in the immortal order and the bots that were engineering the reconstruction of the Life Center's transmitter.

Scotson was low in the ranks, though. What little work he did involved helping make mundane decisions about things like food ration selections for the lower orders or architectural design aesthetics. His afternoons at the office typically mirrored his wife's days at the spa: relaxation, watching shows, and conversing with friends. He'd always spend his mornings at home, staying there through lunch on the days he didn't eat at one of his office building's luxury cafeterias.

His desk faced away from the door. I crept forward and leaned ahead to look in.

The far wall of the den had two high windows and was covered with more framed photos. There was a cabinet of drawers in the corner. The side that I could see of his large wood desk had a small display on it, and a few papers.

With another step I saw his hand braced on the desk's edge. He was standing, his chair pushed off to the side and his face close to the news footage flashing across the larger display centered on his desk.

I went through the door and we both stood a moment there, him bent forward watching images of me smashing up the automats, and I right behind him, my metal bar raised in the air.

He was wearing suit pants, but no jacket. His dress shirt was tucked in, the white fabric stretching tight over his lower back as he leaned forward.

I swung my bar against his right kidney.

He screamed and collapsed backwards, ending up on the carpet against the wall behind him, half sitting, half on his side. He clutched at near where I'd hit him, and looked up in confusion and then, when he recognized me, fear.

The bot ran in from the hall and knelt next to Scotson. "Let me give you something for the pain," it said, reaching around to Scotson's back. "You should get to a med-pod."

I moved in and raised my bar over Scotson's head. "Tell it to leave," I said. "Tell it to get out and stay out, or the next hit will be a lot harder."

"You shouldn't be here! You have no right!"

I raised my bar further, poised to land another blow.

He took a breath. "Get out," he said to the bot. "Get out and stay out."

The bot obeyed and returned to the hall. Scotson stared up at me, waiting for me to act or speak, but, as the newscast continued to drone on behind me, I just held the bar above him until he spoke.

"What do you want?"

"To talk."

"Ok, good. Just stay calm. We can talk."

I continued holding the bar over him, my muscles so tense that it shook and twitched in my hand. "Do you know what I think, Scotson? I think you were never surprised at all that Kiri didn't live through that session with you."

He sighed. "I was. Of course I was. Like I said a the trial, it was a horrible shock to me."

"That doesn't make much sense, being surprised by what happens when you choke someone."

He turned his eyes away, a half-grimace still on his face. I hadn't been able to tell if the bot had treated his pain or not.

"I realized last night how you've done all this," he said. "It was that med-pod ... I made a mistake with the information filters. I haven't told anyone that, and they haven't figured it out yet, but they will."

"Are they trying to look for me? Have they figured out a way to scan for me?"

"At the moment, everyone's in shock. What you did wasn't supposed to be possible."

He glanced behind me at the display on his desk. Someone on the news was saying how all the repairs would be finished by the next night.

"Why hasn't the Administrative Order ever fought back?" I asked. "You must know that you could have longer lives."

He shook his head. "I don't know. We're happy. Most people are, in all the orders."

"Tell that to the ones in my ward who jump from roofs."

"We try to minimize that."

"No, you don't. There's no effort made."

He exhaled and groaned at the same time, half pain, half frustration. "Alright, maybe not. I'm not involved with that sort of thing."

That was the first thing he said that I fully believed, because I knew it was true.

He leaned into the wall and managed to right himself a bit. He was still clutching at his side. "Corim, nothing you do here can bring her back. Remember that."

I looked him over, his awkward, twisted position on the floor incongruous with his fine clothes and shined shoes.

"I think it was part of the thrill for you, knowing she might die."

"Let's talk about why you're here and what your plan is," he said.

"You had thought of her dying before. Admit it."

He shook his head again, desperation across his face. "Maybe I'd had thoughts like that, but it was still an accident."

Even now, giving a calculated reply, he couldn't bring himself to speak with any true remorse about it.

"I wasn't thinking clearly," he continued. "Like I said before, I'm sorry."

"So am I."

He looked up at me as he considered his next words. He was still leaning to one side, and I was still holding the bar over him.

"Corim, think this through, you being here. All you've done so far is cause a little damage. You can still move up in the world. We can find a place for a clever man like you in the Administrative Order. Then you'll have real influence. You'll have a house like this. You and your son and your friends. We can make a deal here."

"Don't try that again. I know you never would've kept the deal with Kiri."

He let out a weak grunt and re-clutched his side. I wondered if I'd ruptured his kidney. When he spoke again, his words were strained.

"There's something you should see. It's about Kiri."

47

"In the bottom left drawer." He motioned to the cabinet in the corner.

Keeping my eye on him, I stepped back and around the desk to the cabinet, and slid the drawer open with my foot. It was full of folders.

"Look for your wife's name. There's a file about her."

I bent down and flipped through the folder tabs, squinting to read their small type. I didn't see any names on the tabs, but instead jumbles of numbers and letters that represented some kind of coding system. All the folders looked very old, and they had a musty odor. As it started to register with me that it would make no sense for him to keep a paper file on Kiri, I heard a faint metallic sound come from the desk.

I turned just in time to see that Scotson was up and coming at me, a knife in his hand. The bot had indeed treated his pain, and I'd been foolish to believe it when he'd acted otherwise.

I raised my bar, but he grabbed my wrist with his free hand, squeezing tight and holding back my arm. I tried to do the same by grabbing the wrist of his knife hand, but I wasn't quick enough to stop the blade from slicing into the center of my chest.

As the pain hit, I managed to push the knife away, but it was still only inches from me, and he was trying to force it forward. I still held the bar, but he was twisting that arm back up over my shoulder. I was pressed against the cabinet, bending backwards over the top of it. I braced against his push with all I had, but he was the stronger man, and he had at least forty pounds on me.

"Drop it," he said.

No matter how much I struggled, no matter how much I tried, he would soon have me pressed down with my back atop the cabinet. I knew he'd then slam my arm against the cabinet's edge until the bar fell to the floor, and I knew he'd then cut into my chest again and again until the life was long gone from me.

It would've gone that way if I had kept bracing myself and fighting against what he was trying to do, but in that one moment when I was still holding him off, I accepted that he was physically stronger, so when he pushed harder I surrendered to it, falling back with the push, ducking the blade, and twisting myself away from his mass.

He slammed into the cabinet, and I pulled my hand free and swung the bar into the side of his knee. He tried to recover, turning and swinging the blade back at me, but I was already taking another swing, this time down at the arm that was holding the knife. The blow landed where his forearm met his elbow, and he let out a cry as the knife fell to the floor.

He tumbled back – the knee I'd hit was failing him. I thrust the end of the bar into his stomach, and as he fell onto his back I took another swing that caught his arm again.

I kicked the knife across the room. It was a small antique dagger – ivory handle, silver hilt, and a blade of folded steel with dark lines from its forging running its length like grains over wood. He must've kept it on his desk as a decoration, and I hadn't noticed it nestled among the papers and displays.

Scotson groaned as he tried to regain his breath, and he clutched at the knee I'd hit.

I staggered back and looked down at the blood spreading across my blue shirt. I reached up to it, scrunched up the soaked fabric, and pressed it against the bleeding. The blade had crashed into my sternum, and I was feeling a pain much like what I'd felt when I'd run through the border. I was dizzy and had to catch myself from falling as I hunched forward. The bar fell from my hand, bouncing against the carpet and rolling against a leg of the desk.

Scotson's eyes widened at the sight of me. He regained his breath enough to let out a slow whisper of a laugh, and he used his good knee to prop himself back up against the wall.

"I was worried I'd get in trouble for my mistake with the med-pod," he said, "but now I'll be a hero for killing you. I bet they'll even restore my full lifespan."

I dropped to one knee. The blood loss continued, a stream running down my arm and flowering onto the carpet below.

"That's right, Corim. Die just like your disgusting wife."

As his words echoed in my head, I pressed my hand tighter against the wound, and when I took in a breath, there was something different about the pain I was now feeling and the pain I'd felt running through the border. I wasn't fighting to breathe – my lungs felt sturdy through the pain. The skin over my sternum had sure enough been deeply cut, but not my lungs, not my heart.

Scotson laughed again from his spot against the wall. I replied by breathing deep, reaching across the carpet, picking the bar back up, and rising above him.

His face dropped. "Stay back."

He squirmed as I stepped toward him. It was clear he couldn't get up, and this time he wasn't faking it.

I took another step. I was over him now. The dizziness I'd felt had passed.

"Get away from me!" he ordered.

"Scotson Yvera, you took the love of my life," I said.

He looked at me with utter distain. "So what? It doesn't mean anything. You people don't ever have real love. You don't even know what it is."

"Do you really believe that?"

"You all live truncated lives in a sterile, closed environment," he scowled. "None of you ever fully develop emotionally."

His hands twitched up defensively as I swung the bar down, but they didn't move fast enough to block the blow that made him go limp. There was no thought or hesitation as I swung the bar again. It was an ugly thing – I had to make it so there would never be a chance of reviving him. This death had to mean death. The brutality of it made me swing harder and faster so it could be done with all the sooner.

I don't know if I stood over his body for seconds or minutes. At some point I started to exit the den, but stopped at the desk when I heard commentators on the news speculating about the methods by which we could've expelled our artificial cells. They seemed clueless as to how we'd actually done it, instead putting forth absurd ideas – one expert was sure there was at least one traitor within their ranks who had helped us.

The next story was about how the Judicial Order was, on the assumption that we had never traveled far from the city, assembling teams to search the woods around Lake Park for our camp, as well as to patrol and fortify the border.

The next segment was about the producers of the news programs for the lower orders, and how they were using what we had done to foster fear and paranoia among the General Order. They showed a control room full of displays, and two men proudly played a video they'd just created that showed Raff, Ian, Uro, and I setting fire not to the Life Center, but to the support beams of a stretch of train tracks. Then came a spectacular shot of a loaded train flying off the burning, severed tracks, the crowded cars crashing into the asphalt below and piling up on each other. The next clip was of us observing it all from a safe distance, joy on our faces as we pumped our fists.

I wanted to keep watching to see what other lies they were creating, as well as to see what else I could learn, but a spell of dizziness reminded me that I was still bleeding. I went back into the hall where the servant bot stood just outside the door, still obedient of its dead master's order not to come in. I again paused to peer into its blank glass eyes before I went down to the kitchen to clean my wound.

It was a nasty arc of a cut, deep and jagged. It would take a long time to properly clot, but I could hold it together for now. I'd unbuttoned my shirt, now soaked with both my blood and Scotson's, and was using the towel I'd found by the sink as a compress.

I poured a glass of water with my free hand, and stood at the kitchen window watching a cardinal move among the low branches of the maple by the house. The glass in my hand was heavy crystal – not the shatterproof, lightweight glasses we were given in the General Order. I was turning it in the light, looking at the red streaks my fingers left on it, when I heard a vehicle pulling up and the sound of the garage door opening.

It had to have been his wife returning home much earlier than I'd anticipated. I'd been hoping to have time to search the house for things that could be of use to us at the beach, or to at least grab some food, but now I had to move. For all I knew, the wife might attack if she saw me, and I had no desire to harm her. With the state I was in, I couldn't be sure I'd win that fight anyway.

I threw the glass down on the counter, picked up my bar, and ran the best I could through the house, leaving a trail of bloody shoeprints over the white carpet. I cut across the dining room with its silver chandelier, then across the larger of the two living rooms, with its ornate chairs of carved wood and embroidered cushions.

I exited out the side patio door where the house was closest to the woods. Within seconds I was behind the cover of branches and leaves, frantically trampling over sticks and weeds as I kept the towel pressed into my chest as tightly as I could.

I cut a wide path to circumvent the front lawn. After I got down the hill in front of the house and came to the road, I paused to make sure it was clear before crossing it. That was when I heard his wife's screams coming from the house. It turned my stomach, but it caused me no regret for what I'd done. I may have brought her great anguish, but I believed, I needed to believe, that my execution of Scotson Yvera was as justified as any execution that had ever been meted out by the Judicial Order, and that it would, one way or another, prevent anguish for many others.

Yet I still tossed the metal bar far into the woods, freeing myself of its weight, if not its memory.

48

I didn't have it in me to do anything more than walk. My mouth was dry, my breathing was labored, and every attempt to quicken my pace left my legs weak. I'd wanted to make it far along the river by nightfall, and maybe even surprise everyone by reaching the beach a day early, but now there was no chance of that.

After what must've been three hours of fighting my way through the wilderness, I'd made little progress. I'd tried to cut a bit west to be sure I wouldn't end up anywhere near the search parties near Lake Park, but now that the sun had started to fall I could see that I'd overcorrected and had spent the last few miles only going west and not at all south.

When I attempted to push through a thicket of shrubs and weeds, a spell of dizziness came on, and I had to sit down and lean against the moss of an old tree.

It was there, feeling the loneliness of my surroundings, that it hit me how much of a fool I'd been to do this on my own. It was such a personal mission for me that it clouded my judgment and made me take awful risks. And when Raff, Ian, and Uro had argued with me about it, I'd used my position as leader to convince them that there was no real risk at all.

I needed to rest, and I needed food and water. Rest and water were hours off, but I reached deep into my pocket and pulled out the last pilfered snack I had left – a chocolate bar. Ian's favorite, the kind with almonds. I'd planned on saving it for him until long after he thought all the chocolate was gone.

"Buddy," I said into the fading light of the afternoon, "I think you'll forgive me if I have this."

I let the pieces melt in my dry mouth, and chewed the almonds an extra long time. I was so hungry I felt like I could've eaten a hundred of those bars, but I stopped myself at the last two pieces, rewrapped them in the foil and returned them to my pocket. Knowing I had a treat saved to deliver to Ian would do me more good than the calories ever could.

When I rose to walk again, a spurt of energy carried me over the next mile, but it gave way as the sun fell farther through the trees. My legs felt like thin sticks supporting an impossible weight, and my knees throbbed in pain. My mouth was so dry all I could think about was getting to the creek, but I was so confused and off-course that I had no way of knowing if the creek was minutes away or hours.

When my calves started to cramp, I stopped for another rest, and to check my wound in the fading light. A great bruise had spread from both sides of my sternum, covering my ribs in a purplish cloud. The cut had stopped bleeding for the most part, though the tender scabs were delicate and would open at the edges whenever I carelessly inhaled deeply enough to stretch the skin.

I found a patch of ferns and dandelions to lie down in. I just wanted to stretch and massage my cramping muscles for a bit, but as soon as I leaned my head against the soil my limbs felt too heavy to move. All I could do was listen to my breaths and stare up at the leaves quivering in the wind as darkness fell like a desperate embrace, quick and primal, insistent and rapacious.

My body numbed, and my mind quieted. I became empty of memories and identity – I was no longer someone who had ever had a father or a son, or a mother or a wife. There was no blood loss, dizziness, or hunger, and there was no beach to return to. There was no destination at all. There was only the silence around me, the stillness of the ground below, and the stars through the leaves above.

I awoke in the night to what I thought was a wolf's howl. Either I'd dreamt it or it had carried from miles off, but nonetheless I was filled with the delirious terror that a pack of wolves was circling me, smelling the blood on my clothes, and on the verge of moving in for the kill. As I fell back asleep I thought I heard far-off voices in the night.

I didn't wake again until the morning was well underway, with the eastern sun already reaching down through the branches. I didn't understand why I'd slept so long, or why it hadn't renewed my strength.

I managed to get up, but I wanted to lie down again after fifty feet of unsteady steps. I stopped to lean against a tree, grasping on just to stay upright. I should've been trying to come up with a plan, but instead my mind wandered to dark places. Was this the most I could hope to recover? That would mean I wouldn't be able to continue on at all, something that seemed more likely with every minute I wasn't on the move.

I cried what few tears I could when I thought of Ian – maybe at that very moment he was standing where the beach meets the river, looking into the mountain gorge in the hope that I'd already be crossing through it to rejoin him.

Pressing my hands against the smooth, gray bark of the tree trunk, I started to hear the distant conversations of men. Even in my delirium, I understood that they could only be the search parties spreading out from Lake Park.

What did they intend to do if they found me? Would they tackle me? Punch me? Tie my hands and drag me away? Maybe they'd take pity on me if they saw the shape I was in. Maybe some would even pretend not to notice if they spotted me, or even help me somehow.

Entertaining such a foolish hope snapped me back into action – the truth was I wouldn't survive any scenario in which I didn't push forward. The only fear I should have was the fear staying still, and if my body didn't agree, then I'd have to ignore it and just keep on putting one foot in front of another.

The voices were coming from the east, so I headed southwest. Being near the search parties meant I was closer to Lake Park than I'd thought, and that I was bound to hit the creek soon. The thought of water helped, as did imagining that Kiri and Ian were walking there next to me. As the thirst burned my throat, and the ends of branches swiped at my half-closed eyes, I almost started to believe it.

The dizziness was so bad that I kept grabbing from tree to tree for support. I didn't let myself stop, but it was slow going and the voices were getting closer. By the time I heard the bubbling of the creek, I was also hearing the footsteps of men along the banks.

I kept my head low and slowed my movements, and then froze altogether when I saw flashes of white shirts moving through the leaves ahead of me.

"Head that way," someone said. It was the first clear voice I'd heard since I'd left Scotson's the day before.

"You two circle back through there," someone else said.

I looked around for pines or a thicket to hide in, but had to settle for a spot in the modest leaf cover provided by the low branches of an alder. I made out more voices, and heard clumsy splashing from the creek.

Suddenly there were footsteps crashing somewhere closer to me, accompanied by heavy breathing and sighs of annoyance. I sat and pressed the back of my shirt – the one part of it that wasn't brown with bloodstains – against the crook of the old alder's trunk, and I wrapped my arms around my knees to make myself small.

I peeked over my shoulder. Forty feet away, leaves were shaking as branches were being pushed aside and released. At twenty-five feet, I saw the faces of two men coming my way. One was maybe thirty, and the other maybe fifty.

I couldn't run, and I was in no condition for a fight, but that didn't stop me from wishing I still had the metal bar, or the dagger that I'd stupidly left on the carpet of Scotson's den. I decided that I wouldn't resist at all, and to remember to never say a word about where Ian and the others were, no matter what was done to me.

They barged closer with big lumbering steps as they glanced around. Then the eyes of the older man were on me, and I waited for him to run at me, or to point me out to his companion, or to shout back to the creek.

But his gaze turned away, and he and the other man continued on, passing by just in front of me. They had been looking for a group or a camp – perhaps my face hidden among the low branches had been so unexpected he hadn't consciously registered it.

I breathed again, the day's dry air burning against my throat, and waited until they were long gone. At least I wouldn't have to worry about lightheadedness for a while the way my heart was racing. Keeping low and staying quiet, I headed west again.

An hour later, although I was still hearing occasional distant voices from the search parties, I made my way to the creek. I picked a spot where the high, narrow banks would offer the best concealment, and moved the quickest I'd moved all day to get to the water.

I knelt in a shallow part of the creek, sunk my hands into the gritty soil below the surface, and lowered my face to let the water flow into my mouth. It tasted better than any meal I'd ever had. I wanted to drink until my stomach was too full to take another sip, but I vaguely remembered something I'd learned about the dangers of taking in too much water without food, and I restrained myself the best I could. The last thing I needed was a repeat of the night Raff and I had tried fish.

I gently cleaned my wound, dabbing at it with my wet sleeves and wiping away what dried blood I could. I crossed the creek and entered a stretch of pines where I was well concealed and my footsteps were muffled by the beds of dry needles. I was safer, but still moving slowly, and it was already the afternoon.

Not a half hour later, I was traversing a hill when I was hit with a crushing headache. Resting didn't make it better, so I kept pressing on. Pain or not, I was encouraged because I'd put the creek at least a mile behind me, and I wasn't hearing any signs of the search parties.

The best moment of the day came when a flat expanse of woods opened up to reveal the river. Dusk was already approaching, and I was so far upstream that I was in unfamiliar territory, but I now had the river to cling to, and I could move along it all night if I had to. I staggered to the water through the lines of long-ago fallen trees that ran along the riverbanks there.

My head was pounding, the sun was sinking into the tree line, and I'd never known it was possible to feel so empty and weak, but I started downstream, slow step after slow step.

49

I woke up confused, with the night hanging over me, and the roar of the river in my ears. I was on my side, on the sandy dirt of the bank, my head resting on one arm. I had no memory of lying down there, but the pain in my left ankle reminded me that I'd rolled it with a careless step.

When I sat up, it was clear that the ankle was the least of my problems. I was in a cold sweat, my empty stomach was nauseous, and my muscles ached from head to toe in a way that went beyond fatigue. Without thought, I lay back down, rested my pounding head back onto my bent arm, and fell into a shallow sleep where I dreamt that the stones of the river were floating over me, and that the two men I'd seen from the search party were dragging me by my feet through a hallway of white-tiled walls and bright lights.

In the morning, I woke up a dozen times before I was able to stay awake. Even then, all I could manage to do was to roll onto my stomach and crawl up the bank enough so I'd have a better view. It wasn't just that I couldn't get up physically – my mind had become so lost that I didn't have any desire to get up.

I was unsure if I recognized this stretch of river or not. The forest was thick on both banks, and while there were some light rapids and scattered islets, there weren't any of the turns, falls, or jutting rocks that there would've been if I'd made it anywhere close to the mountains.

I managed to stay awake, but didn't get up. Even flat on my back, I was seeing stars in my eyes as the rising sun came and went among the drifting clouds. The mosquitoes fed at my hands and neck, and I searched around me as if I might find some salve or elixir among the dirt and stones.

Once again, I had to find a way to move, whether I wanted to or not, whether I was afraid to or not. But when I rolled to my side and pushed against the ground, my arms shook in a useless struggle. I rolled onto my back again. My head was swirling, and my sweat-covered skin was burning.

"One last try," I said. I told myself that Kiri was there at my side, and imagined her reaching down to help me up, her hair falling around her face, her voice calling my name.

But this time no tricks of the mind could help. No optimism, desire, or force of will could lift me off that bank. Whatever strength I'd had left was now gone.

I gave up, and I gave in.

"What have I done?" I whispered through dry lips. I was thinking of Ian. I was thinking of what this would mean for him. Kiri had shown him that she was willing to die if it meant doing the right thing. I supposed I was giving him a similar, if far less noble, example, but I couldn't imagine he'd take any comfort in that.

"I'm sorry," I said to the image I'd created of Kiri standing over me. I let her fade into the trees and water.

The pain persisted, and I surrendered to it as the sun climbed higher and the river flowed away toward the unseen mountains. And then I felt only a tranquil warmth moving through me, like the light that you wake to when you wake up near someone you love. And I would've given myself over to that light if I hadn't seen my son running toward me across the stones of the bank, his tanned skin brown against the white rapids of the river and the green of the forest.

Hands were laid over me, propping me up and wiping the sweat from my brow. All I could make out was that it was Ian and Raff. My head came to a rest on Raff's lap, and Ian tore off pieces of bread and put them to my mouth. They spoke to me, but I had trouble following their words, and when I tried speaking, the words wouldn't come as quickly as my thoughts. My first real communication was unbuttoning my shirt to show them where I'd been cut.

Ian went to the water and filled the wine bottle they'd brought. He had me drink from it, and he poured drops into his hand and wiped them over my face.

Bit by bit, I started to feel some strength retuning, and mental clarity started to follow. It wasn't a dream – they were really there.

I slept – this time deeply – with my head still in Raff's lap. When I awoke, my skin was no longer burning the way it had been.

"I'm ready to get going," I claimed, my voice still weak.

They wisely made me wait and rest. They told me how they'd already started making progress at the beach with building shelters in the woods. They told me about the three men and two women who'd joined us, who they said were starting to accept that they were going to have to live in the wild for a very long time.

In the afternoon, they lifted me to my feet, and with Raff supporting me we began moving forward. My thoughts cleared up with every mile, and I started to get my legs back. I was walking on my own again as evening started to fall and we reached the shadowy gorge where the river parted the mountains.

In the day's last light, the gorge opened up and we crossed into the patch of woods where we'd spend the coming months building a new life. Ospreys were circling over the river where it widened and met the sea.

Uro, his old smile back on his face, came up to embrace me when we stepped onto the beach. Our five new compatriots were there, too. Their faces were the same, but the anguish that had been so visible on them when we'd first met at Lake Park was now gone, and they greeted and hugged me as if they'd known me forever.

I sat down on the beach, and got my shoes off my sore feet. The crowd stayed with me, and someone opened a bottle of wine and passed it around. Ian had disappeared somewhere, but he came running back, sat next to me, and presented a handful of wild strawberries. They were ripe, and a good deal larger than the ones we'd found before.

"We found a better patch," he explained. "You have to taste these."

As I ate the strawberries and the warm breeze rolled over my skin, I started to feel whole again. "They're delicious," I said. "I think we'll do well here, don't you?"

He stared up at me without answering. His blue eyes seemed sharper and brighter than they'd been just a week before. "I thought you weren't ever coming back, Dad. I didn't think we'd find you."

I wrapped my arm around him, and we looked out at the sun setting red over the water, the blood long clean from my hands, and the wound over my heart closing.

"Of course I was coming back, Buddy. You know you'll never lose me."

Printed in Great Britain
by Amazon